The Sizzle Paradox

Also by Lily Menon

Make Up Break Up

The Sizzle Paradox

Lily Menon

ST. MARTIN'S GRIFFIN
NEW YORK

First published in the United States by St. Martin's Griffin, an imprint of St. Martin's Publishing Group

www.stmartins.com

Designed by Devan Norman

Library of Congress Cataloging-in-Publication Data

Names: Menon, Lily, author.

Title: The sizzle paradox / Lily Menon.

Description: First edition. | New York : St. Martin's Griffin, 2022.

Identifiers: LCCN 2022003285 | ISBN 9781250801234 (trade paperback) | ISBN 9781250801241 (ebook)

Subjects: LCGFT: Novels.

Classification: LCC PS3613.E4923 S59 2022 | DDC 813/.6—dc23/eng/20220127

LC record available at https://lccn.loc.gov/2022003285

Our books may be purchased in bulk for promotional, educational, or business use. Please contact your local bookseller or the Macmillan Corporate and Premium Sales Department at 1-800-221-7945, extension 5442, or by email at MacmillanSpecialMarkets@macmillan.com.

First Edition: 2022

10 9 8 7 6 5 4 3 2 1

For Ollie, my golden retriever, who never left my side through the writing of this book.

(The snacks on the table may have had something to do with it.)

PARADOX: A logically self-contradictory statement. Or, a surefire way to make a perpetually single grad student go slowly but undoubtedly insane.

The Sizzle Paradox

Chapter One

LYRIC

My best friend is a serial killer. It's the only explanation for the unconscionable *mayhem* that is his bedroom.

Okay, so scientifically speaking, that's not accurate. There could be many explanations for the mess, and his being a serial killer is probably pretty low on the list. I'd have to check the exact statistics. My point, though, is that the disarray makes it look like his room is the scene of a macabre and violent murder. But in spite of that initial impression, Kian is sleeping peacefully, buried under the covers, snoring softly in the dim light from the closed curtains.

I jump onto his bed, right on top of his sleeping form, and bounce a few times. It's okay, he's a big guy. He can take it. To my point: He doesn't even move, not even when an avalanche of chemistry textbooks and notes slides off and onto the floor, and a leaf from his fiddle-leaf fig plant lands with a sad plop on top of it all. "Yo, Montgomery." I ruffle his curly, dark brown hair—always thick and luxuriant, thanks to his half-Indian heritage, no matter what products he does or doesn't put into it, unlike my own fine strands. "It's nine. Do you think you might want to, I don't know, venture out into the land of the living?"

He grunts and mumbles something almost coherent.

I frown at the top of his head, the only part of him that's visible. "'Jimmy's steak is clean'? Who's Jimmy? Why were you sampling his steak?"

With a mighty groan, Kian turns over, sending me flying backward. Grabbing my elbow, he pulls me up and sets me next to him. There are lines on his face and his thick eyebrows are all kinds of screwy. "I *said*, 'Give me a break, LB.'" His voice is just a sleep-marinated growl.

I laugh. "Oh. So nothing about Jimmy or his steak at all?"

He palms my mouth to stop me from talking, his hand bigger than my entire face. He's a walking veritable giant, but he's my giant, so I let it go. "I went to bed, like, four hours ago."

Pushing his hand off, I lie down next to him, my head on his broad chest as we both stare up at the ceiling fan on full blast. Kian is always hot. Probably because he's, like, 90 percent muscle. Meanwhile, I'm already beginning to get goose bumps in my thin T-shirt and pajama shorts. "Were you working on your thesis?"

"Yep." He can tell I'm cold, so he absentmindedly covers me with a corner of his blue plaid blanket. I snuggle in, immediately ten times cozier. "I need to get everything done. I defend in, what, two months?"

"It's going to be great," I reassure him, patting his giant head like he's my faithful mastiff. "You're the most brilliant environmental chemist I know."

I can hear the laughter in his voice. "That would mean so much more if you knew any other environmental chemists."

I snort but don't say anything. We lie there in silence, listening to the traffic outside our decrepit apartment building, the hum of the fan inside. Kian is the only male specimen of our species—except my dad, but he doesn't count—that I can do companionable silence with. Put me in front of any other dude and I turn into a tripping, panicking, wooden-mouthed idiot. But right now, I'm as relaxed as I'll ever be. In this tiny, messy bedroom that looks like a patio garden and smells like soap and books and sounds like impatient New York traffic, I may as well be in a spa.

Naturally, I'm *very* aware that Kian is an exceptionally aesthetically pleasing male specimen. I'm not an oblivious robot. He looks like he belongs on a movie poster, starring opposite Zoey Deutch in a romantic comedy set in NYC at Christmas. He'd wear a black wool peacoat, his dark hair dusted with sparkling snowflakes, towering over the Christmas shoppers as he gazed at Zoey with warmth and adoration and passion simmering in his brown eyes. Who doesn't want that?

Me. I don't want that.

Because yes, all that's very swoony, not gonna lie. But he's also *Kian Montgomery*. My best friend. My partner in crime.

The friend zone is where we both live and thrive. Take us out of it and we'd immediately perish, our insides mangled and crushed from being in an unfamiliar environment, like those deep-sea creatures that aren't meant to ever see sunshine.

After a moment, Kian speaks. "So, I take it the date didn't go well?"

Okay, contemplative moment shattered. I squeeze my eyes shut, feeling my cheeks warm. I should've known better than to think Kian would forget. "Why do you say that?" I make sure to keep my tone light.

"Because you're in my room bothering me instead of making the dude pancakes or something?"

"Ugh. That's so sexist."

"Sexist? So are you telling me you're *not* the cooking fiend I've known and been best friends with for the last seven years?"

"There's a stack in the kitchen. And blueberry oatmeal, too," I mumble, and then turn on my side to face him.

His eyes crinkle with laughter but he doesn't do more than smile a little. "Mm-hmm."

He waits. I wait. He waits. And then I break. With a sigh, I say, "Okay, okay. It didn't go well. Par for the course for me as of late."

Kian pats me on the shoulder and then puts both hands behind his head, his massive goalpost elbows sticking out on either side. He could impale horses with those. "What was wrong with this one?"

"I don't know, dude. I mean, Paul's so ridiculously hot. As you know."

He scoffs. "How would I know? I saw him at the coffee place when you not so subtly pointed him out, and yeah, he's muscular with straight teeth, but 'ridiculously hot'? I don't know about all that."

I laugh and sit up, wrapping his blanket around my shoulders. It leaves him uncovered in just his sleep shorts, his tawny, well-muscled chest and abs exposed to the air, but he doesn't complain. He's probably already sweating. "Why are straight guys so reluctant to admit other guys are hot? Like, just say it. It's not a ding on your manhood."

Kian raises an eyebrow and says, deliberately, "I can say it. I'll say it no problem."

I make a *go on*, *then* expression.

Kian clears his throat. "Paul was . . . a bot."

I quirk my mouth. "Really?"

"Paul had . . . crotch rot."

I attempt to pinch his side, but he laughs, easily holding my wrists in one steel manacle of a hand. "Okay, *okay*," he says finally, knowing I'm clearly not going to let him rest. "He was hot!"

I nod approvingly and sit back, and he releases my wrists. "See? Did it kill you to say that? Anyway, I have no idea what happened." I pause and lean over Kian's torso to reach the curtains, and, pushing some kind of fern that looks like it should only exist in the mountains of North Carolina aside, yank them open. The room floods with light and Kian hisses, as if he's a vampire. I ignore his melodramatic attempts to get me to close the curtains and plunge us into gloom again.

When he's able to speak like a normal human, Kian says, "So? How'd he rate on the SPS? You know you're dying to tell me."

The SPS—or the Sizzle Paradox Scale—is a scientific instrument I designed a couple years ago to rate my romantic and sexual partners. Measuring things using scientific instruments is second nature to me; in experimental psychology, if you can't measure something, it doesn't exist. And as a doctoral student with a barren social calendar, I have no boundaries between my work and personal life. Which is probably reason 3,456 I'm currently single.

I look down at the cars splashing through springtime puddles on the road below us and sigh. "It started out so promising. A 4 out of 5 on the pre-sex sexual chemistry index and the invitation to kiss portion."

Kian raises his eyebrow. "Not bad."

"Yeah. And then the actual kiss was a 3."

He scrunches up his face. "Ooh."

"Well, it got better . . . the hooking up was a 4 and the actual sex was a 4."

Kian looks impressed. "Not bad."

"Yeah, but get this. The postcoital communication? A 2. And that was me being generous."

Kian's mouth falls open with an audible pop. "A 2? Is that the lowest yet?"

"Yep." I pull the blanket tighter around me, miserable as a cat in a rainstorm. Postcoital communication is what normal people call "cuddling"—you know, basking in the hazy glow, your head on your partner's chest, talking about sweet nothings. "Paul was probably the hottest guy I've gone out with in months and he wasn't horrible to talk to. I really thought this one had a shot at going somewhere. But it's always something. If the sex is great, they bore me to tears. Or if we hit it off emotionally, the sex is tragic."

"Man." Kian appears lost in thought for a moment.

I squirm a little; he's never judged me for not having been with a guy for more than three months (or thirty minutes, as the case may be), but I'm always afraid he's going to start. I mean, *I* kinda judge me. I *want* a long-term relationship that glows with good health. I want it almost more than anything. But I just don't seem to have what guys want and also, I'm probably a picky bitch.

"What was so bad about the postcoital communication part?" Kian pauses. "Also, can I just put in that the term 'postcoital' is disgusting?"

I snort and then shake my head. "After we finished, he burped."

"Burped?" Kian screws up his nose. "Is the bar really that low out there?"

"Apparently." I sigh. "But it's not just that. I think the real reason we didn't last past the night is, um . . ." I consider my next words, wondering how to say it delicately. And then I decide to just press on. This is one of the luxuries of living with Kian—I don't have to watch my words around him.

Pulling a hand out from under my blanket shield, I curl a strand of my dark blond hair around my finger. "Actually, I think it's because he's an MFA student."

"What?" Kian frowns at me and scratches the dark stubble on his cheek. *Scritch scritch scritch.* The sound of so many mornings spent dissecting a sucky date from the night prior. "You're so picky." It's pretty normal for Kian to read my mind and echo my thoughts. We've been friends so long, it doesn't even freak me out. "What's wrong with being an MFA student? You're a psych grad student; I'm an environmental chemistry grad student."

I wave a hand and the blanket slips from one shoulder. "Not the student part—the MFA part. The entire time we were hooking up, I just kept thinking, what would we really have in common besides our shared interest in underground metal bands, anyway? He'd be, like, quoting Whitman at me and stuff, and I'd tell him . . . what? About the sexual chemistry exhibited by newts in the rain forest?"

Kian shrugs and sits up, propping his gigantic self against the wall behind him. Progress. At this rate, he'll be out of his bed by lunchtime. "I mean, you *could* talk to him about sexual chemistry." When I give him a dubious look, he adds, "In *humans.* That would probably be an aphrodisiac. You're doing a literal Ph.D. on it, LB. Share some of that sexy knowledge."

I pull my knees up and prop my chin on them. "You really think guys would find that sexy?"

He shrugs, the muscles in his upper shoulders rippling with the movement. If Kian weren't so sweet, he'd be insufferable. "I would. You should try it next time."

"Okay." I nibble on my bottom lip as two fire trucks go blaring by, making Kian wince. Never a quiet moment in NYC.

But I grew up here, so it doesn't really bother me as much as it does him. "I will." After a pause, I laugh a little, not meeting Kian's eye. "Pretty weird that someone studying sexual fucking chemistry in committed romantic partners hasn't had a committed romantic partner in a year and a half, huh?"

Suddenly, his big, warm hand is over my smaller, cold one. "You'll find someone again. Let's face it, it won't be long before some other dude asks you out." He pauses and when I look at him, he smiles his lopsided, I'm-evil grin that always means he's up to no good. "There's no accounting for taste, I guess."

I pull my hand from under his and smack him. "Shut up."

"Seriously, though. You'll probably have another date by the end of the week. And that's another chance to try. To finally crack the Sizzle Paradox, trademarked by one soon-to-be Dr. Bishop."

"Yeah." I pull the blanket in tighter, not saying what I'm really thinking. It's not *getting* the dates that's a problem for me; it's having them turn into something strong and mutually enjoyable in the long term. And therein lies what I've coined the Sizzle Paradox: The more I'm into a guy—either for his mind or his body—the less chance we have at a healthy, committed relationship. Something *always* goes wrong. But why? Why can't I find both sexual chemistry *and* love?

My entire thesis is devoted to studying how partners in successful relationships manage to keep both sexual and romantic chemistry alive. The reason I was admitted into my doctoral program is because I came up with a "revolutionary" way (that's the word the Columbia psych department uses when speaking to study volunteers and, more importantly, sponsors) to research this in an objective fashion, rather than relying on self-reports from the couples, which can be unreliable.

With the help of the biotechnology doctoral students, I designed software that can analyze people's brain activity using an fMRI machine to measure how strong their sexual and romantic attraction is to their partners. So, in real time, we can see the rate of sexual attraction and romantic love by showing the participant a picture of their significant other. No one's done anything like that before.

The idea is that we then interview couples who score the highest on both measures to see what they're doing right in their relationships. Once we find commonalities among thousands of couples, we can use that information to construct a sound framework for what makes a successful long-term relationship. Psychology has those frameworks now, of course, but they're hypothetical, based on ephemeral feelings and subjective self-reports. This is the first time we've been able to verify the existence of a happy relationship using neuroscience.

It was an idea that excited me when I first got into the doc program. It would help thousands of couples. It would unmask the somewhat mysterious nature of sexual attraction and romantic love. We could take apart healthy relationships and see what made them tick and then I could tell the world about it. I was brimming with excitement.

And now, here we are, five years later and . . . let's just say I'm struggling. Not because of the science; the science is solid and we've amassed a lot of data. It's me. I've lost my mojo along the way.

See, although I *have* been in a couple of serious relationships over the last few years, I've experienced nothing even close to the emotional connection of the thousands of couples I've studied. Therefore, every time I sit down to analyze the data I've collected or write up my "expert opinion" on how couples can make their relationships stronger based on my study findings, I feel like a huge fraud. I'm no expert on committed couples. Why are people looking to me to tell them what to do? Most days, I want to hide under my desk at the lab and cry.

I look at Kian, ready to move on to other, more pleasant topics. "So, when's Kiley coming over?"

He makes a face as he gets out of bed, stretching and lazily scratching his chest like a big, lumbering bear. "Yeah, that's not a thing anymore."

"What?" I throw a pillow at him. It bounces off his back and falls in a sad heap to the floor. "Since when?" I actually liked Kiley. She complimented my risotto once.

There's something closed off about his face all of a sudden. Weird. "Since a couple weeks ago, though she didn't really want to accept that. We made it official last night." He strides to his secondhand dresser, pulls out the Avengers T-shirt I gave him for his birthday two years ago, and throws it on over his sleep shorts.

I hop off his bed, frowning. "Where was I when you came in?"

"Already asleep. Which was a good thing because Kiley was . . . strident about her opinions of me. We stayed up till, like, two A.M. talking. And when I say 'talking' I mean she yelled at me while I sat there and took it."

"Damn. Well, wait five minutes and I'm sure there'll be someone else more than willing to take her spot."

Kian raises an eyebrow at me as he heads to the bathroom. Without saying anything, he shuts the bathroom door, and a moment later, I hear the shower start up.

Definitely something strange going on there. Breakups usually roll off Kian like rain off a tin roof. He's the first person to tell you he isn't looking for anything serious. He's the anti-Lyric in that way.

Well, I think, *I'm sure he'll talk about it when he's ready.*

In the meantime, I head to the tiny kitchen, pick up a pancake, and begin nibbling on it morosely. The faucet drips steadily into the sink, like it's counting down time. It's my own dating life I really need to focus on.

For science.

Chapter Two

*

*

KIAN

I soap myself up in the shower, thinking about Kiley.

Not in *that* way. Not anymore. The thing is, she was fine, exactly my type—funny and sweet, with an inability to take anything seriously. I put the soap away and pick up the shampoo, squinting at the bottle. It's something new, something Lyric obviously picked up. The scent is called "Calm Serenity."

How do you bottle calmness or serenity, let alone decipher how those might smell? Shrugging, I squirt some of the pale purple liquid into my hand and then slather it onto my head, almost immediately feeling calmer and more serene. Witchcraft.

Anyway, even though Kiley was my type, I could tell the relationship was starting to mean more to her than it did to me. And that's just not cool. It was time to cut ties.

There's a voice in the back of my head, though, that asks what number relationship this was, this year alone. It's only March. I just turned twenty-six. Why do I keep going through girls like they're sheets of paper? For that matter, why do they keep going through me?

I shake those thoughts off. Twenty-six is still young. There are plenty of people out there who aren't committed by this age. The last thing I want to do is end up like my parents—miserable, in a marriage that happened because "it was what people did."

By the time I'm toweling off, I feel better. I get dressed, look at myself in the water-spotted mirror, run a hand through my wet hair, and let it fall where it does. Kiley and I were just done, that's all. We came to the end of the life cycle of our time together; it was a natural death. And now it's time to move on.

Whistling, I pull open the bathroom door, the steam escaping in a rush as if it resents being trapped in here with me. And when it clears, there's Lyric, standing in front of me with her giant sunglasses perched on her head, dressed in her usual outfit of a T-shirt and shorts, much like mine. There's a tote bag slung over her shoulder that says, *Just one more chapter.* I'm pretty sure I got that for her at some point.

"Let's go shopping, Montgomery," she says. "I think we could both use it."

I grin and head to the kitchen, where I grab three of her pancakes and begin stuffing them into my mouth. "Let me guess—Target?"

Trailing after me, she slides her pale feet into sandals. "Where else?"

ꝏ

Target is kind of *our* place. When we were undergraduates at Columbia, we made frequent middle-of-the-night trips to the twenty-four-hour one near campus, using our parents' credit cards to buy dollar stationery and ramen and coffee we definitely didn't need. Now, as creaky grad students, we have more sophisticated palates.

"Look at *this*." Lyric holds up a massive wreath in the home decor department. It's probably about fifty inches in diameter, with grotesque fake furry bunnies and birds hot-glued on at regular intervals among the luridly green grass. There are already a few tufts of bunny fur in her brown hair, and she can barely hold the thing up with her matchstick arms. "We need this."

"LB, that wouldn't even fit on our front door. Not to mention, I'd probably have a heart attack every time I came home." I walk farther down the aisle and pick up a set of hammered copper mugs. "Now *these*, on the other hand . . ."

"Oh my God." Lyric is beside me in an instant, the wreath forgotten. "*No*, Kian. How many hammered copper thingies do you already have?"

A middle-aged woman in the aisle gives my hammered copper mugs a look. She clearly wants them. I hold them closer to me and look down at Lyric. "I don't have any hammered copper mugs, FYI. I might have a hammered copper tray and a hammered copper cup collection, but definitely no mugs."

She narrows her eyes and leans against the metal shelf. "What are you even going to use them for?"

I ping one with my nail; it makes a satisfyingly metallic ringing sound. "I don't know. Maybe I'll learn how to make Moscow mules. You know, when I'm in my fancy *new* apartment after graduation. Maybe that'll be my signature, grown-up drink."

I look at Lyric, laughing, but she's got this crushed look on her face, her big blue eyes all wide.

She sinks into a nearby white wicker Papasan chair and I crouch on the floor next to her, frowning. "Hey. You okay?"

Lyric clutches a pillow embroidered with tulips and the saying *Spring in my step* to her. "You—you really think you might leave? In May, after you graduate?" She's attempting to ask it without any inflection, but I know her too well.

Something twists in my chest at her expression, at the way she's trying to mask whatever she's feeling. I tug gently on the ends of her long, dirty blond hair. "Maybe. I mean . . . where we live, it's a student apartment." I keep my voice soft, even though there's a sick feeling in my stomach now, too, at the reality of what we're talking about. We've managed to avoid it until now, but the truth is, I'm graduating in just over two months. And then—then it'll be time for the real world. Lyric doesn't graduate until next year, which means . . . we'll have to be apart for the first time in more than half a dozen years.

In the fluorescent lights of the store, there are shadows under her blue eyes. "Yeah, I know, I just . . ." She clears her throat and attempts a smile. My heart feels like a stone. "You know what? It's going to be great." She pats my shoulder, which is level with her nose. "You'll just have to invite me over all the time."

I scoff. "Invite you? You know I'm gonna have a whole room ready for you to crash in anytime."

Her eyes twinkle. "Really?"

"Really."

We stare at each other, smiling now. "Love ya, Pound," I say, squeezing her small, thin fingers.

"Pound" is a nickname reserved only for when I'm feeling especially affectionate. I came up with it one night during undergrad when I was stoned as hell and realized that her initials, LB, stood for—you guessed it—"pound" in the American lexicon. They didn't let me into Columbia for nothing.

"Right back atcha, Montgomery."

Lyric's cell phone dings. She pulls it out of her bag and sighs before texting back, her thumbs flying furiously. "Dammit, Max," she huffs after a second. Looking up at me, she says, "He needs twenty dollars because he 'bet on the wrong horse,' whatever that means."

I snort. "Or he ran out of beer too early on the weekend."

I stand, shaking out my sore legs while Lyric wraps up her conversation with her wayward little brother, just as a guy comes around the corner. He's dressed in dark jeans that look dressy somehow, and a button-down shirt with the sleeves rolled up to the elbows. I immediately see that his eyes are riveted on Lyric and he's walking straight toward her. I feel a flash of irritation at the focus in his eyes, as if she's something he wants to acquire, but then remind myself to chill. Lyric's a big girl. And she really needs this ego boost right now.

Turning to where she's still lounging in the chair as if she owns it, I wink and speak quietly. "Incoming." Then I move off farther down the aisle, where a gorgeous redhead is looking at pillows, so I can give Lyric—and the approaching man on a mission—some space.

LYRIC

The guy's so good-looking, I want to melt into the chair I'm currently sitting in. He's not classically handsome, not a Chris Hemsworth or a Kian Montgomery. But he's got those slightly intellectual, interesting good looks, like he was born to play the lead in Broadway productions of *Uncle Vanya*. He reminds me of Benedict Cumberbatch, my favorite Sherlock ever. (Kian, on the other hand, calls him Been-a-Dick Slumber-Cat because he can never remember his real name.)

But now is not the time to think of Kian because my real-life Benedict has just walked up to me and said, "You should totally buy that chair."

"Oh yeah?" I try to say the words, but they stick in my throat. All I manage is a wheeze that makes it sound like I'm currently expiring of a rather serious cat hair allergy. I clear my throat and try again, looking up into his blue eyes, much darker than mine. "Why?"

"Because you look cute in it." He's still smiling, pleased with himself. Okay, not a great pickup line. I'd rate it a 2 on my scale, if pickup lines were rated. But he's still cute. There's still an attraction.

I attempt to stand, but unfortunately, I've forgotten how feet work. My foot gets entangled in the chair legs, and I almost fall. Benedict catches my elbow and laughs, not appalled at all by my clumsy social anxiety. I catch Kian's eye at the end of the aisle, where he's managed to attract another woman like a bee to a flower (of course). He mouths something that looks like, *Chill, my dude.*

I don't know why I'm like this. Maybe it's because my brain is more adept at remembering statistics and data and bits of esoteric research than how to interact with actual human beings, especially those of the hot male variety.

"You all right, there?" Benedict asks, and he still hasn't moved his warm hand from around my elbow.

"Yeah!" I squeak, tugging my sandal out from under the godforsaken chair with my big toe while attempting to look casually breezy. It comes free with a wrench and I tuck my hair behind my ear.

Suddenly, my mind goes blank. I cannot think of a single thing to say to blue-eyed Benedict, and the more I think about the fact that I cannot think of a single thing to say, the fewer thoughts there are in my head, until I see them all begin to spiral down my mental drain in a cold, dark, disappointed swirl.

Benedict's smile slowly fades as he probably begins to suspect that I am either not interested in him or cannot do two things at the same time, like breathe and think. But then, for some reason, he rallies. Holding out a hand, he says, "I'm Sebastian."

I snort. "*Sebastian*. Yes, of course you are." It's only when he looks offended that I realize, without context, that probably sounds very, very rude. I take his outstretched hand and hold on to it tightly, to prevent him from running away. "No, only because I thought you—you reminded me of Benedict Cumberbatch. And the names Sebastian and Benedict are so similar in style."

He squints at me and half smiles, as if he's confused or charmed or scared or possibly a combination of all three. "Is that a compliment?"

"Oh God yes," I chuckle, waving a hand in the air. "Benedict Cumberbatch is almost offensively hot."

Sebastian's shoulders relax. He's not very tall, not as tall as the Bigfoot known as Kian, and being five eight myself, I come up to his eyes. This is nice. I won't have a crick in my neck by the end of this conversation, at least. He gestures around him at the Target home decor aisle. "So, I don't know if you had important plans for home renovation today, but if not, maybe we could go get some froyo or something?"

Yesss. Kian was right, here's another chance to crack the Sizzle Paradox. And if I do that, I won't feel like a fraud, which means I'll be able to rescue my flailing thesis that I haven't worked on and that, oh, I need to finish in order to graduate with my doctorate next spring. I smile at Sebastian, ready to accept, when I remember, duh, *Kian.* I can't just ditch him here in—

My phone beeps. My smile turns apologetic. "Just a second." I fish it out of my tote bag and look at it.

Kian: get out of here

He has clearly figured out my dilemma, because by now we can read each other's body language like picture books. Still, I'm not convinced.

Lyric: But we walked here together

Kian: You should go with him, I'm fine.

Lyric: k if you're sure

Kian: do it for science

I put my phone away and smile at Sebastian once again. "You know what, I'd love some frozen yogurt."

Wow. I even managed to say it like a normal person.

Chapter Three

LYRIC

The soulless corporate froyo place Sebastian takes us to is in the same plaza as the Target, with muted beige walls and cheap plastic chairs. He insists on paying for my cookies and cream double scoop, even though I tell him I'm happy to pay my own way. We take a seat by the window-wall in the back, next to a gaggle of giggling thirteen-year-old girls who are clearly immediately smitten with Sebastian, though he doesn't seem to notice.

Sebastian stretches his legs out, and the toe of his shoe (a very nice loafer; living with Kian, it's easy to forget some men like to dress well) touches the edge of my sandal. I wonder if he does this on purpose, and a small thrill goes through me. My hand itches for my phone's Notes app, but I resist. I make a mental note instead: So far so good. A solid 3 on the pre-sex sexual chemistry index.

"So." He eats a big spoonful of French vanilla. A slightly boring selection, but I don't jump to conclusions. "What do you do? For work, I mean?"

"I'm a doc student. My area's experimental psychology—just research, no clinical stuff. Hoping to graduate next spring." If I can get my shit together.

His eyebrows ascend, as most people's do when they hear that. I usually forget it's impressive to some people, because I spend 99 percent of my time around other dorks who are also working on their doctorates (and sometimes their second or third ones). "Nice. You look . . . I mean, I thought you were an undergrad."

I smile as the thirteen-year-old girls begin playing a very noisy game of "be friends with, marry, or kill." One of their froyo cups suddenly clatters to the floor to a chorus of shrieks. "Yeah, no, I graduated high school and college early, so I get that a lot. I'm only twenty-four, but most people in my program graduate around twenty-seven or -eight."

Sebastian whistles long and low as he sets his quarter-empty cup on the table to the side. What kind of dude leaves his froyo unfinished? *No, stop it. Don't think of it that way. Give him a chance.* When he turns back, his eyes bore into mine. "I like a smart lady."

I smile. "Thanks."

He reaches forward to wipe a dot of froyo off my chin. It's a total rom-com moment, but my stupid brain hasn't gotten the memo. Instead, it's focused on blaring one message at me: *Alert, alert! Personal bubble being breached, Lyric! He's touching our* chin! *We hate that!*

I wish I were normal.

Logically, I know I should be charmed or even turned on because he is definitely giving me Bedroom Eyes™ while he does this, but all I feel is a slight niggle of discomfort. I'd rather be at home, watching *Casablanca* with Kian. (It's his favorite movie, but he'd kill me if I ever told any of his other friends that. As far as they know, that honor belongs to *John Wick*.)

I sit back and move my foot away from Sebastian's without really thinking about it. "Um . . . thanks." There's a pause, during which I continue eating my cookies and cream and avoid eye contact because I don't want Sebastian staring at me or trying to wipe my face anymore.

But *why*. Why can't I just let myself be swept up and away? What has my overly analytical brain clocked as being wrong with Sebastian? I can already feel this date shriveling and puckering, pulling its legs up under its body, getting ready to pirouette and fall to the ground, stone-cold dead.

I clear my throat, thinking of my unfinished thesis on my laptop, dying a similar death. "So, what do *you* do?"

"I'm a Realtor."

I perk up a little. "Really? Because my roommate might be looking for a new place soon. He's graduating in May." Ugh. I don't even like talking out loud about Kian graduating. But he said I could go crash over at his new place anytime, and I'm planning on taking him up on it. He won't be rid of me that easily.

The thirteen-year-olds head out, all of them sneaking not-so-subtle glances at Sebastian and giggling. Outside, I watch them get into a silver minivan driven by one of their dads. Oh, to only have to worry about math homework and why your parents won't let you wear lip gloss yet.

Sebastian holds out a business card, breaking me out of my mini-reverie. Slightly confused, I take it. "For your roommate," he explains. Then, he frowns. "You said 'he'? So . . . are you guys involved?"

I laugh so hard I almost choke on a cookie chunk. "Oh my God, *no.* Kian and I have been friends since freshman year of undergrad, and . . . yeah. We would be an absolute disaster together."

Sebastian raises a dark, manicured, clearly skeptical eyebrow. "Really?"

I finish swallowing my mouthful before I answer. "Really. You wouldn't even think to ask that if you saw us together. Believe me, we're about as far away from each other's types as we can be. Dating each other?" I shudder. "No way."

Sebastian seems to relax a little. "So tell me about yourself, then. What are your hobbies, your special talents . . ." He leans forward, so his face is just inches from mine. I can smell milky vanilla on his breath. "Your deep dark secrets." Again, he holds my gaze and I *want* to feel a thrill, a more intense version of the one I felt when he pressed his foot up against mine, but . . .

there's just a little blip of interest, weak and dehydrated, hoping I'll defibrillate it back to life. And dammit, I intend to try.

I force myself to hold his gaze, setting my cup down (which is hard to do when I'm not looking at what I'm doing). "Okay. Well, I'm . . . I'm really into collecting tote bags."

Sebastian's face freezes for a moment, and then he straightens up a little. "Tote bags? Like, actual, literal bags?"

"Mm-hmm." I pick up the one by my feet. "Kian gave me this one for Christmas a few years ago. I love the big ones, you know, with the zipper on top. They're great for carrying around books and stationery, stuff like that."

Sebastian has an expression on his face that is somewhere between amused and pained. "Right . . . cool."

Shit. That doesn't sound enthused or genuine. I remember the one tenet I read in some dating article online—if things are going badly, just ask the other person about themselves. "What about you?"

Sebastian smiles again, though it looks just a tad forced this time. "Well . . . I'm a man of many talents, I think. One of them being the tried and true tying a cherry stem with my tongue."

"Really?" I lean forward, interested. The bell on the door tinkles as two guys walk in—slightly stoned college freshmen, from the looks of them. "That's fascinating because my best friend, Charlie, she's actually a biologist researching the dexterity of the tongue muscle in various mammals. Did you know that giraffe tongues are eighteen to twenty inches long and prehensile, which is why they have way more control over them than we do?"

Sebastian blinks a few times. Then he fiddles with his sleeves. Then he scratches his head. "Cool. . . . So, hey, I actually have to run. I have a one P.M. showing, and it's now almost . . ." He checks his phone. "Ten thirty."

"Oh, okay." My heart sinks like a stone through my body and falls into my foot. Another one bites the dust. We toss our cups into the trash and I walk out with him into the slightly breezy, damp spring morning. "Thanks for the froyo."

He smiles a little distractedly. "Yeah, no problem. I'll see you around. Let your roommate know I can help him out if he wants to find a place."

"Sure." He walks a few more steps forward and then I call out to him on an impulse. "Sebastian?"

He turns reluctantly, his eyebrows raised. I can practically see the thought bubble above his head: *Great. Right when I was on the cusp of escape.* "Yeah?"

I lick my lips, my hands clutching the strap to my tote bag like it's a life preserver and I'm floating away in a stormy sea. "Can I kiss you?"

He stares at me blankly, like I'm speaking a different language. A highly awkward moment passes, then another. I wait for him to compute my request. "You . . . want to kiss me."

I nod and press the toe of my sandal into the sidewalk. Feelings of the extremely excruciating variety are zipping through my body like lightning bolts. "Please. It's—it's kind of for research."

Sebastian walks back to me, his posture uncertain. "Okay . . . ?"

"Really. That's not a line." A breeze blows my hair all over my face and I use the hair tie on my wrist to tie it back in a bun. "My research is on romantic and sexual chemistry. And I need help. On many levels."

At this, Sebastian's eyes begin to sparkle. He steps even closer, his hands going to my waist, his voice husky. "Really?"

Oh my God, he's turned on. Kian was right! Kian's a genius! I've fucked up the ability to rate the invitation to kiss on the SPS because I propositioned Sebastian. But that's okay. There's still the kiss. I tip my head back a bit and look at Sebastian's lips. They're thin, a little on the dry side, but not wholly unattractive. "You'd be doing me a big favor."

We're standing between two busy shops—the froyo place and a cell phone store. But right now, there's no one outside to be scandalized. And this kiss should last maybe ten seconds, tops. *For fuck's sake, Lyric. Don't* time *it.*

Sebastian brings his lips down to mine. His mouth is hungry, devouring, the dryness of his lips slightly chafing mine. He wasn't kidding about the dexterity of his tongue. That sucker's darting in and out, up and down, practically doing the Macarena in my mouth.

But that's not a thought someone caught up in the moment would have. I refocus, trying to let myself sink in, letting myself get swept up in it all.

But by the time Sebastian pulls away, his eyes bright, his cheeks flushed, all I can think is, *I wonder if my nail polish delivery came.* I sigh inwardly. A 2 on the scale. Fuck. At this rate,

I'll *never* be able to connect with my data and finish my thesis and graduate on time.

I'm starting to hyperventilate a bit.

He grins at me, obviously congratulating himself for my quickened breath. I think about asking him if he has a paper bag handy. "So. Did that help your research?"

"Oh, yes." Forcing myself to calm the fuck down, I nod seriously and step back. That's not a complete lie; this kiss has helped me realize I'm farther away from my goals than ever. His hands fall off my waist. "Definitely. Thank you for your service to science, sir." I give him a mock salute because I am an awkward potato and this is what awkward potatoes do. I am horrible at goodbyes.

He looks at me askance, his smile fading. "Yeah . . . all right, then. Can I call y—"

"No." I say it before my mouth can catch up with my brain. "I mean, that's . . . that's okay, really. I think we both know it won't work." I begin to walk away, a wet blanket of disappointment wrapping around me. Another one that showed promise and just . . . fizzled out, like a firework in the rain. "See you, Sebastian."

KIAN

Mariana the Bartender is quite possibly the hottest girl I've ever kissed. Plus, the environmental scientist part of me really likes the fact that she's named after the deepest trench in the sea. But no way in hell am I going to tell her that.

I wrap my hands in her thick red hair, so shiny it's glinting like metal under the overhead lights. She's pressed up against the wall in the hallway of her tiny apartment, which she has invited me into. She's got one smooth leg wrapped around mine like some kind of sexy flamingo. Her tongue ring scrapes my lips, my teeth, my tongue, and her hands are traveling over my pecs and abs, down to the waistband of my jeans.

My body is definitely digging this. My goddamn traitorous mind, on the other hand, is thinking about the stack of my notes at home, waiting to be studied. I have to defend my dissertation soon. Very soon. Kissing random hot women I met in Target is probably not the most responsible thing I could be doing right now.

I wrench my mind back to the present, to the very beautiful woman in my arms. She smells good, too, kind of fruity, like strawberries or something. Speaking of strawberries, I meant to get some at Tar—

"Hey."

I blink and realize she's ended the kiss and is now squinting up at me. Her leg is no longer wrapped around mine, and her hands are on her voluptuous hips instead of on my body. Shit. "Yeah."

"Where'd you go?"

"What're you talking about?" I play for time and try to pull her closer to me. She resists.

"Are you hung up on someone else or something? Because

you definitely weren't into that kiss. Like, at all. And I know I'm a *very* good kisser."

I flash her my trademark, patented, panty-dropping Kian Montgomery grin. "And so modest, too."

She doesn't return my smile. Her panties stay firmly on.

I push a hand through my hair and step back. "No, I'm not hung up on anyone else." I think of Kiley, our breakup, and the only thing I feel is sad for her. But I don't miss her. I don't wish it back. "I'm preoccupied about something else, sorry. You really are a phenomenal kisser."

"Right." Mariana gets a container of Tic Tacs out of the pocket of her tiny shorts and pops one in her mouth. I guess we're done kissing. "Listen, I can give you my number. Maybe we can do this again some other time, when you're done being 'preoccupied' or whatever." She does the air quotes with her fingers, her many rings gleaming.

I force a convincing smile as I realize I've been dismissed. "Yeah, that'd be great." I hand her my phone and she puts her number in, along with her name: Mariana xx. "Thanks."

I walk to her front door, and as I open it, she grabs my T-shirt in a fist and pulls me back for one last, lingering kiss that tastes of minty freshness. It's a great kiss—fucking hot, to be honest. But my heart's just not in it.

So where *is* it, exactly, my heart? I have no fucking clue. Once we say goodbye again, I walk down the apartment building stairs, making my way home. Knowing I need to figure this out.

I check my cell phone, but there's not a text from Lyric. I just hope she's faring better than me with Target dude.

Chapter Four

KIAN

But when I get home, she's already there, lounging on our ratty tan couch, wearing one of my T-shirts with her sweatpants. It falls off one shoulder, exposing creamy white skin and a pink bra strap.

Lyric has really pretty shoulders, but like everything else good about her, she doesn't realize it. She's the most unassuming person I've ever met. In my weakest moments, I think life would be a lot easier if I just dated Lyric. But obviously, that would be a disaster of civilization-ending proportions. We've been friends way too long.

I toss my key on the little table she salvaged off the sidewalk last year and walk in, kicking off my shoes. "Uh-oh. That's your 'the world's going to shit and I need comfort' outfit. Did Loafers not make the cut?"

Lyric sighs and pauses the TV, which is playing some documentary about trichotillomania in the seventeenth century. Snooze. "No." She pulls her legs up on the couch. "This is fucking ridiculous, Kian. He was perfectly handsome and nice. I should've gotten more mileage out of that one than a single kiss."

I take a seat next to her and she immediately leans against my chest, pulling my arm proprietarily around her narrow shoulders. "Did you tell him you were an expert on sexual chemistry?" I ask.

"Yeah. In fact, I used that to get him to kiss me. You were right, by the way, it really does work on guys."

"Mm-hmm." I begin brushing my fingers through her silky fine hair, like I know she likes. Maybe it'll relax her muscles, bunched up like bungee cords in her body. To be honest, it relaxes me, too. Something tight unknots in my chest, and a pleasant warmth radiates through my body. I feel right for the first time all day. "So? How was the kiss?"

"I thought about nail polish during."

"What?" I can't help the laugh that bursts out of me. Nail polish is a new one. Usually she at least thinks about the *kiss*—dissecting the softness/firmness ratio of the guy's lips, his use of tongue, how much saliva was in play.

She uses her free hand to backhand my chest. "Don't judge! My OPI order's coming today."

"I don't know what that is, but man. Poor dude." Not that I can talk. I wasn't exactly invested in my kiss with Mariana.

"He was a Realtor."

I make a face. Realtors aren't really Lyric's type. But then again, maybe that's what she needs to break the Sizzle Paradox. Someone she wouldn't usually date. "He was cute, though," I allow.

She sighs and leans her head against me. "He was, wasn't he? My Sherlock Holmes, gone forever." After a moment, she says, "Hey, what happened to the Target redhead?"

"Mariana. She gave me her number."

Lyric twists around on the couch to look at my face, a mischievous grin on hers. "Ooooh. So is she the new Kiley?"

I try a smile, but it lands somewhere south of smile and north of grimace. "I don't know."

Lyric disentangles herself and turns around to face me fully, her legs crossed. Out on the street, two cars honk at each other like angry geese. I fucking hate traffic noise, which is a bummer when you live in New York City. "What happened? Was she weird like that one girl with the chicken altar in her loft?"

I push a hand through my hair and let my head fall back as I stare up at the familiar beige ceiling of our apartment. There's that crack Lyric swears looks like a lawn gnome with a top hat on. "Not at all. I think the problem might be me."

She scoffs and kicks my thigh with her socked foot. "Shut up."

I lift my head and square a look at her. "I'm serious."

Her smile fades slowly. "That makes literally no sense. You've had, what, like forty girlfriends since undergrad?"

"You might be exaggerating a *tiny* bit. . . ."

"My point is that you've never had a problem with girls. And when I left Target, that woman you were talking to definitely seemed into you."

I scratch my jaw, feeling a surge of frustration. She's right. I'm Kian fucking Montgomery. I don't *have* girl problems. That's not a thing in my life. This is entirely self-created; this is me being a dick for no reason at all. Most guys would kill to be in my position. "I know she did. And I was into her. But when I was kissing her? I thought about buying strawberries. And defending my dissertation."

Lyric gasps and claps both hands over her mouth. "Have you caught what I have?" she says in a muffled voice.

Doing a combination laugh-groan, I lean forward, so my elbows are on my thighs. "I don't know. I think I'm—" I stop short and stare into her blue eyes.

She lets her hands drop slowly. "You're what?" Her voice is a stage whisper, and she sounds so much like a little kid waiting to be let in on a big secret, I want to laugh.

Instead, I say matter-of-factly, "LB, I think I'm fucking bored." It's something I thought about the entire four-block walk home. And I'm pretty sure I've cracked the code to my inability to engage lately.

Lyric shoots me a dubious look. "Bored of *women*? You?"

I reach into my pocket and pull out my cell phone. "No, bored of doing the same thing over and over. Look." I open my

Instagram and scroll to my followers, most of whom are either girls I'm currently flirting with or have gone out with in the past. "Kiley, Melody, Grace, Lucy, Sierra, Zara." I look up from my phone. "The hot bartender, Mariana. Do you see what I see?"

Lyric frowns and stares over my shoulder at my screen. Her shirt (my shirt) gapes open at the front while she leans in, and I look away quickly. "They could all be swimsuit models?"

"Yeah, they could. But that's not what I'm talking about. I've been going out with the same kind of girl for a long time. I was thinking about that in the shower this morning, actually. I have a type: carefree, fun, adventurous."

"Basically you in girl form." Lyric smiles.

"Exactly. But maybe it's time for me to stop casually dating and take a breather." I study her expression, waiting for her to laugh at the idea.

But Lyric doesn't laugh. She leans against the back of the couch and taps her feet on the floor. "I thought the whole reason you wanted to casually date was because . . . you know. Your parents and all that."

She's not wrong. When I was able to escape the confines of my catastrophic-as-a-thirteen-car-pileup childhood, I realized one thing. I never wanted to become my father, a chronic philanderer. He takes his cheating career so seriously, he should have business cards made.

I also didn't want to turn a girl I loved into my mother—a weak, quiet, shadow version of her former self, afraid of speaking up, terrified of her own voice. The solution to me, at eighteen, was clear. I'd only ever date casually, not even thinking about a serious relationship until I was inching closer to middle age. And I've been faithful (pun intended) to that course of action so far.

Now, I lean back against the couch and consider my best friend. "Yeah. But taking a break isn't giving up on casually dating. It's just . . . taking a break. I'll reevaluate later."

Lyric doesn't look convinced. "Really? Kian Montgomery's just going to *stop* dating? That's never going to last. Have you met you?"

I raise an eyebrow. "I was looking for more support from my best friend and roommate, jeez."

Looking contrite, Lyric goes up on her bony knees to hug my shoulders, although her arms can barely fit around me. She smells like brownie batter. "Sorry, sorry. You know, I actually think a change of pace will be good for you."

I look up at her, my heart lifting a little at her words. "Yeah?"

She studies me for a moment. "Yeah."

Before I can say anything else, the doorbell sounds. Lyric pops up from her seat. "That's probably Zoey. I told her she could come over today to pick up a book."

A minute later I hear the front door, and Lyric's friend Zoey's slightly husky voice. They walk into the living room together and I raise my hand in a wave directed at Zoey. She's a couple inches shorter than Lyric, with curly brown hair the color of wet dirt. She always has hipster glasses perched on her nose and shiny balm slicked on her lips. She's got on a yellow flower-printed strapless dress today that shows off tanned shoulders.

As Lyric follows her into her bedroom, she pauses, then looks at me with her eyebrows raised, a big-ass, dopey smile on her face.

I frown. "What?"

Zoey pokes her head out of Lyric's bedroom. "Um, you coming?"

Lyric hurries to her. "Yep. Here I am." But before she disappears into her bedroom, she gives me a thumbs-up.

I narrow my eyes. What is she up to now?

A moment later, I hear them talking about some statistics project they have to do. I saunter to the kitchen and grab a Coke from the fridge, pop the tab open, and listen to the fizzing for a minute as I stare out the window at the Columbia science buildings in the distance.

My mind drifts to my conversation with Lyric about taking a break from dating. I gave her a hard time about not supporting me, but she was right, I realize. I don't know if I can just *not* date. That doesn't seem like me. I like relationships; I like the give-and-take of it, the happiness that comes with seeing someone smiling at you when you walk into a room, their eyes lighting up. Do I really want to just completely give that up because I'm bored?

Zoey and Lyric come back out of her bedroom and head to the front door. I hear them talk for another minute, and then the door closes. Lyric reappears, practically bouncing on the balls of her feet. "I have it. The definitive solution to your problem!"

I set my Coke down. "What."

A smile spreads across her face. "You just need to shake things up, Kian. There's no need to give up dating altogether." It's like she read my mind. "You just need to date a different *kind* of girl." Looking toward the front door, she says, "Like Zoey."

"Zoey *Jones* Zoey?" I make a face. "Seriously?" I mean, don't get me wrong, Zoey seems nice enough and she's cute in a nerdy librarian sort of way. She's just not on my dating radar and I highly doubt I'm on hers.

"Yep." Lyric paces around the tiny living room in tight little circles, her eyes bright like they always are when she's got a new idea. "You're bored because you're doing the same thing over and over, just like you said. Well, Zoey would be a breath of fresh air. She's serious, she's nerdy, and she's cute. She's obviously the kind of girl you need at this juncture of your life."

I walk closer to her, not convinced. "Really? But, I mean, would Zoey want to go out with a guy like me?"

Lyric shrugs and makes her way to her bedroom, and I follow, ducking under the big crystal wind chime hanging right inside her door. I've learned from past experience that fucker hurts when it slams into your cranium.

"See, now, that's where it gets complicated. Zoey's kind of a tough nut to crack. She's only dated, like, one guy and one girl the entire time she's been in grad school. She's definitely selective, so it's gonna take some doing." Lyric rummages around in her old whitewashed wooden desk for a notebook. She turns around to look at me. "But I know we can do it."

"I don't know, LB. Seems like a long shot, and I'm not even

convinced we're a good match." Narrowing my eyes, I lean against her doorjamb. "Why do you want to set us up, anyhow?"

"Because I'm in a severe dating rut and I want to derive some vicarious happiness. And also because if you and Zoey get serious, then you'll have an excuse to come back to NYC even after you graduate."

I study her, softening. Even though she said it as a joke, there's a hint of vulnerability on her face. I put my arms around her and squeeze her to my chest. "Don't be an idiot, Pound. I'm gonna come back for you anyway. You don't need to find me an excuse."

She sniffs a little and pushes me away, saying mock severely, "I'm gonna hold you to that."

"Deal." I smile and look around her room, gesturing to her windowsill, where several crystals are lined up, winking in the sunlight. "Hey, did you get more?"

Lyric clutches her notebook to her chest. Her face and ears turn a deep pink. "I may have. Every Witch Way was having a sale."

I snort as I walk to the window, ignoring the stink eye she's attempting to intimidate me with. Picking up a yellow-orange stone, I turn it over in my hands. "This is nice. What is it?"

"Um, citrine."

"And what does it do?" I hold it up to the light and it shines, as if it's battery powered.

"It's supposed to encourage confidence and manifestation." She clears her throat, her hands still in a death grip around her notebook. "You know. To help with my thesis."

I grin at her as I set the stone down. "Is it working?"

She silently threatens to stab me with her pen. This is Lyric's greatest shame: that in spite of being a damn good scientist at an Ivy League university and one of the most logical minds I know, she still collects and believes in the highly unscientific, definitely not peer-reviewed power of crystals. In fact, I'm pretty sure I'm the only person who knows this about her. Everyone else who's been in her room thinks they're a gift from her tarot-reader mom, and that Lyric keeps them just to be nice.

"Shut up!" she exclaims, and then, in a quieter voice, "But yeah, it works."

"Excellent." Still grinning, I go over to her bed and lie down on the rose-printed comforter, my arms spread out, my legs dangling off the edge. "Your room is so neat. And your bed smells like actual roses."

She snorts and I hear her rummaging in her desk again. "It's because I actually organize and clean my stuff. You should try it. Folders and hangers and detergent are all the rage now." After a pause, she adds, "So, anyway. What do you think about coming over to the lab on Monday so I can introduce you to Zoey?"

"This Monday?" I ask her, sitting back up because Lyric's bed always makes me sleepy. It smells like her—soft and comforting.

"The very one." She sticks a pen and a pencil into her bun and grabs her laptop off her desk. "Come on, Montgomery. Just give it a shot. If there's nothing there, you don't have to pursue it. I'll even talk to Zoey about it beforehand. I think she'll be into it."

"Really?" I raise an eyebrow. "She's never expressed interest in me before, has she?"

"No," Lyric allows, but then she gestures at me. "But has any girl ever turned you down?"

I give her my best Kian Montgomery smile. "Nope."

Lyric rolls her blue eyes. "Give it a rest. And come by the lab at noon." She leans forward and pins me with a steely gaze. "Noon *sharp*. And make an attempt with your clothes."

I sigh. "I hope you understand I'm only doing this because I love you."

Lyric gives me a satisfied smile. "Good. Now. Want to study together?"

I heave myself off her bed. "Yep. Let me grab my notes."

Chapter Five

*

LYRIC

The guy in my bed is under the covers, down between my legs. He's just a big lump in the near dark; the only light coming in is from the lamppost on the street outside, bathing everything in my room Creamsicle amber. The crystals on my windowsill seem to glow as the guy kisses each of my inner thighs in turn, his stubble rough and delicious, a promise of what's to come.

I gasp as his hot breath fans across me, in places that feel electrified, on fire, like they haven't been in so long.

"I can't wait to taste you." I can hear the smile in his voice; he knows I'm practically writhing with want, already on the cusp when he hasn't even started yet. "Do you want me to?"

Everything about him is an aphrodisiac: his voice that's barely a rumbling growl in the dark like thunder on a steamy night, the way his hands have pinned my thighs, spreading me open, wet and hot and at his mercy. And I *like* him, too. He gets me; he makes me laugh.

I have finally cracked the Sizzle Paradox. He's about to take me over the edge in so many ways, and I answer, my voice a breathless gasp, "Yes. Please. Yeah."

A rough thumb swipes over me, up over my most sensitive part, and my back arches of its own volition. I moan, my fists tightening on the covers, and in response, he plants chaste, featherlight kisses over the trail his thumb just covered, pausing extra-long on the spot that causes me to let go of the covers and grab his hair instead, pushing him down into me. He chuckles and obliges, his tongue pressing harder as he licks me, going agonizingly slow, dipping into every crevice, relishing every part of me.

"Oh my God." My eyes close, every nerve ending in my body focusing on the pleasure emanating from that one point.

"Lyric. You taste so fucking good." His hot breath fans over me as he kisses me down my upper thighs, and then slowly loops back up to my slick wetness. My thighs quiver, and sensing how close I am, he picks up the pace, his tongue circling my clit now, his mouth fixing around it firmly. He begins to suck.

That's all it takes. I buck into him, crying out as I come, wave after wave after wave of the most delicious orgasm crashing into me. He holds me steady, won't let me go as his mouth keeps working, determined to coax out every last tremble from every nerve and muscle.

Finally, when I am spent, when all that's left is a warm,

golden glow in my limbs, the man I can't see climbs out from under the covers. "Thank you," I whisper, running a shaky hand through his hair as he lays his head on my bare chest. "That was . . . Wow. Thank you."

He looks up at me, his dark eyes meeting mine in the dim light. He smiles. "You're welcome, LB."

I jerk awake into my bright, sunlit bedroom, wet and tangled in my sweat-softened sheets. For a long moment I'm completely disoriented, the light of day at odds with my dream, which is already fading like mist.

Wait, what was I dreaming about, exactly? And why'd I start awake like that? I scrunch up my face and take note of my body. I'm thoroughly, completely sweaty, and my muscles feel like jelly—all the classic signs of a sex dream. My heart is pounding, though whether from the dreamgasm or something else, I don't know.

Wisps of the dream come back to me: a guy I felt a definite bond with, under the covers, big hands pinning me down. My thighs quivering as I hovered on the brink of an earth-shattering orgasm. The guy lying on my chest after. Him looking up at me, and—

I sit bolt upright in the bed, one hand clasped to my mouth as the comforter pools around my waist. My pulse is flying.

Oh

my

God.

Did I just have a sex dream about *Kian*?

My gaze catches on the full-length mirror across from my

bed. My eyes are wide, my hair's sticking up in twenty-six directions as if I really did have sex, my hand's still clamped around my mouth. I let it drop, slowly, and concentrate on taking a few deep, slow breaths. They rasp in and out of my throat, my entire body feeling shaky.

What the fuck. What the actual fuck! I had an oral sex dream about my best friend. My roommate. Montgomery, who isn't even *close* to being a viable partner. Where the hell did that come from?

I reach over and grab a crystal from my window—larimar, to restore a feeling of calmness and serenity. I hold the blue stone in my palm, my fist clenched tightly around it, trying to feel its peaceful vibes. Looking at myself in the mirror once I'm marginally calmer, I whisper, "Kian Montgomery, Lyric? What the fucking fuck?"

Bit by bit, as I continue holding the larimar and taking deep breaths, my mind clears. I stop freaking out and shake my head at myself. *You're just stressed. Don't read anything more into this.*

This line of reasoning makes sense, actually, now that I think about it. Kian was the last person I spoke to last night, and I'd been talking with him about the Sizzle Paradox and my thesis. That's it. That's all this was. Just my subconscious putting together a few things that were floating around in my brain. I'm not a pervert; I haven't secretly been harboring desires toward Kian without knowing it.

Setting the larimar aside, I fling off the covers and stand, pulling my hands overhead and doing a light stretch as I check the time.

Be that as it may, I might just eat my breakfast really quickly and head out before Kian wakes up.

Before I leave my room, I get my phone and text my sister Opal.

SOS. I may need you to do a tarot reading for me

She doesn't reply because she's probably still asleep. Opal's not a morning person. Sighing, I square my shoulders to face this already fucking weird day.

Opening my bedroom door, I tiptoe out, looking toward Kian's room—thankfully, the door remains firmly shut.

"Hey, LB."

I jump about two feet in the air. Kian's on the couch, drinking a cup of coffee and scrolling through his phone. Setting it aside, he smiles at me. He's shirtless as he usually is when he wakes up, but today my eyes skim across his broad chest and over his abs to the big hand curled loosely around the handle of his Kylo Ren mug before I force my eyes away.

"Oh, um, hey." I smooth my hair back into a bun and hurry into the kitchen.

"Sleep well?" He looks at me over the back of the couch, smiling.

"What?" I ask the question a little too loudly, spinning around to stare at him from behind the tiny kitchen island. "Yes, why? I slept really well, so deeply I didn't even dream. Although, you know, even when you think you don't dream, you *do* dream, you just don't remember it. The dream." I fold my arms over my chest in what I hope is a casual way, because I've just realized I'm wearing a thin white cotton tank top through which my nipples can almost certainly be seen.

Kian looks nonplussed, his coffee forgotten. "Everything okay? You're acting kind of weird."

"I'm not acting weird, maybe you're acting weird. Weirdo." I laugh in a really high-pitched, definitely weird way and then turn around to stare blankly at the cabinets. "You know what?" I spin around and begin to speed walk back to my room. "I'm just going to—I need to get to coffee with Charlie. I'm late. I'll just eat there."

Without waiting for a response, I shut my bedroom door and change into tan shorts and a T-shirt featuring Anna Freud, grab my purse, and fling the door open again as I rush to the front door. Thankfully, Kian is in the shower now; I can hear the water running. Shutting the door behind me once my feet have been shoved into my tennis shoes, I sprint all the way down the stairs and to the coffee shop.

I wait for my other best friend and fellow Ph.D. drudge Charlie Yang at our usual table in Thanks a Latte. It's at the end of the block from the apartment and the baristas don't care how long we linger there, talking or studying, because they're students, too. Because of my desperation to leave the apartment and Kian behind, I'm forty minutes early, but I fill them up by drinking cup after cup of Americano.

By the time Charlie walks in, her silky black hair damp from the misting spring rain, I'm jittery and have freaked myself out once again and am careening wildly between *It's fine! The sex dream meant nothing!* to *I'm a pervert, a horrible, depraved pervert who deserves to be locked in a special prison for horrible, depraved perverts.*

Seeing me (and being completely oblivious to my manic internal roller coaster), Charlie waves enthusiastically and makes her way forward. "Hey." She scrapes back the metal chair across from me and sits, puffing out the scent of rain and exhaust. "Sorry I'm a few minutes late. You know how Sundays are."

"Yep! No worries!" I hand Charlie her usual latte, which she takes with a sigh of contentment, and force myself to attempt a semblance of normalcy. "Was church busy?"

Charlie, in addition to being a phenomenal data scientist, is also the pastor of her LGBT Korean church. "Oh, yeah. We always get an influx of new people once it begins to warm up. Which is great, but also a little hectic for a grad student who has a million things going on in the spring." She looks at me and makes a face.

I stare at her unable to respond, feeling like a giant stick with no feelings except one, mired in my deep shame.

Frowning, she sets her coffee down. "Are you . . . okay?"

"Yes!" It comes out like a squeak. I down half my Americano, set it down with a clatter, and then look at her, my feet tapping wildly on the floor. "Why?"

Charlie raises one thin eyebrow. "Because you're acting like you took a hit of meth before you came here?"

"I may have gotten here forty minutes early and drunk my weight in coffee," I confess in a rush. I can tell my eyes aren't blinking, but feel powerless to remedy that.

Charlie puts one cool hand over mine, stilling it. I didn't realize I was tapping the tabletop with my fingernails until she does. "What's going on, Doc?" She's using her nickname for me, which is a clear sign she's either feeling especially fond of me or is concerned out of her skull. I'm going to go out on a limb and say it's the latter right now.

I open my mouth to say the words and then stop when they get stuck somewhere in my throat. Pulling my hand from under Charlie's, I take a desperate sip of hot coffee in the hopes it'll jar the words loose. A small group of undergraduates in the corner begin to argue about statistical inferences and confidence intervals but I don't even have the heart to fully listen in.

Looking Charlie right in her compassionate, soft eyes, I say, finally, "I had a very graphic sex dream about Kian." And then I put my forehead on the table with a *thunk* and decide I will live in this position from now on.

It takes Charlie a full five seconds to process what I've said. I can tell when it hits her because she gasps long and loud. "You *what*?"

I roll my head back and forth, still refusing to look up. My face is on fire. "Yeah. It's . . . not great."

"Lyric." I wait for her to continue. "*Lyric*."

Slowly, I sit up and force myself to meet her eye. My skin is probably a lovely shade of second-degree burn right now.

"Is there something there? I mean, do you have . . . feelings for him?"

Charlie is so serious, I burst out laughing. "Oh my God! *No!*" I continue laughing for another minute while Charlie stares, clearly wondering whether to utilize one of her giraffe tranquilizers on me. I dab my eyes with a napkin and lean forward. "*No,* Charlie. It was just a sex dream. That's it."

She relaxes a little at whatever she sees on my face. "Okay. So what's the big deal, then?" Picking up her latte, she takes a sip.

I squawk indignantly as an ambulance races by outside. "Are you serious? This is *Kian* we're talking about." I lower my voice when I say his name; the baristas all know and love him.

Actually, I wouldn't be surprised if that group of undergrads know him, or even the paramedics who just passed by in their ambulance. Kian's a minor celebrity wherever he goes—everyone wants to either date him or be his BFF. It's sickening. "He's my best friend. And my roommate, for Christ's sake." I take another sip of my coffee. "It's fucking awkward is what it is. I had to practically hide and run out of the apartment today; I couldn't face him after."

Charlie laughs. "Chill, Doc. It's not that big a deal. It's just a sex dream. It's not like you can control your subconscious. I mean, you're a psych scientist; you know that better than I do."

I make a face. "I guess."

"No, seriously. You've been obsessing about the Sizzle Paradox so much. It's only natural that your brain's going to latch on to the most available male around."

I consider her over my mug. Hadn't I thought that very thing this morning? It was a desperate attempt to reassure myself I wasn't a pervert, but still. Charlie coming to the same conclusion gives me a lot of hope. "You really think so?"

"Mm-hmm." She nods firmly, her bangs falling forward with the motion. "Stop overthinking it. I'm sure a bunch of stuff just got entangled in there and came out as this sex dream. It probably has nothing to do with Kian."

My shoulders relax for the first time since I woke up this morning. I even manage a smile. "You know what? I just offered to hook him and Zoey up, so maybe that had something to do with it. And I remember thinking something about the Sizzle Paradox during the dream."

Charlie slaps the table with her flat palm, making the napkins jump. "There you go, classic stress dream. Your brain just inserted Kian in there because you'd talked to him last, probably, before going to bed."

I nod before she's even done speaking. "Exactly. *Exactly.* We were studying together until pretty late in the night."

Charlie gives me an *I'm a genius* look and pretends to buff her fingernails. "Yep, told ya. Nothing to freak out about."

I relax so much I'm sure I look like a deflating balloon. "So . . . I'm not a depraved, sex-crazed maniac?"

"Hell no." Charlie leans back in her chair. "You're a woman with a healthy sex drive and a stressful career. Nothing wrong with either of those."

I blow out a breath and smile. I'm okay. Everything's fine.

Charlie lifts her cup to her lips and then pauses. "Seriously, though? You're gonna set him up with Zoey?"

"Yeah, why? What's wrong with Zoey?"

"Nothing. She's really cute." Charlie waggles her eyebrows. "I just don't see the two of them together is all."

I shrug. "Yeah. Kian kinda said the same thing. But he's in a dating rut and as his best friend, I think it's my duty to help him out of it."

Charlie nods and takes a sip of her latte. "Well, if you ever want to help me out of mine, please do. But I'm only looking for a relationship that can exist outside of the confines of the twenty-three hours a day I spend on my career."

I snort. "I hear you. How's the thesis coming along?"

"Oh, same old same old. Man, I can't wait to graduate in two years. It'll be here before I know it." Charlie grins. "I'm lucky my advisor let me expand on my master's thesis. It's saved me so much time on data collection." She sobers up when she sees my expression. "I'm guessing you're still having problems moving forward?"

I put my elbows on the table and my head in my hands. "So. Many. Problems. I feel like a total fraud, Charlie. I'm seriously starting to wonder if I'm in the wrong field altogether. I mean, what makes me the expert on something I *clearly* have no experience with? I'm supposed to be giving people *advice* on how to make their relationships stronger? What a joke."

Charlie gasps. "No!" Leaning forward over our table, she says, in this fierce voice I love her for, "Don't you even *think* about quitting, Lyric Rae Bishop. You're just over a year away from graduating. Don't go soft on me now."

I look up at her, my shoulders sagging. "I know. But Charlotte Alexandra Yang, I'm floundering here. If I can't make a go of it at a real relationship, one where I feel the romance *and* the sexual chemistry, am I really the scientist who should be analyzing data about couples who've found it? What if I have unconscious biases that flow in there and disrupt my interpretation of the data? What if I end up hurting people instead of helping them?"

She considers me over her cup. "What happened with Paul, the hottie Scottie?"

"Gone." I wave my hand in the air as two middle-aged people walk in, brushing the rain out of their hair. Probably professors. "I also met some other dude at Target yesterday—a Benedict Cumberbatch look-alike—but he's gone, too. I have had two serious relationships, ever: one that had amazing sexual chemistry and very little emotional connection, and the other that had all the romance but none of the heat. It seems having both at the same time is completely impossible for me."

Charlie shakes her head sadly as she takes another sip of her coffee; she hasn't had a girlfriend in almost a year. As her close friend, I'm somewhat offended at women and their refusal to see the obvious—Charlie's cute, brilliant, and extremely loyal. "You know what the problem is? We nerds are schooled in everything from the theory of relativity to plate tectonics, but not on how to cultivate a healthy, well-balanced relationship that can go the distance."

I scoff and wipe a drop of spilled coffee with my napkin. "Then I guess Kian didn't get the memo. He has absolutely no problem finding relationships that could go somewhere. They're only short-lived because he wants them to be. Case in point: He told me yesterday that he and Kiley broke up. She didn't take it well. I bet Kian could be married by now if he really wanted to."

Charlie considers me. "Wouldn't it be great if he could impart some of his knowledge to you? If you had, like, even a third of his knowledge, your love life would be a lush garden of delights."

"Right? If only."

We change the subject and begin to talk about the tongue muscles of the tube-lipped nectar bat and how it relates to Charlie's research.

On my way back home after coffee, my phone pings with a text.

Opal: Hey. You still want that tarot reading?

Smiling, I text her back. False alarm. Everything's good.

And it is. For a while.

Chapter Six

*
*

LYRIC

On Monday, at the lab, I stare at the back of Zoey's head for way longer than is normal or acceptable in human society. I know I talked a big game to Kian, but now that the moment is actually here, I'm a little nervous.

Unfortunately, she looks up at me while I'm midstare. Her face freezes, like she's not sure what to do now that she's figured out her labmate is a psychopath. "Hey?"

I put on a grin that, in hindsight, probably only serves to freak her out more. "Hey! Whatcha working on there?" I gesture to her computer, on which she has been typing away diligently (I could really learn a lot from Zoey Jones).

"This freaking software." Zoey grumbles under her breath

and jabs at her computer. "I can't get it to run this analysis, for some reason. Do you know what's going on with it?"

I get out of my chair and walk over, leaning to look at her screen. "Oh, you've got the t-test option checked. You need to run a one-way ANOVA."

"Ahh, thanks," Zoey says, smiling up at me, both relief and gratitude shining in her eyes. "I know inferential statistics is all part of the job, but sometimes it makes me want to jab my eyes out."

"No worries." I brush her off, then realize now would be the perfect time to bring up what I really need to bring up, since Kian's going to be here later this afternoon, thanks to my encouragement. "Um, actually . . . I kinda wanted to ask you something."

Zoey raises her thin, plucked eyebrows. "Oh?"

"Yeah . . . so, are you seeing anyone currently?"

She looks unimpressed. "I thought you were straight."

"Huh?" The realization that Zoey thinks I'm hitting on her—and that she's clearly not interested—dawns on me. Awkward. "Oh, yeah, no, I am. I, actually . . . I'm asking for my roommate."

"Oh." She frowns. "Who? Kian?"

I nod. "Kian Montgomery. He's a really great guy and he's currently unattached, which, let's face it, is pretty rare for him." I snort at my own joke, then take note of the fact that Zoey doesn't look remotely amused. "He really is amazing. And, I mean, you've seen him, right?"

Zoey nods slowly, twirling her pencil between two fingers. "Yeah . . . he's definitely hot." She shrugs. "I don't know, though.

I mean, I've dated my fair share of people I had absolutely nothing in common with. I'm not in the market for another one."

I laugh and sit back down in my chair, basking in the unhealthy glow of the fluorescent lights overhead. "Tell me about it. But Kian's really smart, and he's a great conversationalist. You guys will probably have a lot more in common than you think. It'll be good for him to date someone like you. And who knows? You might find true love yourself."

Zoey smirks. "If I do, I promise I'll let you scan me in the fMRI machine."

"So you'll meet him?" I sit up straighter. "You'll give him a shot? Because he's coming by the lab this afternoon. You guys could chat."

She cocks her head and studies me. "Sure, I'll give this a shot. What do I have to lose?"

I grin at her. "Excellent. I promise you won't regret it."

When she turns back to her workstation, I pull out my phone and text Kian.

You're in. WEAR SOMETHING NICE

KIAN

I visit Lyric on Monday afternoon as planned. I've made an effort per her instructions, dressing nicely in a newish *The Office* T-shirt and shorts that don't have rips in them.

She's at her desk, as usual, in the run-down grad student

office (generously called a "lab" by the experimental psych department) she shares with two other harried psych grad students, one of them Zoey. They each have their own desktop computers on which they run statistical software, analyze data, and—I know from having watched Lyric all these years—spill frustrated tears.

This afternoon, the lab is empty except for Lyric. She spins around in her chair when I knock on her door. "Hey."

"Yo, LB." I duck slightly to get through the doorway, step in, and survey the two other empty chairs. "Where are the others?"

"Ahmed is TA'ing a class and Zoey's—" She stops, her laser gaze narrowing in on the package I hold in my hands. "Wait. What's that?"

Grinning, I hold out the greasy white paper bag. "I figured you wouldn't have stopped for lunch."

"Oh my God." Lyric snatches it greedily and opens it, inhaling deeply. "Aaaah. Bless you, Kian Montgomery." She sinks back in her chair, apparently in a blissful scent coma. "The fragrance of greasy, heart-attack-inducing calzones from Poppa's is better than sex, I swear."

I snort and sink into Ahmed's empty chair, stretching my legs out, eating up almost the entire floor between us. "You haven't been having sex with the right people, then."

There's a weird flicker of something on Lyric's face, and her cheeks get very slightly pink as she studiously avoids eye contact with me, but the moment passes before I can ask about it. Recovering, she points at me. "You're not wrong, my friend, you're not wrong. But I don't even care right now. I kid you not, my mouth is already filling with saliva. The only thing I've eaten today is a toasted bagel from that sketchy vendor on Eighth." After a pause and extremely reluctantly, she puts the calzone back. "But this is going to have to wait. We have a mission to undertake."

I sigh. "Yep. Zoey Jones."

Lyric levels a look at me. "You could sound *slightly* more enthusiastic."

Immediately, I put on a giant smile. "Is that better?"

She raises an eyebrow. "A little creepy, but I'll take it. Just keep an open mind, okay?" When I raise my hands in surrender, she stands, sets the bag gently on her desk, and pats it. "I'll be back soon, baby. I promise."

I roll my eyes and follow her out of the office. "You really need to get out more."

We walk down the cement back stairwell, passing a cluster of suited professors as we go, none of whom pays us any attention. On the first floor, I pop open the exterior door with the heel of my hand and hold it for Lyric.

As she steps past me into the outside air, she says, "Zoey's probably at the picnic table she likes to eat lunch at while she reads a book."

I glance down at her in surprise as we begin to walk together, cutting across the green lawn. The day is gloriously sunny, with just a hint of crisp coolness around its edges. "She doesn't eat with other people?"

"Nope." Lyric gives me a look. Harried undergrads pass us, their backpacks bigger than they are. One of the girls does a double take at me, but I'm too focused on Lyric to give her my trademark cocky smile. "There's nothing wrong with eating alone, Montgomery. You should try it sometime."

"Right." I nod. "Got it. I'll add that to the running 'Lyric Bishop's self-improvement tips' list I'm keeping in my head. One day I'll publish a book."

Lyric punches me lightly on the arm, her fist small and ineffectual against my tricep. "Wow, what a total dork. Oh look, there she is."

Zoey's in a green dress with her hair in a complicated-looking braid today, and she's sitting at a picnic table under an old elm tree. She seems to be reading a nonfiction book about the Black Death while picking at a sensible kale salad.

Lyric strides across the grass with me in tow and smiles when Zoey looks up, frowning slightly, the lenses of her glasses glinting in the sun.

"Hey!" Lyric says. "Here he is! Kian Montgomery himself! In the flesh!"

What the fuck? *That's* her idea of a smooth in? I give my idiot best friend a withering look, and she gives me a not-so-subtle wink, as if she's super pleased with herself.

I stifle a sigh and turn to Zoey, who looks understandably nonplussed by this dumbass introduction, her fork hovering in the air. "Um . . . hi?" she says.

"Isn't he so cute?" Lyric beams at her and Zoey stares blankly back.

Good God. Time to make my move before she totally torpedoes my reputation on this campus.

"Thanks for the most awkward introduction ever," I whisper, just loud enough for Lyric to hear, and nudge her aside with my fingertips. And then I step forward, my most brilliant Kian Montgomery smile on display, the one that makes my dimple prominent. "Hey, Zoey! It's good to see you again."

"Right, yeah, you, too." Zoey sets her fork down and smiles up at me, though it is definitely rictus in quality. Honestly, who can blame her?

I kind of just want to leave. But Lyric's standing there, looking all excited and pleased with herself, and I can't bring myself to just walk away. Plus, it'd be rude to Zoey.

So I rally, turning the wattage up on my smile and gesturing at her book. "So the Black Death, huh? Are you in the plague camp or the hemorrhagic fever camp?"

Zoey blinks down at her book and then back up at me. "Um, the hemorrhagic fever camp, actually." She pauses, her eyelashes fluttering. "You know about the alternate theory of the Black Death?"

"Oh, yeah," I say easily. "Epidemiology is one of my other interests. I almost considered getting my degree in that instead of environmental chemistry."

"That's cool." Zoey pushes her glasses up with her free hand.

I wait a beat, my smile still bright, but I can feel the tepid energy between us evaporating in the sunlight. Zoey obviously feels it, too; after a beat, she goes back to her book and her salad.

Lyric turns to me, confusion written all over her face.

I grab her by the elbow and say, to Zoey, "Talk to you later."

Zoey raises her fork-holding hand without even looking up at us.

When we're far enough away that she can't hear us anymore, Lyric asks, "What *happened*? It was going so well! You guys were bonding! Black Plague, death, epidemiology! She was into all the weird shit you're into!"

I wrap an arm around her shoulders and sigh as we make our way back to her lab. "Nothing happened, Lyric. That's the problem. What you witnessed was a supreme lack of sizzle."

ტ

Lyric's still in disbelief when we get back to the lab. She tucks into her Italian calzone morosely, hot grease and sauce spurting all over her chin.

I spin in half circles in her absent labmate Ahmed's chair. "I just don't think it's going to work."

"But she was impressed," Lyric counters. "I know she was; I saw it! And that's no easy task." After a pause, she adds, "I'm sorry if it's disgusting listening to me talk while I eat, but I don't care. This calzone waits for no woman."

I wave my hand in the air; I know how Lyric gets about food. "This one isn't gonna go anywhere, Lyric. That happens sometimes. Even with a stud like me." I grin.

She dabs her mouth with a napkin and rolls her eyes. "No, it's just . . . I know we can make this work. You guys just need to give this another shot."

I pick up a pen and roll it around my palm. "I mean . . . is there a reason I need to? If neither of us are feeling it, neither of us are feeling it."

Lyric shrugs, takes another bite of her calzone, and chews thoughtfully. Once she's swallowed, she says, "If you absolutely don't want to give this a try, I'm not going to force you. But I saw the way you were this weekend, Kian. I think you just need to shake things up, try something different. And I talked to Zoey today; she was definitely willing to give it a shot, too. Just because this first meeting didn't have fireworks and sparklers doesn't mean you can't have that in the future."

I consider her words while I click the pen open and closed. She's not wrong. This weekend with Kiley and then Mariana was a low point. I don't want to feel like that forever, like a romantic failure, like something's wrong with me.

I lean back in Ahmed's chair with a mighty squeak. "You know, you could probably teach me a lot about going out with someone like Zoey. I've never dated someone like her, but you guys have a lot in common."

Lyric looks at me over her steaming calzone, which has been demolished by her appetite and unrelenting jaws. "Mm. It's funny you say that. Charlie told me yesterday that you should be my tutor to help me crack the Sizzle Paradox."

I half smile. "Except I'm kind of suffering from it myself now." It stings to admit it.

"So what?" Lyric argues. "At least you have game. Do you know what I'd give to have your gifts? I could probably crack the

Sizzle Paradox like that"—she snaps her fingers—"if I could just learn how to interact with hot guys in a normal, human fashion."

I toss the pen up in the air and catch it, thinking about what she's saying. Mariana, the bartender, was into me. Kiley's still into me. "You're right," I say, feeling a rush of relief. "I still have the Montgomery magic. I just need to channel it correctly to get out of this slump I'm in."

She nods and tucks into her calzone. "Exactly."

LYRIC

I'm about to finish off my calzone—alas—when there's a knock on my lab door. I look up to see Dr. Livingstone, my thesis advisor, leaning in. As usual, he's wearing a button-down shirt with a tweed bow tie. His thick glasses are perched at the end of his nose, and his curly white hair is in a pouf around his head. "Miss Bishop."

"Dr. Livingstone." I feel the usual twist of sickening dread in my stomach when I see him. Don't get me wrong—Dr. Livingstone's been my hero for a long, long time. He's published more than any other professor in the psych department. He was one of the first Black professors to get tenure in the psych department. The day I got the letter saying he'd accepted me to be his only doc student for that particular academic year was probably the happiest of my life.

But all that goodwill has long since shriveled and dried up, on both our sides, and if I'm being fair, the fault is all mine. It's been *months* since I've turned in anything thesis-related for him to look at, because I haven't made any progress. I'm stuck on the Sizzle Paradox, on my utter failure at being in a committed relationship that has both romance and sizzle. And until I can find a relationship like that, the last thing I want to do is work with data on couples who *have* found it. Unfortunately, Dr. Livingstone has no time for my sciencey dramas and existential crises. He's the director of the experimental psych program *and* still manages to publish several papers a year. I'm his greatest disappointment.

When he doesn't say anything, I attempt a weak compliment. "I like your bow tie."

Kian darts me a *do you seriously think a sartorial compliment will make him overlook your scholarly failures* look, but I ignore him, and Dr. Livingstone ignores me.

"You missed another deadline," he says, stepping fully into my office now, bringing a smell of cloves and leather with him. He nods at Kian, who nods back, and then turns the force of his disapproval back on me. "I presume you have a very good reason and the pages you were supposed to turn in are making their way through the maze of servers to me as we speak?"

I wipe my hands on my napkin and avoid eye contact like the coward I am. "Well . . . not exactly."

There's a weighty silence. "Ms. Bishop, do I have the facts right? You did, in fact, apply to the experimental psychology doctoral program five years ago? The expectation being that, were you to be granted admission, you'd then embark on and complete a thesis in time for graduation in six years. And that six years expires next spring."

I give him an anemic smile, wanting to melt into my chair. Kian has gone very quiet as he watches this exchange. "Right so far."

Dr. Livingstone continues, not to be interrupted now, when he's finally caught me in my lab. "And that thesis, which *you* chose, Ms. Bishop, is a brilliant, proprietary study of your own design: measuring the levels of oxytocin and dopamine in the brain as study subjects gaze upon pictures of their partners, which in turn inform us of their sexual and romantic attraction toward said partners. Your intention was to further study those who have the strongest attraction—both sexual and romantic—to their partners in order to see what helpful information we could glean from *them*. Do I have that correct?"

"Yes, you do." I try not to sigh.

"Quite ambitious of you. I remember saying that to you when I admitted you into the program. But you were optimistic. You said it wouldn't take long at all to undertake a project of this caliber. As I recall, your exact words were, 'Six years will be *too many*, Dr. Livingstone. You'll see.'"

He glares at me sternly and I try not to squirm.

"And as I understand it," he continues, "you have collected data, which I have indeed seen. Thousands of samples, in fact. But you promised me a *paper* discussing the analysis of that data and . . . where is that, Ms. Bishop?"

I look up at him and begin to pull apart a Post-it pad like a dog with separation anxiety. Except for me it's anxiety at being too close to Dr. Livingstone. If they had a Geiger counter for anxiety and waved it near me, it'd be screaming right now. "It's . . . temporarily held up. I'm having some trouble with it."

"I see." Dr. Livingstone's brown eyes pierce me as if I'm a balloon. My conscience and self-esteem both make high-pitched whistling noises of distress. "And what's the trouble?"

"I . . . ah, am having trouble connecting to the data. It isn't talking to me."

Dr. Livingstone turns an alarming shade of crimson. "It isn't *talking* to you? You aren't connecting with it? Are you trying to *write* your thesis, Ms. Bishop, or date it?"

I concentrate on the neon yellow Post-its in my hand. "I know how it sounds. Believe me." My voice is a croak. "I'm just . . . blocked, I think."

A long, slow exhalation as Dr. Livingstone practices his yoga breathing. "All right. Well, I need *something*. It doesn't have to be the whole thing, but I want to see some forward progress. So have some pages to me in three weeks—perhaps an abstract, or an outline of an abstract, even. *Three weeks* or I'm going to have to take remedial action. Do you understand?"

I meet his eye, my stomach sinking into a pool of acid. "Yes. I understand."

With a firm nod, he turns on his leather heel and is gone.

Fuck.

Chapter Seven

LYRIC

I toss the ruin of Post-it Notes in the recycling bin and glance at Kian, who's staring at me. "I know. You can say it. I'm a train wreck."

"LB . . ." He pushes a hand through his hair, looking stricken. "I had no idea things were this bad. Why didn't you tell me? I could've helped."

I look at him with an eyebrow cocked. The fluorescents overhead buzz grimly; that incessant noise is the background music to my life. "I have the data collected. I've even interviewed the couples who scored the highest. I have everything I need to take on this thesis. But . . . I just can't sit there and pretend to be an expert on something I'm so terrible at myself, Kian."

Reaching into my desk, I pull out a stack of printed papers and toss them on the desk between us.

"What's this?" Kian asks, frowning.

"I fMRI'd myself when I was dating Hamish and then again when I was dating Samuel." Kian picks up the readouts and studies them. "Hamish and I had an amazing emotional connection. We stayed up late talking, liked the same documentaries . . . he even liked cooking as much as I do. We talked about taking cooking classes in Paris one day."

Kian traces a bright green line on one of the graphs. "I see that here. Your oxytocin levels reflect your bond."

"Right. But look at the dopamine levels. They're indicative of sexual attraction."

Kian's finger traces a yellow line. "They're low."

"Below average. I worked on raising my sexual attraction to Hamish for months. But eventually, I realized I'd friend-zoned my own boyfriend, and that's when we ended it."

Kian traces the graphs from my fMRI during my time with Samuel. "And it's completely inverted here."

I nod. "Right. All sexual attraction, no emotional connection. I worked on that with Samuel, too, and it went nowhere. I've had only two committed relationships over the past five years, and both of those completely failed. I've never had the kind of data that Dr. Livingstone wants me to analyze. So how can I, in good faith, wax on about something I have no fucking clue about? People are looking to me as an expert on this because I designed this study, but I'm no expert."

I take a breath, trying to calm myself. "So unless you can

crack the Sizzle Paradox and help me find a committed partner who I feel both strongly romantically *and* sexually attracted to, I don't know how you could help me."

Kian blinks, long eyelashes batting like palm fronds on his golden-brown cheeks. "What if I did?" he says slowly.

I glance over my shoulder at my computer screen when it pings with an incoming email. Oh, great. Just Dr. Livingstone, reminding me of his three-week ultimatum. As if I need it. As if it isn't already burned into my auditory nerves. "Did what?" I ask distractedly.

"What if I tutored you on how to find someone you're sexually and romantically attracted to, just like Charlie said?"

I jerk my head around to look at him so fast I almost get whiplash. "What? How would you do that? I don't think this is something you can teach through sketching me out a blueprint."

He kicks my foot with his giant one as I reach for my water bottle. "I know that. I'm talking about taking you out on dates."

It's the most unfortunate time for me to be midswallow. I almost choke on my water, and Kian has to reach over and pound on my back. When I'm done coughing, I hold up a hand.

"Okay, okay, I'm good," I croak, looking at him through watery eyes. "Are you serious? You and me—on *dates*?" A brief flash of sex-dream Kian lying on my bare chest and smiling up at me comes to me and I push it firmly away. *No*. Bad brain.

He scoffs and leans back, making the poor chair suffer and groan. "Not actual dates, obviously. But, like, fake dates. Dates that are just designed to point out what you might be doing wrong and how you can correct your behavior. So you can stop sabotaging yourself before you even give a guy a chance. It's a data exchange, one scientist to another." He gestures between the two of us.

I study his serious expression. "So what you're saying is, this would be a purely academic exercise. Nothing else."

"Exactly." He crosses his leg in that way guys do, ankle resting on top of knee. "I want you to graduate on time, you know, so you can come join me out in the real world sooner rather than later."

I quirk my mouth in a half smile. "Thanks. I think. But what are *you* gonna get out of it?"

Kian shrugs. "I don't really need anything."

I think hard, not pleased with his answer. "That doesn't seem fair." Sitting up straighter as an idea occurs to me, I say, "Hey. What if I coach you on the right and wrong things to say to get to Zoey? Like you said, she's more like me than any other girl you've ever dated."

He rubs the back of his head. "Ah, I don't know. . ."

"Come on," I press. "Do you want to be in this weird no-woman's land forever?"

He doesn't look convinced, but he shrugs. "Ah, what the hell. If it's time spent with you, I guess it's not a waste even if nothing comes from it."

I reach into my desk drawer, pull out a notepad and pen, and turn back to him. "Okay. So. If we're going to do this, I think we need to establish some ground rules."

"Ground rules?" asks Kian, who has never met a rule in his life that he hasn't shattered to smithereens. "Like what?"

"Well, who's going to bankroll these dates, for instance? We're both poor grad students."

He waves a hand in the air. "Some poorer than others." Kian's job as a part-time environmental chemist in a for-profit lab pays way better than mine as a TA. "I'll pay for the dates."

"No, no, no." I waggle my pen at him. "I want this to be egalitarian. Why don't we split the expense of the dates? You'll do one and I'll do one."

"All right."

I write that down. Then, not quite meeting his eye, I say, "And naturally, this doesn't need to be said, but . . . no physical stuff like a real date has."

Kian laughs heartily. "That definitely doesn't need to be said."

I scowl at him; he doesn't need to make it sound like I'm some repulsive species of sea cucumber. "And how long will we be doing this experiment?"

"Your deadline's in three weeks, so at least that long, I think. Long enough for you to be able to begin connecting with your data again so you can give Dr. Livingstone something to appease him."

"Yeah." I tap the pen on my chin. "But three weeks is probably not going to be enough to get everything down pat and find me a viable partner."

"Probably not," Kian agrees.

"So I'll send Dr. Livingstone a little bit of something in three weeks, but can we keep working on this for, say, a month and a half?"

"Sounds good to me."

I write down the time line for our fake dates on my notepad, then sign it at the bottom. "Here." I pass the pad and pen to my best friend. "Sign it. Let's make it official."

He takes them from me, solemnly scribbles his signature, and hands them back. Then he holds out his hand.

I put the pad and pen away and take his big, warm paw in mine. Looking him seriously in the eye, I say, "Let the dates begin."

KIAN

My buddy Eli and I hike an almost vertical thousand feet up the mountain before we speak about anything substantial. That's the nice thing about Eli—he doesn't feel the need to shoot the shit 24/7 like some of our other friends. And I say that knowing fully that I have been a card-carrying member of the "shoot the shit" party at many points in my life. But sometimes, it's nice to just . . . chill.

It's Tuesday morning, and both Eli and I have it off thanks to the vagaries of a doc student's schedule. I look around at the natural beauty surrounding us—mighty oaks and towering pines, grasses and thick foliage I couldn't name even though their greenness seeps into me. I feel like I can finally breathe here, like my lungs have the oxygen they spend all their time craving when I'm in NYC proper. We're hiking Mt. Tremain, with the sun soaking into our skin and the birds tweeting merrily over our heads. I pause for a minute on the edge of a cliff face; below us, there are miles and miles of trees and streams and dots of color that are people, also out hiking. In the far distance, I see the sparkling steel city, beckoning me back. But it's not time to return yet.

"You ever consider you were meant to be an organic farmer and not an environmental chemist?" Eli's beside me, sipping water from the bladder strapped to his back. His blond hair is matted to his forehead with sweat, but his cheeks are pink with good health.

I chuckle. "Many, many times." Glancing at him before turning back to the vista, I ask, "So how are things with Ava?"

Eli recently got engaged, and he and his fiancée, Ava, have not been able to agree on what kind of wedding they want to have. Every time I've seen them together lately, they've been fighting. Ava wants a big destination wedding with hundreds of guests, but Eli is uncomfortable beginning their wedded life in a mountain of debt. Neither set of parents are in a financial position to pay for it, so it's all up to them.

He clears his throat, clearly uncomfortable. "You know . . . not great."

I nod as a squirrel darts out from the bush on my left and then leaps onto a nearby sycamore. "Still can't decide on a course of action?"

"Hell no. Since a wedding is—hopefully—a once-in-a-lifetime

event, she thinks we should go all out. She wants the memories and the pictures to be special. But I think they can be just as special if we get married in a courthouse in the city. I mean, we're both students, for Christ's sake."

I suck my teeth but don't say anything. This is for Eli to figure out. "Well, I'm glad you're here right now anyway."

"Yeah, me, too." He stretches and his back pops. "Feels good to get out of that damn lab." Eli's a doc student in the chemistry department, too, but he's studying nuclear chemistry and graduates next spring.

"Soon we'll be out for good." I turn and begin to walk again, and Eli follows. He's a good eight inches shorter than me—at six six, I'm used to being the tallest guy in most places—so I make sure to keep my stride shorter so he can keep up.

"Yeah, can you believe it?" He shakes his head and runs his hand along a bush we pass. "I mean, I'm not sure I'm ready for real life."

I laugh. "I feel like I can't *wait* for real life. Being a student is fine when you're a certain age, but I'm in my midtwenties. Time to grow the fuck up."

Eli snorts. "Really? I never thought I'd live to see the day when Kian Montgomery said he was ready to grow up."

I think about my recent realization about my dating life, but wait until a woman and her barely controlled springer spaniel have passed to tell Eli. "Yeah . . . I'm kind of burned out on the same old dating routine. I told you Kiley and I broke up, right?"

"Yep."

"So after that, I realized my problem is that I need to date a different kind of girl, you know?"

Eli fakes a gasp. "You mean you're not going to pull from the undergrad pool anymore?"

"Hey, Kiley was a grad student." I laugh and step over a giant tree root poking up through the ground. "First year, but still."

Eli shakes his head, still smiling. "So who do you have your eye on?"

"No one, actually. But Lyric really wants me to date Zoey Jones."

He frowns, thinking. "Don't know her."

"She's one of Lyric's labmates in the experimental psych department. I've only talked to her once, but Lyric seems to think I should give it a shot." I'm aware I sound totally unenthusiastic, but can't bring myself to lie to Eli.

"Huh." Eli scratches his jaw.

"What?"

"Nothing, just . . . why don't you go out with Lyric?"

I belly laugh.

"What?" Eli asks, hopping up on a boulder in our path and then off again as I go around it. "Lyric's hot if you like tall girls. Which I'd think you would." He makes a show of craning his neck to look up at me to make his point. "And you guys obviously get along great. You're practically an old married couple at this point."

"Nah, man." I shake my head and then tip it back to catch the sun's rays on my face. "Lyric and I . . . we're buddies. Nothing more than that. We've seen each other's awkward undergrad puking-after-you-drink-too-much days. She's gorgeous, yeah, and I've never met someone I enjoy being around so much. I'd be lying if I said I *never* thought about it, but . . . it'd be too weird to date her at this point, I think." I pause and cock my head. "Although I guess I technically will be soon."

"Huh?" Eli looks confused.

"We have a deal—I'm gonna tutor her to help with her thesis."

Eli has this cocky half smile on his face that I don't really like. "Tutor her on her thesis on *sexual* chemistry? Mm-hmm."

I give him a withering look as we hug a narrow switchback, winding our way steadily higher. "Yeah, not so much. I'm gonna give her some pointers on the social part of dating."

"Seriously?" He looks at me, incredulous. "So you're gonna be taking her on dates and shit? Your best *girl* friend?"

"We're gonna take each other, yeah. It's not a big deal. I'm just taking her to Pepper Tony, our usual pizza place, this weekend. I'm like her coach. As Lyric put it, it's 'purely an academic exercise.'"

Eli doesn't look convinced. "Okay. Just be careful, man. If you really have no interest in dating her for real, you don't want to make things weird, being roommates and all. You still have to live with her for a couple more months."

"I'm aware." I catch at a piece of dandelion fluff floating through the air. A couple more months. And then the era of Lyric and Kian will be at an end. Just like that.

We fall silent then, as the incline ramps up to take us to the summit of the mountain.

LYRIC

I'm walking home from the lab at dusk. This is usually my favorite time of day, when the day's work is done and I know a nice hot plate of something yummy and an episode of *New Girl* (my ten thousandth rewatch; I love it so much I splurged and bought all seven seasons so I can watch it whenever I want) are waiting for me at home. I say "usually" because my phone has just rung, and the cacophonous custom ringtone of birds and rainfall means it's my mother on the other line. And she only ever calls (instead of texting) when something's gone fucky with my aberrant little brother, Max.

"Mom?"

"Lyric, oh, I'm so glad I caught you," she says, all breathless. I can picture her in some floaty tunic with a billion bangles jangling on her wrists and her mala beads clacking together.

"It's Max, isn't it?" I adjust my messenger bag and try not to sigh as I wait for the light to change so I can cross the street. Beside me, a throng of grad students and assistant professors with earbuds scroll on their phones.

"How did you know?"

I snort. "What do you mean? What else could it be except the resident black sheep of the family?"

"Lyric Rae Bishop, you know he's just trying to find himself. It'll happen in the blink of an eye and our Max will be all grown up."

"Our Maxie Pad will never grow up if you don't push him out of the nest," I counter, as I begin to walk across the street. Down the block, two taxis honk like angry geese. I wait until it's relatively quiet to speak again. "What is it this time?"

"Nothing in particular . . . he's just been acting peculiar. You know, distant. Not coming home to get his laundry done. Turning down home-cooked meals to go do Goddess knows what." She sighs. "I wonder if it's a self-esteem issue. He swears he's fine, but a mother knows these things. I told him today, I said, Max, I drew the Knight of Wands for you. That means you're about to go on an exciting adventure, a new beginning. Keep your eyes open for that. But does he listen? No. He never does."

I make a noncommittal noise and go around a dog walker with about thirty exuberantly happy dogs. "All I can say is, I hope his new adventure doesn't involve more jail time. He should get better hobbies. Has he considered training guide dogs?"

My mom makes a groaning sound in her throat. "Anyway, that's enough of him. What's my Lyric up to?"

For just a moment, I consider telling her about my tutoring session with Kian coming up. But then I realize she'll probably want to pull out her tarot deck and do a fifty-card spread for me right here over the phone, and I decide to keep that little tidbit to myself. "Ah, nothing. Just, you know, heading home after

TA'ing three undergrad stats courses today. I'm pretty tired." Out of nowhere, a giant yawn overtakes me.

I can hear the smile in my mom's voice as she responds. "Well, I love you, honey. Don't work too hard, and get some rest. We'll see you soon, okay? Amethyst and Willow were saying it's been too long since we've all been together at once."

"Yeah, it really has." Mostly because wrangling my four adult siblings and eighty-five of my extended relatives who all live within a ten-block radius of each other is a full-time job.

"Dad sends his love, too. We're proud of you, you know. Our Ivy League scientist."

My cheeks warm at the undeserved compliment. Little does she know what a train wreck my career really is. "Oh, Mom. Love you both. I'll come home soon." I end the call and turn on to the street where Kian and I live.

I think about what she said, about Max acting weird, and hope he isn't into drugs. But no matter what's going on, I decide, I'm going to be there for him and the rest of my family.

Chapter Eight

*
*

KIAN

Saturday night is a 10/10 as far as perfect date-night setups go—crisp and clear. The buildings in the city shine like lit torches, and lights from the constant traffic shine like neon streamers. I stop and look at the blazing brightness for a moment as I walk home from the bodega on the corner. NYC can turn night into day like no other place in the world. If this were a real date, it'd be pretty damn romantic. Eli's warning flashes in my brain and I push it mentally away. Lyric and I are fine. We both know the rules, we both know it's *just* us doing each other a solid. It's what friends do.

I walk in the front door and look around for Lyric, but then notice that her bedroom door is closed. She's probably getting dressed; we're supposed to leave in fifteen minutes for the pizza place. She insisted on paying for this one, so I bought her a present instead. You know, to get her into the date mindset.

I knock on her door.

"What!" she yells, her voice muffled as if her head's stuck in her shirt.

I shake my head. "I am your date," I say in a slightly affected formal way. "And I'm here with a gift."

A few moments later, the door is wrenched open and Lyric stands there, her hair staticky and her expression confused. "Huh?" She looks me up and down. "Wow. You're all dressed up."

I'm not; I've just exchanged my usual faded T-shirt for a well-fitting, simple black T-shirt and jeans and combed my hair. I take in her disheveled state. "And you're . . . not."

"No." She points to the wine bottle and small bouquet of yellow roses in my hands. "What's that?"

"I always like to bring a little something for my first date with a woman." I hold them out and smile my charming, patented Kian Montgomery first-date smile (the secret is that it's really part smolder).

"Oh, um, wow. Really?" Lyric is looking at the flowers and wine as if I'm asking her to take two poorly assembled bombs. Then, after a moment, she snatches them out of my hands. "Thanks." Giving me a lopsided, slightly nervous smile, she adds, "Do you know that sending a hundred million roses, the amount purchased on the average Valentine's Day, produces around nine thousand metric tons of carbon dioxide emissions from the field to the florist?"

I narrow my eyes. What's happening here? Why is she acting

so stiff and awkwa— And then it occurs to me. She's in date mode now. This is how she acts on dates. Oh, dear God. "LB . . ." I cock my head. "Maybe just a 'they're so beautiful' will suffice?"

She looks down at the flowers, apparently dumbfounded by the suggestion. "Oh. Right. Sure." She turns and sets the bottle and the flowers on her dresser, which is already piled high with textbooks, notebooks, Post-it Notes, markers, and various tote bags. They're all in neat piles, though. If we didn't live in a dollhouse-sized NYC apartment, she'd probably have specific places for all these things.

I take in her faded Columbia T-shirt and sweatpants. "Is that what you're wearing?"

She looks down at herself and then up at me. "Yeah. Why? It's just pizza, right?"

"Yes, but this is a *date*. You have to put in effort."

"Yeah, but it's a fake date with *you*."

I shake my head and walk to her dresser, yanking open the drawer I know she keeps her shirts in. "Uh-uh. If we're going to do this exercise or tutoring or whatever you want to call it, you have to respect the spirit of the thing. Dress and act like you really would on a date. Here." I pull out a slithery, filmy teal tank top with sparkly straps. "Wear this."

Lyric scoffs. "*That?* I bought that for a skit the psych department put on last Christmas. I was a mermaid."

I'm barely listening while I rummage through her pants drawer. "And these jeans." I toss her a pair of dark-wash skinny jeans and turn to survey her hair. "And wear your hair down. You have really nice hair."

She picks up her slightly bedraggled ponytail and looks at the end of it as if making its acquaintance for the first time. "I do?"

"Yep. It's this pretty honey color and you have natural blond streaks. I had a girlfriend who'd spend hours at the salon to get that." When Lyric darts me a spiky look, I hold up my hands. "I didn't ask her to. She just wanted to. Looked good, though."

Lyric relaxes and studies the clothes in her hands. "Okay. Meet you out in the living room in ten?"

"Yep." I turn to go.

There's a gentle, cool evening breeze as we walk to Pepper Tony about five blocks away, with Lyric stumbling into me every so often. She decided to wear her black ankle boots with three-inch heels that she'd forgotten she'd bought when she was shopping with her sister Opal a few months ago.

I steady her for the fourth time as we pass a group of young professionals—bankers, from the looks of them—waiting to get into a crowded oxygen bar. "Well, it's good you're learning how to walk in these in case you want to wear them on an actual date sometime soon."

"Do they look good?" She adjusts the small purse on her shoulder and shakes her hair back.

"Yeah, really good. They make your legs look two miles long."

She smiles, satisfied. “Excellent.”

“Yep.” I pause, wondering how to phrase the next part delicately, without hurting Lyric’s feelings. “But I think there’s a tiny bit of room for improvement with the, ah, social side of things.”

Her smile fades a little and she sighs. “Why do I seize up and become a stilted colt when hot guys are around, Kian?”

I snort and stick my hands in my pockets. A Tesla passes us slowly on the street, windows down, blaring nineties pop. The driver, a creeper in his late forties, gives Lyric a *hey girl, what’s good* look, but she doesn’t notice. I glare at him until he catches my eye and faces forward. “A ‘stilted colt’? Yeah . . . you’re gonna need to explain that one.”

“You know.” Lyric begins to stumble around even more than she already is, folding and extending her legs as she goes. It’s the most ridiculous thing I’ve ever seen. She turns to me after a few seconds of this, apparently done with her impassioned performance. “A stilted colt. Like a baby horse with really skinny long legs who has no coordination and is defined by its awkward nature.”

I raise an eyebrow as we continue to walk. “Right. Well, you *definitely* nailed that one.” She hits me on the chest and I laugh and put my arm around her. “Don’t worry, LB. We’ll figure it out.”

She glances up at me. “You really think so?”

I squeeze her shoulders. “Yep. The Sizzle Paradox is as good as gone.”

LYRIC

Pepper Tony is packed tonight, but we come here often enough that Antonio, the owner, immediately leads us back to "our" seat in the corner, under a kitschy hanging light shaped like a red pepper with pepper-shaped cutouts in the red plastic. Kian looks pink in its glow, his golden skin seeming to shine with good health even more than usual.

"Thanks, Antonio," he says, as the man hands us the menus. Even though we don't need them. We always get the same thing—half-Hawaiian (me), half-pepperoni (Kian), with one piña colada (me) and one Coors with a lime cork (Kian).

Once Antonio confirms we want the usual, he takes the menus and is gone. I sit back in my narrow booth and smile at Kian, nudging my boots off under the table. Not the most comfy footwear I could've picked, but at least they look hot. "So far so good, right?"

"Yeah." Kian rests his elbows on the table. "But let's not break the fourth wall anymore."

I raise an eyebrow. "Meaning?"

"Meaning, let's pretend this really is a date from now on until we get back to the apartment. So no talking about the Sizzle Paradox or your thesis or any of it—let's just keep it to what we'd say on actual dates."

"Okay." I prop my chin on my fist, look at him from under my eyelashes, and ask in a smoldering voice, "Do you eat a lot of pizza?"

Kian stares at me for a long moment. "I . . . do." I can see him rallying before my eyes. Did I say something wrong? No, according to *Cosmo*, asking a guy about himself is definitely the way to do these things. He looks around Pepper Tony. "This is a nice place." Turning to me with his dashing smile, he adds, "You look cute in peppers." He points to my bare arms, which are covered in little pepper reflections from the hanging light above us.

I laugh, impressed. "Hey, that was a good one! Flirty but cute—" He holds up a big finger as a warning and I remember the fourth wall. Clapping my hand on my mouth, I say, "Oh, sorry." I clear my throat and put my hand down on the table, trying to reset. "Right. Ah, thanks. You . . . look cute in peppers, too?" For fuck's sake. Why is it so ridiculously hard to talk to guys when I'm date-Lyric?

Thankfully, before I can see the disappointment in Kian's eyes, the waiter brings over our drinks. Eagerly, I suck down a quarter of my giant piña colada. Social lubrication. That's what I need. Kian, meanwhile, takes his time sipping on his Coors, looking completely at ease on his side of the booth, even though he takes up almost all of it on his own. "So, tell me about yourself, Lyric Bishop."

I dab my mouth with a napkin to play for time while I think about what I can say that won't add to my awkward potato status. Kian narrows his eyes a little, as if he knows what I'm up to. I put the napkin down, feeling the warmth from the piña colada seeping into me, easing some of my social pain. "I'm a doc student in the experimental psych department at Columbia." Hey, not bad.

"Oh, how cool." Kian leans forward, his brown eyes big and bright with faux interest. "What do you study?"

"Sexual chemistry."

Kian raises a saucy eyebrow. "Really?"

I take another sip of my piña colada, encouraged by his interest. "Yep! Speaking of sex, did you know that ducks have a corkscrew penis?"

Kian stops on his way to take a drink of his beer. "Okay."

"Yeah, it's really neat. And in pigs—"

Kian gives a nearly imperceptible shake of his head. He's breaking the fourth wall to give me some much-needed advice.

"Right." I nibble on my lip and watch a couple at the other end of the tiny restaurant. She's leaning into him, talking quietly, and he's looking at her with shining eyes. Why can't things be that easy for me? Turning my attention back to Kian, I say, "Sexual chemistry is the study of that potent physical connection between two potential sexual partners."

He chews the inside of his cheek, as if weighing whether to say something.

I set my piña colada down; my shoulders slump forward. "I'm shit at this, aren't I?" I don't even care that I'm breaking the fourth wall anymore. These are dire circumstances.

Kian sets his beer down, too, and leans forward to pat my arm. "It's not *that* bad. . . ."

I snort. "Yeah, really convincing, Montgomery."

"You just need some finessing. Here." He sets his hands on the table. "Try asking me what I do, but instead of just asking it, graze the top of my hand with your fingers while you speak."

I squint at him. "And that's good? Sounds hella annoying."

He shrugs. The three students seated beside us laugh uproariously at something, and he speaks over the sound. "I'm telling you, it'll get any guy's attention. Minor physical touch is a total turn-on on first dates."

"Okay." I shake my hands out and look down at his hands, placed oh so casually in front of him on the table, palms down, fingers slightly overlapping. I meet his eye. "What do *you* do?" I try to graze the back of his hands, like he said, only I end up jabbing him with my fingernails.

"Ow." He blinks at me. "Try that again."

"What do you do?" I touch the back of his hands.

"That's more like a grandma pat. We need a sensual *grazing*, LB."

I throw my hands up. "I don't know what I'm doing!"

"Okay, okay, let me. You put your hands on the table and I'll show you."

I do as he asks and wait for him to work his magic.

He leans forward, his eyes going all melty and soft, just a hint of a smile at his lips. "What do you do, Lyric?" As he speaks, his big fingers come to rest lightly on the back of my hand, like butterflies alighting on my skin. He moves them just a touch, softly but surely awakening the nerves there.

I sit up straighter. "Holy shit."

Grinning, he picks up his beer and takes a swig. "Right? I'm telling you, it works."

"That was really good." I look down at my hands, which are

still tingling. Completely out of nowhere, a vision of my sex dream slams into my brain.

"What's up?"

"Hmm?" I look up at Kian, my cheeks heating.

"You got so serious all of a sudden." He frowns. "You okay?"

I take a deep sip of my piña colada. "Yeah, of course. Why wouldn't I be?"

Kian studies me for a long moment, as if he isn't sure he should believe me.

The waiter brings our pizza then and we thank him, each of us getting a slice (or three, in Kian's case) to put on our plates. "Can we be done now?" I ask, taking a bite of my divine Hawaiian. "Please? I'm tuckered out."

Kian laughs. "Okay, let's take a break. We can review after-date procedures once we get back home."

I relax against the booth. "Good." Once I've swallowed my mouthful, I ask, "So? Do you have any questions about Zoey?"

He picks a pepperoni slice off his pizza and chews it thoughtfully. "Not really."

Dissatisfied at his apathy, I decide to offer him some unsolicited advice. "So the hand thing is good, but you're gonna need more than just that to impress Zoey. I think it'll be best if you guys can get a spark going on something intellectual before you ask her out. That comment you made on her plague book was good. You just need to do more of that. Don't force it. You're a smart guy, Kian. She'll like that."

"Great," he says, trying on a smile that doesn't go anywhere.

I shake my head and take a sip of my piña colada. "You sound super enthusiastic."

He sighs. "I know. I'm sorry. I really do appreciate your help. Maybe I just need some more time to warm up to Zoey or something."

"Yeah, that's probably it. Your system's just in shock because she's so different from every woman you've ever dated." I sit up straighter as an excellent idea occurs to me. "Hey! Maybe we should set up, like, a get-together and give you guys another chance to connect."

Kian nods as he demolishes his second slice. "Not a bad idea. And maybe I can invite some fresh meat for you to ask out."

I make a face. "Ew. Don't say 'fresh meat.' But other than that, yeah."

"We should definitely polish up some of your skills, though."

I sigh. "Okay. Tell me what I've done wrong so far. What was so bad about the duck thing?"

Kian makes a face and wipes his mouth with a napkin. "LB, there's so much hot stuff you can say about sexual chemistry without ever having to utter the phrase 'corkscrew penis.'"

"I think it's interesting!"

"It's a real testament to how horny guys are that you've managed to maintain a steady stream of dates and two serious relationships in spite of having no game at all." Seeing something on my face, Kian leans forward and puts a gentle hand on mine. "Your lip's dragging on the floor, Pound. Cheer up; we'll figure all this out. It's basically just a case of training, and you're one of the most hardworking people I know."

I quirk my mouth and look up at him. "Yeah, you're right. I got this."

"You definitely got this." He sits back and picks up his beer again, regarding me thoughtfully. "You know what Eli said to me when I told him we were doing this?"

I shake my head and continue tucking in to my pizza, feeling comforted both by Kian's words and the familiar warm bustle and chatter of the restaurant.

"He thinks we're setting ourselves up for failure."

"What do you mean 'failure'?" I ask around my mouthful of pizza.

Thankfully, Kian is used to deciphering my "can't stop won't stop eating" conversational puzzles. He puts another slice of steaming hot pizza on his plate. "Eli thinks we're going to develop feelings for each other or something."

I almost choke on a pineapple chunk. "What?" Laughing, I take another healthy sip of my piña colada. My body's pleasantly buzzing now. "That's ridiculous! Did you tell him how stupid he is?"

Kian raises a bushy eyebrow. "Not in those words . . . but yeah. I told him things are totally different between you and me. We don't even see each other as potential partners."

I shudder theatrically. "God, no. How big a train wreck would that be?"

Kian grins while he eats his pepperoni slice. "A pretty gigantic one. Not to mention, you're my best friend. Why the hell would I want to potentially ruin what we have by growing feelings for you?"

"Exactly." I slam my palm on the tabletop. "That's *exactly* how I feel. This is the best friendship I've ever had. Ever."

Kian smiles at me and cuffs me gently under the chin. "Aww."

"Shut up." I glare at him for a moment to make sure he understands I am not cute. That done, I continue to eat.

KIAN

By the time we're back in the apartment, Lyric is her usual self and hasn't mentioned the unique male anatomy of any non-human species in an hour, which I take as a win.

I set my wallet and keys down on the table by the front door. "So."

Lyric kicks off her boots and turns to me. "So what?"

"Let's talk about end-of-the-date moves." I step closer to her and she tips her head back to look at me. "Do you have any?"

She scoffs. "Do I seem like the kind of person who'd have any?"

"Okay, good point. Well, I do. Want me to show you?"

Lyric hesitates. "Sure. But, I mean . . . you're not talking about . . . ?"

I raise my eyebrows. "What?"

"*Kissing*, are you?"

I hold up my hands, although my eyes automatically drop to her pink, bow-shaped lips. Just habit from previous dates with other women, obviously. I force them back up to her eyes. "*No.*"

She smiles and spreads out her arms. "Cool. Show me what you got."

"Okay." I take a breath, trying to get back into end-of-date mode, and step close to her, so close that our bodies are almost touching, but not quite. She smells like lemon sugar, thanks no doubt to one of her many foodie-scented lotions. The smile on her face fades as she looks up at me. "I had a nice time," I croon, pitching my voice low, gazing into her blue eyes. Then, very deliberately, pressing the silky fabric of her camisole against her back with my fingertips, I graze my fingers from between her shoulder blades down, following the curve of her back, and stopping at the waistband of her jeans.

We stare at each other for a long moment in silence, Lyric breathing deeply, my fingers lingering on the small of her back. Then I step back and clear my throat. "So? What'd you think?"

She blinks and adjusts her top, not looking at me. "Oh, that was great. Yeah, really good. Good moves."

I smile. "Yeah?"

Lyric does meet my eye then. "Zoey'll really like that, I think."

I pause. "Cool." Turning to go, I say, "Well, I'm gonna hop in the shower, wash the pizza smell off me."

"Kian?"

I turn to face my best friend. "Yeah."

"I had a nice time, too." She smiles as she tucks a lock of hair behind her ear. "Let's do it again soon."

"You got it, LB."

Chapter Nine

KIAN

The next week, I'm back at the greenhouse, tool belt on, surveying the work before me. The various environmental studies departments at Columbia have tasked their doc students (biologists, chemists, and architects, among others) with one project on or around campus to make the campus more environmentally friendly and reduce its carbon footprint. Nothing like free doc student labor, am I right?

Anyway, mine is this large "greener" greenhouse at the Morningside Campus. It's better for the environment than traditional greenhouses, and the idea is that, once it's done, the university can grow its own sustainable organic produce that can then be used by the dining and nutrition programs. I'm not opposed to contributing my time to help the Columbia machine save money as long as it's for a good cause.

I'm kinda geeking out about this new material I'm using for the frame of the greenhouse. It's called Ferrock, and it was invented by an unsung hero and genius—an environmental chemist in Washington State. Why don't people like him get millions of followers on social media? I think what he's done is way more impressive than rich, beautiful people getting even richer and more beautiful, but maybe that's just me.

Anyway, Ferrock is way better for the environment than cement, which accounts for five percent of the world's carbon dioxide emissions (I'm aware I sound like Lyric), and even better than aluminum, which is extremely commonly used to frame in greenhouses. This will be the first Ferrock greenhouse in New York and it was a bitch to get Columbia to let me buy some, so it's vital I pull it off to protect my honor and reputation around these parts.

I've already built a wire mesh frame and hand-filled it with Ferrock to make the walls eight inches thick (not going to make a dick joke here; I'm working on being more mature and well rounded, after all). The roof is reinforced with steel and wire, so it's exceptionally strong. I'm also burying the foundation of the greenhouse so it'll never get below freezing, even in the coldest winter months. This way, Columbia can continue using it all year round. Needless to say, the project is tremendously—some might even say stupidly—ambitious . . . and time-consuming as fuck.

I hope it's all going to be worth it, though. Projects like these are one of the things the recruiters at the New York State forestry department—my dream job is to be a scientist there—keep their eyes open for. They have a few projects of their own I could spearhead in this vein; if I nail this one, I'd be a fierce contender for one of the positions on their team. And then I wouldn't have to take my dad's offer to be a scientist and C-level executive at his multimillion-dollar firm.

Look, I know most guys would jump at the opportunity for a sweet gig like that right out of grad school. But I'm not most guys. And most guys don't know my dad. We have . . . let's just say vastly different life philosophies. His greatest ambition in life was to be a millionaire by the time he was thirty. My greatest ambition in life is to have a job where I get to be outside most of the day. He viewed marriage and having a kid as a way to portray himself as a steady, stable family man to his more conservative, rich clients. I'm committed to my noncommitment because the last thing I want to do is end up like him. So when I'm done at Columbia, I'm going to take a job that my dad would never have touched with a ten-foot pole. Because this is how I prove to myself that I am a Montgomery in name only.

I wipe the sweat out of my eyes and breathe out. It's hotter than hell in the greenhouse on this spring afternoon, so I peel off my shirt and adjust the tool belt around my hips as I survey the window cutouts on the south side of the structure. I pull my hammer out of its holder and am about to begin smashing stuff (okay, so technically I'm "framing the windows," but phrasing it as "smashing stuff" makes this so much more fun) when I hear a female voice calling my name.

Hefting the hammer in one hand, I turn. Kiley's picking her way across the grass, her face bright and eager as it always is. She's wearing a short white dress that shows off her tan skin and her long legs. I raise the hammer in greeting. "Hey. What's up?"

She walks into the greenhouse and looks around at the mess of wire and wood and Ferrock dust. "It's so hot in here."

A rivulet of sweat rolls down the side of my face, as if highlighting her point. "Yeah, no kidding." I slide my hammer back into its loop on my tool belt, waiting. I'm pretty sure she didn't come here to make conversation about the weather.

She steps closer, and it hits me how tiny Kiley is. Way smaller than Lyric, at five foot two. She fiddles with her braid, a black rope cascading down her shoulder. "I've missed you," she says, reaching for me. Her arms slide around my waist before I can say anything, and I resist the urge to step back. "I think we're making a huge mistake, Kian." She runs her hands down my back, toward my ass.

I catch her arms gently but firmly, stopping her. "Kiley. No."

She pulls her hands away from my ass, but keeps her arms around my waist. "Seriously. I miss you." She grabs my face and pulls me down toward her, standing on her tiptoes to kiss me.

Kiley was always a good kisser. Her lips are soft but sure, her little pink tongue darting out to lick me, her mouth curving up into a smile. "See?" she croons, stroking the front of my pants, which have a definite bulge to them now. "You miss me, too."

I pull away at that, and take a step back. Her eyebrows knit together. I shake my head. "This is a bad idea."

"Why?" She asks it kind of aggressively, putting her fists on her hips. "What are you so afraid of, Kian Montgomery?"

"I'm not afraid." I rub the back of my sweaty neck and take a breath. "I just don't think we're a good match. We're in very different phases of our lives."

Her angry fists stay planted on her hips. "Well, I think you're totally wrong."

I don't know what to say to that, so I shrug. "Okay."

"*Okay*? That's all you have to say?" Her frown grows deeper.

"I'm sorry I hurt you," I say quietly, holding her gaze. "I wasn't trying to. I just think—this is for the best. You deserve better. And when you find him, you'll thank me for ending things and freeing you up."

She scoffs. "Whatever, Kian." She turns to go, then whips back to look at me. "Are you dating someone new? Is that what this is about?"

"No. I'm not dating anyone." In the distance, I see Lyric approaching the greenhouse, dressed in a I AM NOT A-FREUD OF ANYTHING tank top and shorts. Beside her is Zoey, in a plain tan jumpsuit. I turn my eyes back to Kiley. "But I am *fake* dating someone. Does that count?"

She rolls her eyes. "You are *so* weird. And just FYI, when you come crawling back to me, I won't be there. You missed your chance."

I nod solemnly, though everything she's saying just reinforces my decision. "Okay."

She glares at me and then stomps away, her face puce. I blow out a breath and turn to watch Lyric again. And Zoey, of course.

"Hey, ladies," I call, when they're close enough to hear me. "Welcome to my humble abode. Actually—" I look around the space, my eyes narrowed. "It might be more like 'crumble abode' right now."

Lyric groans as she enters and pushes me on the chest, laughing. She's always been a big fan of my dad jokes.

Zoey doesn't crack a smile. "What are you doing?" she asks instead, looking around with interest at the mess.

"I'm building a 'greener' greenhouse," I explain, my spiel whenever anyone asks me about this project. "It uses a material called Ferrock instead of cement or aluminum."

"I see." Zoey goes over to one of the Ferrock frames and examines it, then bends and examines the foundation. Then, looking up at me, she asks, "And you're burying the foundation for climate control? To keep the greenhouse usable through the winter months?"

"Yeah, exactly." I dart an impressed look at Lyric, who gives me a smug smile before making a shooing motion with her hands to encourage me to keep talking to Zoey.

Rolling my eyes, I hook my thumbs in my tool belt loops. Lyric narrows her eyes at me and then says, "Hey, Zoey. A bunch of us are going to the concert in Central Park tomorrow night. Do you want to come? It starts at eight and it's going to be so much fun!"

Zoey continues studying the Ferrock frame and doesn't

rush to answer. Or meet my eye. Not a great sign. I have a feeling Zoey's about as into Lyric's big plan to set us up as I am.

Finally, she stands and brushes her hands off. "Mm, I might come if I have some time to kill."

Ouch. I turn to look at Lyric, wondering if she can see the shattered ruins of my ego crumbling to the floor amid all the other dust and rubble. I may not have been super excited about Zoey coming, but I still don't want to be rejected like that.

"Okay, cool," Lyric says, cheerfully. Apparently she doesn't care that Zoey just ran over my self-confidence with an eighteen-wheeler.

Zoey turns to Lyric. "Yep. I need to get back to the lab. See ya."

Lyric nods, raises her hand, and Zoey turns to leave. But right at the door, she looks at me, her face serious like it always is. "Thanks for showing me your greener greenhouse. It's pretty cool." A hint of a smile hovers at her mouth. Then she turns for real and walks off across the grass.

I turn to Lyric, who's looking at me with her blue eyes as wide as they'll go. "I don't think Zoey's interested. Maybe you should stop trying to make this happen."

Lyric laughs and shoves me, though I don't move at all. "Ugh, like pushing a wall," she says, before adding, "Oh, come *on*! Did you hear what she just said? 'Thanks for showing me your greener greenhouse. It's pretty cool.' Coming from Zoey Jones, that was practically a 'hey, baby, I'm totally into you.'"

"If you say so." I look after Zoey, who's now a pinpoint in the distance. If she's feeling a little bit of interest . . . should I take her up on it? My insides feel gnarled and confused.

Lyric interrupts my short reverie. "I'm pretty sure she's gonna wanna see your Ferrock samples soon, if you know what I mean." She does the dorkiest laugh known to man and elbows me in the waist.

I give her a dry look. "Never say that again. And definitely not to any guys whose pants you want to get into."

She sobers up and picks up a trowel, turning it end over end in her hands. "Point taken. Hey, but who all's coming to the concert tomorrow night?"

I turn back to surveying the window frames. "The usual suspects. Eli, Ava, Templeton, and Jonas."

"Oh." Lyric twists the toe of her sandal into the ground. "Right."

I give her a sidelong glance before returning to my work. "Why? What's wrong with them?" Lyric's hung out with them plenty of times before. "Oh, and you can bring Charlie, too, if you want. You know that."

"It's not *that*. It's just that I've known Templeton and Jonas forever."

"Uh-huh . . . ?"

"So I can't exactly flirt with them. I was hoping to practice some of what I learned on Saturday."

"Ah." I turn to her, a drill bit in my hand. "So you want me to bring an eligible bachelor?"

"Not super eligible. Just somewhat eligible. I'm sure I'll

mess up, so I don't want it to be someone I can try with later, you know? And then you can eavesdrop and give me constructive criticism later."

I grin. "All right."

"And if Zoey shows up, I'll do the same for you."

When I nod, she holds her small fist out for a fist bump. After we do, she looks around at the greenhouse, her eyes bright. "You're doing a good job, Montgomery."

"Thanks, LB."

"I just hate that all this means you're going to be leaving me."

I set my drill down and put my arms around her.

"Ew!" She wriggles. "Man sweat! Get off me!"

Laughing, I let her go. "Okay, okay. Now get out of here. Some of us have to actually work."

Sticking her tongue out at me, Lyric walks out. Shaking my head, I watch her go.

Chapter Ten

LYRIC

Opal and I sit in the front row of the small, dimly lit, otherwise empty theater and wait for Arthur to come onstage. I turn to my second oldest sister, my eyes glinting. "So. Have you thought any more about letting Arthur have his moment to shine in front of our family?"

Opal sighs dramatically and hangs her head half off the back of her theater seat. "No. He asks me about it every night, though. It's become our routine—dinner, an episode of *Game of Thrones*, sex, and then, 'When are you going to introduce me to your family?'"

I poke her in the shoulder. "Too much information. But also, the man has a point."

This is the most interesting thing in my life right now: Opal and Arthur's romantic saga.

See, Opal is thirty-six years old. She owns her own beauty salon and is an incredibly talented hair stylist. She's supported herself since she was seventeen and dropped out of high school, against our parents' wishes, to go to beauty school. She's nothing if not practical and orderly; everything she does, she does with pragmatic purpose. She's had Excel sheets to organize her life since she was fifteen. And now, to my utter delight and her utter dismay, she has fallen in love with a twenty-six-year-old magician.

Yep, you heard me right. He's ten years younger than her *and* he's a magician. Oh, and he's absolutely lovely. I've begged her to tell Mom and Dad and the rest of our siblings so I can finally talk freely about it. But Opal refuses. She's convinced she's going through an early midlife crisis and that a horrible breakup is imminent. She says there's no reason to tell everyone if she's just going to have to untell them. She brushes me off when I point out that they've been dating three whole years now, and have been in domestic bliss that entire time.

Opal glares at me, her blue eyes—with just a tiny bit more emerald than mine—glittering in the overhead lights of the grimy theater we're in. It's where Arthur can afford to rent out space so he can practice his magic tricks on us before he debuts them at the clubs and bars that hire him.

My sister jabs a ring-stacked finger at me. "Every time I've done a tarot spread about this, I get the Tower card. Or Death; that's another frequent flyer. Tell me that wouldn't freak you out."

I shrug. "Both of those cards can symbolize transformation and change. Which *will* happen if you tell Mom and Dad." I pause and narrow my eyes at her. "Wait a minute. Is that what you're scared of? That things will change? Maybe this doesn't have anything to do with Arthur or your supposed midlife crisis at all! Maybe you're just scared of what life will look like if you actually commit to him publicly."

My sister stares at me, her mouth opening and then closing again. Then she turns to the stage, her cheeks bright pink. "Shh. Look, Arthur's coming out."

I grin as I turn to face forward. Arthur's wearing a T-shirt and jeans—and a cape. He says it helps him get into the mindset when he's practicing, even though he doesn't actually wear it during his real shows. He waves at me and I wave back. "You can run from this as much as you want, Opal, but you know you can't hide forever. Arthur's not going anywhere. I'm surprised Mom hasn't caught on yet. You know how she's got that weird sixth sense about all of us."

"Speaking of Mom and her sixth sense," Opal murmurs as Arthur clears his throat, a sign he's about to get started. "She told me she feels there's something big coming from Max soon."

I cut my eyes at my sister. "Yeah, I got that phone call, too. 'Big' like what, though? A manslaughter charge?"

Opal snorts as Arthur pulls a soft felt heart from his sleeve (that's always his first act when Opal's in the audience watching him. He says it's to symbolize how he wears his heart on his sleeve for her—I know; they're hopeless). He tosses it to her and she catches it, laughing and shaking her head. There are happy lines at the corners of her eyes and I know exactly what she's thinking: *It would be so easy to grow old with this man.*

But first, she's got to get out of her own way.

ꝏ

The Great Lawn in Central Park holds some of my favorite (and also most excruciating) memories. The next evening, as I walk toward the vast expanse of green grass in the twilight holding a rolled-up blanket, I think back on a memory from my undergrad days: hooking up with this guy Roderic I liked sophomore year while the New York Philharmonic played in the background.

I'd been into him for months and months, staring at him moonily through my sociology class until my professor threatened to fail me. Finally, after eons of me boring a hole into the back of his head and pleading with my tarot decks and all the Goddesses for help, he picked up on my vibe and asked me out.

We hid behind a couple of gigantic pine trees at the very edge of the Great Lawn so as not to inadvertently flash anyone—or get arrested. I didn't think either of us were particularly interested in the music that night, although now, as a person of the older-wiser variety, I'm aghast at my youthful disrespect for such phenomenal music.

Anyway, after we were done, like, forty-five seconds later (luckily for Roderic, I didn't have the SPS back then, because if I did, he'd have scored a 0.5 at *best*), he sat up and looked over at the stage. "Check out that chick playing the cello. She's hot. I think I can see some side boob action."

And instead of smacking him upside the head with the bottle of champagne from our picnic basket and inviting him to rub a bottle of capsaicin lotion on his untalented dick, I turned bright red (not that he noticed) and mumbled, "Oh, yeah. Definitely. Super hot." We split the bottle of expensive-for-me champagne I'd bought, Roderic smoked some pot (that he most definitely did not share with me), then he left me with a "see ya." He never even spoke to me in class after that. Worse, he didn't even *pause* to listen to the philharmonic on his way out.

I walk along the border of the Great Lawn, the slightly damp grass tickling my feet through my open-toed gladiator-style sandals. The sun's bidding adieu to this part of the world, her golden tresses trailing over the trees, turning their leaves to burnished ingots. This is my favorite time of day—when the world takes off her business suit, lets her hair down, and puts on a rose-gold dress, a coy smile painting her mouth pink. There are already a few dozen people here, ready for the concert that starts in an hour, but I remain near the bordering trees just breathing the pine-scented air and letting my mind float back to sophomore year.

The day after Roderic so inelegantly dumped me, Kian brought me back to Central Park. I was a total brat about him dragging me out of the house; all I wanted to do was lie in bed and watch movies where girls kick ass and decide never to date boys ever again. But Kian, as usual, was unperturbed and sunny, and when he showed me the picnic he'd laid out on the Great Lawn to "erase the negative association" from my mind, complete with a new bottle of champagne, a bag of Swedish Fish—my favorite candy—and an iPad queued up with all the movies I was going to watch at home, I promptly burst into tears. He was horrified for a second, until he realized I was crying happy/touched tears, and then he gathered me in a bear hug, the kind where my toes barely scrape the ground.

It seems like every great memory I have in this city involves Kian in some way. It's going to be really weird when he leaves; I'm not even sure what a Lyric without a Kian looks like, to be honest. Frowning at the thought, I pull my cell from my pocket and text Zoey.

I'm here!

Her response comes back a moment later: Almost there.

Excellent. Next, I text Kian: Z's on her way. Are you bringing your guy?

His response takes a minute. Yes ma'am. You're gonna like him—psych nerd like you

Who is it?

But Kian is in an extra-aggravating mood tonight and only sends back three winky-face emojis. Sigh.

A psych grad student, though? I chew my lip as I make my way onto the lawn proper to roll out the blanket I've brought. That means I probably know him pretty well, even if he's a different year than me. Is that a good thing or a bad thing?

"Irrelevant, Bishop," I mutter to myself as I smooth out the blanket and plop down on it, my Stevie Nicks T-shirt and cotton shorts already rumpled, in spite of my best efforts. "This is practice. End the evening with a kiss you don't zone out on and we'll call it a success."

A kiss I don't zone out on. That's a pretty low bar, even for me. I can manage that. Smiling with a sense of bravado I most definitely don't feel all the way inside, I hug my knees and settle in for some people watching while I wait for the rest of the group to arrive.

ꝏ

Zoey and I lounge back on our blankets, watching the stage crew set up for the band. "Who's playing again?" she asks, sipping golden chardonnay from her plastic wineglass.

"A band that's just gotten big in the indie rock scene, apparently. Kian's more into them than me. They're called The Third Nipple."

She gives me a look—half-disparaging, half-disbelieving—and, oops, I realize this doesn't paint Kian or his judgment in the best light. I reach for a grape and talk quickly, trying to make up for my fumble. "Um, they're really very good, actually. I listened to a bit on YouTube. Don't judge them by the name."

"Right." She doesn't sound convinced, but I take note of what she's wearing: a boho-chic maxi dress with a low-cut, sexy twist back. Dressing to impress, maybe? I bite the inside of my lip to keep from smiling. Heh, heh. Good job, Kian. You got through to her at least a little bit, you charismatic bastard.

I can only hope his choice for me, whoever it is, is equally open to the possibility of some sizzle between us.

"I don't go out much." Zoey interrupts my train of thought, looking down into her chardonnay. "It's so hard to meet people as a grad student."

"I know." I sigh and pour myself a glass of pinot. "We're not *just* broke, we're critically overworked, dangerously stressed, *and* abjectly broke. It's the world's shittiest three-for-one deal."

"Totally." She meets my eye and offers up a small smile.

Oh my God. Are we bonding? I have to leverage this moment. For Kian and his big, giant, wounded-bear heart.

"Kian's really been a lifesaver for me," I add casually, swigging my drink and feeling its warmth soften the edges of my social anxiety. "Don't know what I would've done these past seven years without him. He balances my neuroses out quite nicely, like a fine wine with stinky cheese." I glance at her. "I'm the cheese, obviously."

She studies me with interest. "You guys have been friends for seven years?"

"Ever since I was a freshman and he was a sophomore. I was only sixteen when I came to Columbia, so he kinda took me under his giant wing. I think he felt protective of me or something." I snort fondly, thinking back to how he'd even written me out a little manual consisting of dining hall foods and college guys to avoid, how to schedule my classes so I always had Fridays off, and which professors were most likely to give me an easy A because they were secretly disenchanted with the entire teaching franchise and were day-drinking in their offices on the regular. "He's an only child, but I think he missed his calling as a big brother."

Zoey raises an eyebrow. "Sounds like he has a thing for you. Or had one, anyway."

I wave her away, used to this kind of response from, oh, everybody. "No, no, we're just friends. Kian and I would be a disaster together." I've said it so many times it rolls off the tongue very easily and Zoey looks assuaged. Naturally, I'm not going to tell her about our date tutoring. Kian can disclose that whenever he feels comfortable.

"And uh, you said your friend Charlie was coming, too, right?" Zoey checks her nails as she says this, and I'm surprised she even remembers Charlie. I don't think the two of them have said more than three words to each other the whole time I've known them.

"You know Charlie?"

Zoey takes a sip of her drink. "No, I don't *know* her, per se. I just . . . know of her." She tucks a strand of hair behind her ear.

"Oh, okay. The plan was for her to come, but she texted me earlier today and said she had some kind of sermon crisis come up at the church where she's a pastor."

"Oh."

I smile encouragingly at Zoey. "Don't worry, though. Kian's bringing all his other friends in case you want to meet more people."

She gives me a small smile. "Great."

As if on cue, Kian and the rest of the group appear: I can see Eli and Ava (both of whom look uncomfortable and terse, like they've been arguing), Jonas, Templeton, and a Black man I don't recognize, at least not from this distance. That must be my mysterious eligible bachelor. "There they are," I say, noting the nervous edge to my voice. I down the rest of my pinot quickly and catch Zoey's eye over my glass. Awesome. She probably thinks I'm an alcoholic now.

But then she also quickly downs her drink and we catch each other's eye again and smile. Game on.

"Hey, LB." Kian leans down and gives me a hug, almost choking me with his massive upper arms.

"Hey," I squeak out, my eyes on the new guy, who's busy setting his adorable plaid blanket down next to mine. He even brought a freaking wicker picnic basket. I love it all. I wave to the others I already know, grinning with pure joy at the prospect of a fresh start.

"Hi, Zoey," Kian says easily. He sets down a large tote bag and shakes out his own ratty picnic blanket so it's somewhat close to Zoey's, while the others find spots.

The new guy takes a seat next to me and holds out a hand, a winning smile on his face. "Hi. I'm Daniel Fuhrman."

I take the very charming Daniel's hand. His grip is dry, firm, and warm. Perfect. "Lyric Bishop. Nice to meet you."

Daniel's brown eyes, framed by the thick fringe of his lashes, crinkle in mirth. He's got on a gray T-shirt with one horizontal yellow stripe running through the center. He's about six feet tall and built like a runner or a swimmer—long and lean. Lyric likes. Lyric likes very much. "Yeah, you, too. Although I have to confess, I already kinda know you."

I blink in surprise. "You do?"

"Sure. You're in Dr. Livingstone's lab, right?"

"Yeah . . ." Shit. Why don't I recognize him?

"I do some data entry for Dr. Prince down the hall on the weekends. I've seen you around."

I frown and slap at my ankle, where a mosquito has been energetically sucking my life force out of me. "Data entry? But that's for undergrad assistants."

Daniel's smile doesn't dim one watt. "Yep. I'm a junior."

A junior. An undergraduate. Daniel Fuhrman is a *kid*. I look over my shoulder at Kian and glare at him with the force of a thousand angry wasps until he feels the sting and looks up. I widen my eyes and jerk my head in the universal *Can I have a word with you, you absolute moron?* signal.

While Kian excuses himself from the no-doubt-scintillating conversation he's having with Zoey, I turn to Daniel, the smile back on my face. "Give me a sec?"

He nods and reaches for his picnic basket.

Stomping off to the side, I wait for Kian to catch up. When he does, I look up into his face and jab a finger into his chest. "Is this who I am to you?"

He looks slowly down at my finger and then back into my eyes. "Huh?"

"An *undergrad*, Kian? He's a kid. A child. An infant."

Kian blows out a scoffing breath. His breath is minty; he always brushes right before an outing. And in spite of my irritation, I notice that he's dressed pretty nicely, in a pair of lightly distressed jeans and a button-down shirt with sleeves rolled up to his massive elbows. Not bad at all. I hope Zoey appreciates the effort. "Stop being so judgy, will you? He's a junior. Which means he's only, like, three years younger than you. Daniel's a great guy."

I narrow my eyes. "How do you know him, anyway?"

"We met on my weekend basketball league. He's one of the best point guards I've ever seen."

I give him a big sarcastic smile. "Boy, do *you* know what women want!"

He chuckles and scratches his chest, all slow and manly. "Give him a chance, Bishop." Slinging a heavy arm around me, he ruffles my hair, which manages to be both obnoxious and endearing somehow. "It's going to be fine. You guys have a lot in common. He even works in one of the other psych professors' labs! Plus, you told me not to get you a *super* eligible bachelor, remember?"

I sigh. Kian has a point. "Yeah, true." Glancing over at Daniel, I see him making easy conversation with Charlie, Jonas, *and* Templeton, and Templeton has historically been very mistrustful of strangers. "Okay, I'll be more open-minded."

"Good."

We fist-bump and then Kian lumbers back to woo Zoey, while I saunter awkwardly back toward Daniel, the baby bachelor.

Chapter Eleven

KIAN

"Sorry about that. Lyric had a question about . . . rent that couldn't wait." I hand Zoey a small plate of grapes.

"No worries." Zoey smiles. She's been smiling more and more as the evening wears on, and I can't tell if that's because she's genuinely warming to me or the liquid libations or both. Either way, I'm not totally against it. I mean, Lyric set this up and Zoey wanted to come. Who am I to say no? To quote Lyric, I'm willing to see where the universe takes me on this one.

She gestures at me with her wineglass. "So you were telling me about the plague museum you went to in England."

"Right, right." I pick my beer back up and take a sip. "The Eyam Museum. It was pretty cool. The entire village of Eyam quarantined themselves in 1665 when the plague broke out and helped contain the spread, which was pretty forward thinking for back then. Mm." I set my beer down again and reach for the backpack I brought with me. "That reminds me. I found something at my place when I was cleaning up that you're welcome to have if you want."

"Oh. You mean like a present?" Zoey looks a little taken aback, but also curious.

"Well, only if you want it." I pull out a framed page and set it between us. "It's an eighteenth-century copy of the old satirical engraving by artist Paulus Fürst. I found it at a flea market in the UK on the same trip."

Zoey picks up the frame and studies the picture of the doctor in the beaked plague mask, her fingers tracing over the lines, a small smile at her lips. "It's called *Doctor Schnabel von Rom*," she says, and I'm not surprised she knows what this is. Zoey Jones appears to be about as weirdly obsessed with the plague as I used to be. "Loosely translated as: Doctor Beaky from Rome. This is so cool."

I chuckle, pleased. "Well, it's yours."

She looks at me. "Are you sure?"

I wave a hand. "Yeah. I never hung it back up when Lyric and I moved into our current apartment and now I have to move again in a couple of months. It's just going to sit and gather dust. I'd rather it went to someone who'll get some enjoyment out of it."

Zoey sets the frame down next to her and pats it lovingly. "I'll take good care of it, I promise."

We smile at each other, and there's nothing forced or awkward about it. Zoey Jones is someone I could easily be friends with, even if it never progresses to something more. And there's something pretty cool about that.

LYRIC

I reach surreptitiously into my shorts pocket while Daniel and I talk. Not because I'm a pervert, but because I have two small crystals there—chrysocolla and rose quartz—to enhance communication and any feelings of romantic love that may be lurking like sulky, antisocial teenagers in our hearts. I intend to pull them out, eye-rolling and sighing, into the light.

Yes, I am an Ivy League–educated scientist with a pocketful of crystals. It is my burden to bear.

The band is almost ready to come out and I feel a renewed sense of urgency as nighttime wraps its inky cloak around us. Couples all around snuggle closer to each other on their blankets, and the singletons are getting progressively more drunk. I need to get things moving faster.

So far, I find Daniel plenty attractive on both an emotional and physical level (really gorgeous smile, super attentive communicator) and from the way he keeps glancing down—at my legs? in shyness? I need a Kian Montgomery to help me decode—it's probably true of his feelings for me, too. But in spite of that initial spark, all we've done is talk about Dr. Livingstone for twelve whole minutes. BTW, Dr. L's colorful bow ties and perpetually disapproving gaze? Not exactly a mood maker.

I'm opening my mouth to change the subject when Daniel interjects another gushing thought as he sets his now-empty plate of cheese and crackers down. "He's such a visionary. Man. I know I said that before"—yeah, he did, four times—"but it's an honor just to be *near* his lab, even though I'm not working for him. To be honest, I would've settled for emptying Dr. Prince's trash cans every night just to be near all that genius." He chuckles, his eyes far off and moony, and I wonder if Daniel might want to ask Dr. L out on a date instead of me.

But at the exact moment of my dispirited thought, Kian and Zoey laugh, heads bowed together. I feel a renewed sense of empowerment as I watch them. If Kian can do this—burrow his way into Zoey's skeptical heart, I mean—then I can definitely get someone as open and willing as Daniel to agree to another, real date. I'm not going to let all Kian's hard work and tutoring go to waste.

Leaning in closer to Daniel, I brush a fingertip down the back of his hand, just like Kian taught me. Daniel's gaze immediately refocuses on me. "I'm so glad you came here tonight," I say, making my voice as throaty as it'll go while simultaneously hoping I don't sound like a toad with a mean case of laryngitis.

Daniel's eyes are practically shining. "Oh my God, me, too."

I feel a warm ember of happiness in my chest. It's working! Thank you, Hecate and Aphrodite and Durga and any other Goddess responsible. "Really?"

"Absolutely." Daniel squeezes my hand. So what if he's a junior? He's clearly mature and sweet and hot and into me, and plus, we'll have so much to talk about all the time, what with our shared interest in Dr. Livingstone's research and all (well, my current interest in Dr. Livingstone mainly consists of how I can wrestle him off my back, but still—maybe Daniel can help with that, too). "You're the main reason I agreed to come tonight. I was so excited when Kian invited me."

My smile widens. "I had no idea you really knew who I was. I thought you were just saying that."

"Are you kidding? If Dr. Livingstone picks a doctoral student to mentor, you can bet your ass I'm going to know who it is!"

My smile begins to wane, in danger of closely resembling one of Dali's melting clocks. "Huh?"

"You're going to think I'm nuts, but I have an Excel sheet full of each of Dr. Livingstone's mentees from the last three years: their GRE scores, their résumés, their research areas, their undergraduate stats. I want to maximize my chances of getting into his lab once I graduate, and this is the best way I've found how."

Oh . . . my . . . God. Is this . . .

Has he been *interviewing with me* this whole time?

I open my mouth to ask but the words just won't come out. I can't speak. I want to curl up in a fetal position and stuff my face with all the cheese in Daniel's wicker basket, but I can't move.

It turns out I don't really need to ask. Reaching into said wicker basket, Daniel pulls out an immaculate waterproof folder from which he extracts a crisp sheet of paper that he then hands to me. I take it because I don't know what else to do.

"My résumé," he says, a little shyly. "I hope that's not too forward of me. I'll be applying to Dr. Livingstone's lab as a grad student next year. If you could put in a good word for me, that would mean so much." He holds up his hands, eyes earnest. "Only if you think I deserve it, of course. No pressure at all. I'm just so grateful you spent all this time talking to me tonight."

There are no words. There are no feelings. There is nothing in the entirety of this world except for the molten lava of mortification that has buried me and perfectly preserved my pathetic, ashen smile like some sad relic of Pompei. "Of course!" I chirp as peppily as I can, skimming my eye over his résumé.

Damn, he's good. I can see that even through the haze of my flagrant humiliation and self-flagellation: 3.9 GPA, a handful of graduate-level psychology courses, psychology honor society president, founder of four social justice clubs on campus, second and third author on a couple of published papers. And before he worked in Dr. Prince's lab, he worked in another professor's for two years.

"This is really good," I say more calmly. "*Really* good." I look up at his hopeful face. "You have a really solid shot even without me putting in a word, but I'd be happy to anyway. Every little bit helps, right?"

Daniel claps his hands over his heart and mimes falling backward. "Oh my God!" he laughs, his hands now going to the top of his head. "Seriously? You think so? Oh my God, thank you! Thank you!"

I wave a hand, laughing at his effusiveness. "Hey, I remember what it was like trying to get into Dr. L's lab. He's a legend. But you're a shoo-in, Daniel. I wouldn't worry about it."

Daniel looks like he might cry. "You have no idea what that means to me. Holy shit. Thank you."

"Yeah, sure."

The band comes onstage to a swell of cheering and clapping and I look over at Kian and Zoey. They're facing the stage now, sitting close together, their shoulders almost touching. Kian says something and she nods and laughs.

I turn to Daniel and speak over the sound of the first chords the lead guitarist plays. "Excuse me a second?"

"Sure," he says, his eyes on the stage.

I crawl over to Templeton's blanket. He looks over at me and nods a greeting, his dark hair in its usual mohawk. I don't feel much like talking anymore, and Templeton's the quietest person in the group.

I cross my legs. "Hey, Templeton. Mind if I hang out with you for a bit?"

"Nope."

"Thanks."

My cell phone buzzes in my pocket and I pull it out. "Huh. It's Max."

"Your little brother?" Templeton asks, and I nod and get to my feet.

"I'll be back soon."

There's no way I'm going to ignore this call. Max only reaches out when he's about to be thrown in jail or beaten up. The pleasures of coming from such a large family—Max rotates who he calls when he's in trouble so no one person has *all* the info on the shit he's up to.

Jogging past all the people on their blankets, I make my way to the edges of the lawn, by the trees. Plugging my ear with a finger, I answer the phone. "Max? Are you okay?"

"Lyric?" he says, his voice high and excited. Oh, boy. I brace myself for whatever he's about to throw at me next. "Lyric, hello? Can you hear me?"

"I'm at a concert, but yeah, I can hear you if you speak up!"

"Lyric . . . I'm engaged! Mom's throwing a big party tomorrow—you'll come, right? Your Maxie Pad's getting married!"

My mouth falls open and the world begins to spin out and around, as if I'm on a crazy carnival ride. I put one hand out on the rough trunk of a pine tree to steady myself.

My delinquent, unemployed, pothead baby brother is going to be sending out crisp, calligraphed wedding invitations soon (side note: who the hell is he marrying? last I checked, no girl wanted to get close to him). Meanwhile, the most eligible bachelor I've met in ages just gave me an invitation to his LinkedIn profile.

Yeah. I'm definitely going to die alone.

Chapter Twelve

KIAN

I glance at Lyric as we ride the Staten Island Ferry to her parents' house the day after the concert. The spring air is cool and wet, a fine mist of it hanging in our faces as the sun reflects off the sparkling water. Lyric sits stoically in the worn plastic seat next to mine, facing forward. She appears to be checking out the other boats on the water, but I can tell by the way her jaw is clenched hard enough to shatter her teeth that she's stressing. Plus, her hand is buried in her hoodie pocket and I can tell she's rubbing away at whatever poor crystal she's brought along for the ride.

I attempt a lighthearted tone. "So! Max getting married . . . wow. Who would've thought, huh?"

Lyric gives me a look that shrivels my balls. "Yeah. Who would've thought."

We haven't really talked about it. She told me last night when I got home that Max had called with the news. But when I opened my mouth to unleash a barrage of questions—the first one being, was she sure this was Max Paddington *Bishop*?—she held up one hand, said, "I don't want to talk about it," and walked off to her bedroom and shut the door. I had walked Zoey home after the concert and hadn't had a chance to ask her or Daniel about how they hit it off, either, so that told me Daniel was a nonstarter.

"It might be a good thing," I say gently now, attempting to cheer her up. "Maybe this'll be the kick in the pants he needs to turn his life around. They say love changes everything."

"What do you want to bet he met her in prison?" Lyric bursts out before I'm fully done speaking, her hand aggressively moving in her pocket. "She's probably a complete psychopath. Maybe she thinks we're rich or something." Lyric snorts at the thought.

"Max has never been to prison," I say mildly as I look out over the water at the approaching island. "Jail isn't prison."

Lyric snorts again.

Woof. This is going to be a fun visit.

LYRIC

I'm trying to fix my mood with the cleansing energy of the black onyx ball in my pocket, but it's not working this time. And it *always* works. Just goes to show how powerful of a malignant energy Max's new fiancée must have. The more I think about it, the more determined I am to protect my little brother from the biggest mistake of his young life. And that's saying a lot, considering he's been held at knifepoint or had a bone broken more than half a dozen times. (Let's just say he likes to bet on things. A lot. And he doesn't exactly have the cash to back it up when he loses.)

Kian and I step out of the Lyft onto my parents' rain-soaked street. I was purposely vague about what time we were getting here; otherwise, about seven different family members would've turned up at the ferry to give us a ride, peppering us with a thousand questions a minute, and thoroughly exhausting me before I even got to my parents' place. Normally I don't mind so much, but today I'm on a mission.

I've whittled my agitation down to a fine, sharp, razor-focused point. I'm going to deploy every psychological tactic I can to bring Max's fiancée down. I'm going to expose her for what she is—a fraud and a fake, someone clearly taking advantage of my idiotic, hapless little brother in some way. I don't know exactly how yet or what her end goal is, but that's what I'm here to find out.

I pull my Columbia hoodie around me and stride purposefully up the drive, toward the house, where a worn statue of Pan the Horned God greets us from the small table on the front porch. Mom and Dad are Wiccan, have been since I was in elementary school. But the Horned God's benevolent expression irks me today, and I glower at him.

"You're not going to start something, are you?" Kian says

from beside me. He's keeping pace with me easily, his long legs eating up the distance in half the time I'm taking.

"What do you mean?" I stand with my hand poised to knock and turn to him. "Why do you say that?" Am I that obvious?

"You're just that obvious." It's possible Kian and I have been living together for too long. "Come on, LB. Just relax. Get to know her. What if you end up liking her? What's her name, anyway?"

"That will *never* happen." I glare at him and finish knocking. "And her name is irrelevant."

"Irrelevant," Kian muses, a sparkle in his eye. "I like it. Very avant-garde."

I have just enough time to finish sticking my tongue out at him when my mother, dressed in one of her ubiquitous embroidered tunics and chunky metal triple moon necklaces, opens the door and gathers the two of us into a bear hug, dragging us into the unending, cheerful uproar and familial chaos that is the house I grew up in.

ꙍ

"Can you believe it? Maxie's getting married!"

This time it's my aunt Colleen who interrupts us, her round, happy face beaming with joy. Over the course of the last ten minutes, though, I've been stopped by at least eight different relatives who've all said variations on the same thing. Kian, my mom, and I are attempting to navigate our way into the kitchen, where my mom has promised hyperpalatable, death-hastening snacks and the inevitable meeting with Max's calculating fiancée, but everyone is just. so. excited. about this turn of events. I don't want to be a total stick in the mud (yet), so I'm smiling and laughing and nodding and making all the right faces. But soon. Soon I will unmask her.

Kian pinches the back of my arm as Aunt Colleen and my mom begin to discuss wedding invitation calligraphy.

"Ow." I scowl at him. "What?"

Using his paddle-like thumbs, he smooths out my eyebrows, then smiles, satisfied. "There. Now you look like you're walking into your brother's engagement party instead of to break up a puppy kidnapping ring."

My mom tugs on my arm and we continue our march to the kitchen. There's a tremendous hubbub there—the kitchen has always been the gathering place for my family—and I can hear Max's high-pitched laugh. My heart tugs with exasperation and affection; as much as I bemoan my little brother's extremely boneheaded choices, I do still love him to death. I'd do anything for him, including stopping him from making the biggest mistake of his life, no matter how much he might hate me afterward. I steel myself as my mom pushes her way through the boisterous crowd and uncles and aunts and cousins clap me on the back and welcome me home as if I've been at sea battling pirates instead of studying an hour away.

The inner circle in the kitchen consists of my immediate family: my white-bearded dad, who gathers first me and then Kian in a very similar bear hug to the one my mom gave us, and my four siblings—my older sisters Amethyst, Opal (sans

Arthur, as usual), Willow, and in the center of it all, being heralded as a homecoming hero, my little brother Max, dressed in a Grateful Dead T-shirt and what look like his old high school gym shorts.

Next to him is a full-figured, short-statured Hispanic woman with long black hair and enormous brown eyes, wearing a flowy black skirt, a pink camisole, and chandelier moon earrings. She's right around Max's age and looks a little like a kindhearted witch who'd brew you a love-spell tea, only it'd make you fall in love with yourself instead of that asshole you probably shouldn't be into anyway. I have to resist a tug of affection toward her that she didn't earn. She's beaming even bigger than the rest of my family, her round cheeks pink and her lips slicked with gloss.

Max catches my eye and lets out an ungodly shriek as he lunges forward and wraps his arms around me. We're both the same size and so we end up bumping foreheads. "Oh shit, sorry, sis!" he chortles, holding me at arm's length. "Can you believe this, huh? Can ya?"

Before I can answer, he tugs me forward to the good witch. "This," he says, his voice trembling with emotion, "is Camellia Martinez. Isn't that just such a perfect name?" He gazes at her as if she invented the concept of names. Coming to, he continues, "Camellia, this is my other sister, Lyric. The one I told you about."

Camellia looks up at me, a nervous, hopeful smile on her face. "Hi." Although I'm not actually offering a hand, she somehow manages to take mine anyway, and sandwiches it between two of her small, soft, warm ones. "Max does *not* stop talking about you. You've done so much for him, and I can only hope to be half the woman in his life that you've been."

I blink at her. Then I blink at Max. My mouth, I'm pretty sure, is open. "I, um . . ."

My little brother laughs. "Lyric's speechless! Dude, I don't think I've ever seen that happen! Usually she'd be telling me ten thousand things I'm doing wrong and need to fix."

Letting go of my hand, Camellia swats him gently on the arm. "Well, then, you probably deserved it." She grins at me. "Right?"

"Right," I reply, before I can even compute that I'm agreeing with her. The enemy. Although . . . looking at them now, holding hands, her lovingly telling him off and him with his eyes crinkled in absolute joy . . . I have to say, Camellia Martinez doesn't at all appear to be the devious cradle-robber I was expecting her to be. "So, Camellia," I say, rallying. "How did you guys meet?"

"At NYPL about eight months ago. I'm a librarian," Camellia replies.

I narrow my eyes at Max. There, that's it. I've caught them in their first lie. "Really. What were you doing in a library, Max?"

He laughs. "I know, right? I went in to use the bathroom. And then, before I knew it, I was walking out of there with a library card and a stack of books. Guess who's a big Ruth Ware fan now?"

I stare at him. "You . . . you're reading Ruth Ware." I have tried for *years* to get him to read a single book. Even a chapter book. Even a wordless picture book.

"And I'm introducing him to Tana French next week," Camellia puts in, smiling fondly at him. "We do a little book club with two other couples."

"Oh, oh, and guess what else, Lyr?"

I turn to Max, stunned. "What?"

"I got a job. An actual nine-to-five—well, sorta. I'm a house painter for Camellia's dad's company. So I get to not work in an office, which, let's face it, I need, *and* I get to mostly do my own thing, too."

I rub a hand over my face. "You're serious?"

He beams at me. "Yep. Are you proud of me? You've been telling me to save money and get responsible for years and now I finally am. It comes with health insurance and everything."

I can't speak. Suddenly, I'm choked up and blinking back tears. Camellia has done in eight short months what my family and I have been trying to do for *years*. And you know what? Thank the God and Goddess for her.

I gather Max in a hug and squeeze him tight, my eyes closing. "I am *so* proud." Then I open my eyes and smile at Camellia. "Congratulations, you two. Let me see that ring."

Laughing, she holds out her left hand. On it sits a thin gold-tone ring, with the sculpture of a tiny camellia flower on it. I smile up at the happy couple, who are both waiting eagerly for my reaction. "It's perfect, Max," I say, shaking my head. "Holy shit. I don't even recognize who you are anymore."

He laughs uproariously and slings an arm around his fiancée. "Right? She did a number on me."

"Thank you," I say to Camellia, totally meaning it. "And keep doing it, please."

They laugh together this time and then are accosted by Uncle George, who for some reason wants to know if Camellia has strong feelings about unicycles. I watch them go with a smile, and then feel a tap on my shoulder.

I turn to see Kian gazing smugly down at me. Guess he extricated himself enough from my family to have heard some of my conversation with Camellia and Max.

"So," he says. "Gave her a chance, did ya?"

"Shut up." I elbow him in the ribs and reach for a caramel brownie.

A couple hours later, my mom, sisters, and I are sitting around the kitchen table grazing on Nutella fudge and sipping coffee. The rest of the family has drifted outside into the backyard where my dad is grilling, and through the window, I watch Kian give Amethyst's three-year-old daughter Lapiz a ride on his shoulders. I laugh when Lapiz attempts to crack Kian's skull open with her sippy cup, but he takes the assault gamely and continues galloping around like a horse.

Amethyst follows my gaze and smiles tenderly. "He's great with kids, isn't he?"

"He's a natural-born dad," my mom, an early Kian adopter,

puts in proudly, as if he's her own son and this is the singular measure of his worth in the world. I guess it's important to her, since she did have five kids.

I carefully select another square of fudge from the pan. "Yep. Someday he'll make some girl happy." Hopefully someday soon, if Zoey works out.

Opal gives me a look. "Any chance that girl might be you?"

I glare at her over my fudge. "We've had this conversation. Kian and I would be—"

"A disaster," my entire family choruses.

I pause and look around at them all. "Well, so long as we're all on the same page."

"Are you dating anyone?" Opal asks, sipping her coffee. She knows the answer to this question. Why's she acting like we don't talk nearly every single day? Also, does she think I'm about to let her put me on the spot like this without repercussion?

"Not at the moment," I reply carefully, though my eyes are slinging daggers. "And you? Wasn't there some guy you were telling me about recently?" I screw up my nose like I'm deep in thought. "Ar . . . Arnie? Adam? Something like that?"

Even the tip of Opal's nose turns red. "Nope. Not me." And then she chugs her coffee, probably scalding her throat in the process.

No one else except me notices Opal's seeming overreaction. Then again, I'm the only one privy to information about her romantic life she hasn't shared with anyone else.

But she doesn't need to explain to me why she doesn't want

to tell our family about Arthur. Besides not wanting to accept the inevitable because it'll throw her entire life into chaos and shatter the careful identity she's built for herself, Opal's showing all the classic signs of fear of judgment. And she has a point—my family can be boisterously, noisily, annoyingly open with their opinions.

Although *why* she even cares, I don't know. Everyone lost their shit when Amethyst married Brandon at nineteen, but that all turned out fine. Similarly, Willow almost gave my dad a heart attack when she announced she and her boyfriend Deacon were opening a vegan dog bakery in Manhattan, but that's worked out super well and no one says anything about it anymore except to ask if she can bake their dog's birthday cake.

Opal's a self-made woman in love with a self-made man. Who cares if what he does isn't practical? Who cares if he's a decade younger? Do you know what I'd give to have someone look at me the way Arthur looks at Opal?

Also, why are all my siblings now happily in love while I stand out alone in the rain like some loser with a montage of sad love songs playing on repeat?

I blink to dispel the thought just as my mom starts to speak to me. "What happened to Paul? Weren't you dating someone named P—"

"Yes, but that was, like, three guys ago, Mom." I sigh and pick dispiritedly at another fudge square I heave onto my plate. Maybe I can just date fudge. That would be such a happy life. "Paul's gone. They're all gone." I think again of Daniel Fuhrman and his exquisite résumé. How I got that instead of a kiss.

I will not sob at my mother's kitchen table.

"It'll happen for you." Willow pats my hand, looking all big sisterly and protective, and somehow that makes me feel even worse. It's glaringly obvious here, at our little brother's engagement party, that I am the black sheep of the Bishop family. Not Max, as I'd deluded myself into thinking. It was me all along.

"It'll happen quicker if you just stomp your pride and date Kian," Amethyst puts in, all no-nonsense in her mom bun and sensible flats. "Really, Lyric. He's gorgeous, he's well-mannered, you know each other really well, he's on his way to getting a great job. And he's so good with women, you tell us all the time."

"Oh my God." I rub my face and then stop—I'm already close to combusting and I don't need any more kindling. "Look, Kian's great with women, I'll give you that. He's the perfect guy on paper, also true. That's why he's tutoring me on how to do what he does, except with the gentlemen instead of the ladies."

"Wait, wait, wait." Opal looks up from her phone where she has no doubt been secretly texting Arthur. Those two can't go five nanoseconds without sending kissy faces to each other. "What do you mean 'tutoring'? You didn't tell me about this."

I fill them in on the date situation. "It's just temporary, until I can get a handle on things and get Dr. Livingstone off my back." Talking about my perpetually disappointed mentor makes me hyperventilate. I should be working on this shit instead of going into a hyperglycemic coma eating sugar-dusted sugar with sugar on top with my pushy family.

"So . . . you're getting 'tutored' by Kian because he's the perfect guy for literally almost every woman out there . . . but just not the perfect guy *for you*. Did I get that right?" Opal asks flatly.

"Pretty much, yeah." I shrug. "You know. It's *Kian*. Best friend. Roommate. Plant-obsessed, pancake-gobbling nut. I know him too well to date him. But once he's done with me, I know I'll find someone great." I paste on a big, bright smile, but from the looks I'm getting (ranging from pitying to disbelieving to disapproving), I'm guessing it's not working.

I feel a wide, empty hole open inside my chest as I look around at the women closest to me. We're all so similar in appearance—blondish hair, willowy build, blue eyes fringed with pale lashes. But the similarities between them and me end there; they all have happy, stable, long-term romantic relationships and I have . . . a Dr. Livingstone who hates me, and a Kian Montgomery who's leaving me soon. So why can't I get this right? Why can't I get any guy to stay?

Well, there's no answering that or filling the void inside me with love right now. So I cram in another fudge square, hoping to fill it with chocolate instead.

Chapter Thirteen

LYRIC

My social gas tank is running pretty low later that evening when Aunt Colleen suggests everyone drive to the local Kohl's so Max and Camellia can register for gifts. Of course, in the Bishop family, this is an extended-family event and not just reserved for the happy couple.

"Oh, I want to go!" Amethyst says and then pulls a face and turns to her husband Brandon. "But one of us will have to stay here, honey. Lapiz is asleep upstairs."

"Oh, shoot." He frowns. "I wanted to pick up a dress shirt for work."

"I can do that for you!" Amethyst chirps hopefully.

"No, no. You don't know the difference between lavender

and mauve, and it has to be a mauve shirt. Lavender washes me out."

You see what I'm dealing with? This is what constitutes a "problem" for my happily married family members. I sigh. "I'll stay here in case Lapiz wakes up. I don't think I'm up for a Kohl's run anyway."

Both Brandon and Amethyst look at me as if I've just announced I'm their guardian angel, descended from heaven. "Wow, thanks, Lyr!" Brandon pats me on the shoulder and Amethyst squeezes my waist on the way out.

Kian flops down on the couch beside me. "I'll stay, too."

"There's plenty of food in the fridge if you get hungry," my mom says, ostensibly to the both of us, but she's really just talking to Kian and we both know it. The man's a relentless consumption machine. Hungry Hungry Hippos? Yeah, that was inspired by Kian Montgomery.

"Thanks, Mrs. B." He grins gratefully up at her, no doubt already planning his next meal.

My mom nods toward the now-empty kitchen while eyeing me meaningfully. "Lyric, can I talk to you really quickly about . . . our candy delivery service?"

Kian gives me a confused look, and I shake my head. I'll explain later. My mom always comes up with outlandish excuses when she needs to talk to a family member in private.

"Sure, Mom." I follow her into the kitchen, where she stops by the lemon squares. Mm. Lemon squares.

"Stop thinking about dessert for two seconds because I have

something for you." My mom reaches into the pocket of her palazzo pants and pulls out a rough-hewn pink crystal. "Rose quartz that was specially mined on St. Hana in the Pacific. I got it when Dad and I took our vacation there last year. It was blessed by an elder of the island, and it's supposed to be one of the most powerful stones to attract love into your life." She tries to press the crystal into my hand, but I move my hand away.

"Mom, no. That sounds rare. And expensive. You should keep it."

She frowns. "But I've already found my lobster, Lyric." My mother is an incorrigible *Friends* fan. "Now you have to find yours."

The last thing I want to do is divest my mom of a very powerful, ancient, expensive crystal for something that, at this rate, is never going to happen. "I can't, Mom." Leaning in, I kiss her soft, vanilla-scented cheek. "But thank you."

Sighing, she pats me on the back. "I love you, Lyric. Believe it or not, something beautiful is waiting for you right around the corner. I can feel it."

In spite of my rapidly multiplying misgivings, I smile at her. "Thanks, Mom. Love you, too."

"Oh, did you see this?" She walks over to a hanging frame on the wall in the attached dining room. "It's your latest paper about the role of dopamine in sexual chemistry, in the *Journal of Experimental Psychology*. But you know, at the rate you publish, I won't have any more room left on the walls."

I laugh and hug her. I know what this is: a consolation prize. This is my mom saying, *Well, you're shit at relationships, but at least you're good at being an academic!* And maybe I should be offended. But truthfully, she's right. At least there will always be academia. Even if, currently, academia and I are mortal enemies, thanks to my struggling thesis. "I'll try to slow down for the sake of your home decor."

"That would be nice." Winking, she melts back into the chaos of the living room.

I wander back into the kitchen, looking down at the array of desserts on the counter. "Welp. She wasn't wrong about something beautiful waiting right around the corner," I mumble, picking up three lemon squares on napkins—one for me, two for Kian—and head back to him and the comfort of the couch.

After a few circus-like moments of family members forgetting keys, wallets, coupons, toupees (don't ask), and then coming back in to get them, the front door finally closes on all twenty-six thousand Bishops and it is blessedly, peacefully quiet.

Setting my lemon square down, I lean my head back against the couch and close my eyes. "Ahhhhh."

Kian chuckles. "I thought you liked the chaos of a big family." While waiting for my response, he stuffs both lemon squares into his mouth in quick succession.

I crack open an eye and look at him. "I do. But I also like my peace and quiet. Living with just you for the past five years has ruined me."

Kian studies me for a moment as he chews and swallows, his face serious. Then he points to the fireplace. "Mind if I turn that on and turn out the lights?"

"Nope."

He flicks the switch that sets the gas fireplace alight and then plunges the room into darkness. Firelight flickers along every surface, casting deep pools of shadow in the corners of the room. When Kian sits back down, I snuggle into his chest, take a deep breath, and sigh. He smells like smoke from the grill outside and soft cotton and boy. A safe, masculine, comforting smell.

Wrapping a lock of my hair absentmindedly around his finger, he says, “You okay, LB?”

I still for a moment, watching the fire. “Yeah. Why?”

“You seem . . . I don’t know. A little down. Is it Max and Camellia?”

I wait a beat or two, hoping my answer won’t make me sound like the petty bitch I am. But who am I kidding? Besides, this is Kian. He isn’t allowed to judge me. It’s in the best friend contract we both had to sign. “Yeah, kinda.”

“I thought you liked her.”

“I do.” I sigh. “And somehow, that makes it worse. Max actually went and found someone *good*. Like, really good. I can see them married with kids in twenty years, living in a nice two bedroom not far from Mom and Dad, complaining about how the HOA won’t let them paint their house the exact shade of greige they want.”

Kian chuckles, the sound deep and rumbly in his chest. “That’s a very specific picture.”

“You’re welcome.”

He tugs gently on my hair. “But why does that make it worse?”

I throw a hand in the air. "It's *Max*. My Maxie Pad. He's not supposed to do something as serious as get married, especially not at twenty-two! I thought I had at least a decade to get my shit together before he'd even consider any of that domestic stuff."

"Didn't realize you were in competition with Max," Kian says lightly, and, as predicted, there's no judgment in his voice.

"I'm not," I mumble, my cheeks heating in spite of Kian's chill vibe. I'm ashamed of the way I'm acting. And I still can't help it. "I don't know. The 'date' with Daniel last night that ended up with him giving me his résumé. Max's engagement. Dr. L breathing down my neck. My complete and utter inability to crack the stupid Sizzle Paradox or bring myself to work on my stupid thesis. It's all just starting to take its toll on me, I think."

Kian pulls back so abruptly I almost fall over. "Wait. Daniel gave you his *résumé*? What the hell?"

"Yeah . . . he was excited to meet me because I work in Dr. Livingstone's lab. He wants to apply next year." I shrug. "But his résumé was actually impeccable. I'm gonna put in a good word."

Kian pulls me tight against his chest again and I go willingly. "Damn, I'm sorry, LB. I had no idea."

"No, it's okay. You had no way of knowing," I say, meaning it. "Besides, I'm happy to help him out. He seems like a good person." After a pause, I ask, "So how did things with Zoey go last night? You guys seemed like you were having a good time."

I feel Kian shrugging under me. "Yeah . . . we had a good time."

Turning up toward him, I frown. "I can smell that 'but' a mile away."

Giving me a look, he adds, "I don't know. It felt more . . . fraternal than romantic, to be honest. Like she's someone I'd take out for a couple of beers and we'd talk about the Black Plague together and then go home to our significant others." He pauses and I let him think. Finally, he says, "But it's probably just the fact that I'm used to relationships where things got hot and heavy way too fast."

"Mm, good point." I pat his flat stomach in commiseration. "You'll get there. Just don't give up."

Kian strokes my hair for a few moments and we sit in companionable silence, the fire hissing softly in the background.

"Okay. I have a proposition that might cheer you up," Kian says finally, into the quiet room.

KIAN

Honestly, I hadn't even really been considering it. But seeing Lyric so downtrodden, so down on herself . . . it's not like her. She's been bummed about boys before, disappointed about things not working out, sure, but this . . . this feels more serious somehow. Like she's actually wondering if there's something deeply wrong with her life, and . . . I don't know. I can't stand to see that.

Not to mention, everything I said about Zoey is true. It's a little more disconcerting than I let on to Lyric. Zoey and I have a lot in common on the surface but when we're together, the chemistry is way off. The more we talked, the more I found I wanted to just hang out with her. Like a friend . . . or a sister. Someone I respect and like, but not someone who gets the fires going. And the more we hung out, the more it seemed like Zoey felt that way, too. Which, obviously, is a problem. Maybe some more "date" time with Lyric will help me figure this out.

I hold up my phone. "Eli and Ava just announced they're eloping two weekends from now. No wedding planner, no big wedding. They just want to have a destination wedding in London with their closest friends. Get married in a little chapel, nothing big, but have a nice party afterward. And it's during spring break, so all of us academia nerds can go. It's gonna be a mad rush to get everything booked and ready, but I think we can do it."

I whistle. "Wow. That's huge. I mean, isn't that what most of their fights have been about until now?"

"Yup. Maybe that's why they're doing this. It's a little bit of what Ava wanted—a destination wedding—and a little bit of what Eli wanted—a smaller price tag." I shrug.

Lyric considers this and then nods appreciatively. "I like that. They're already compromising like a married couple. So what's the proposition?"

"Well, Eli wants to invite me, Templeton, and Jonas."

"Of course." Lyric picks up her previously abandoned lemon square and takes a big bite.

"And I thought you could go with me as my plus one."

She stares at me and then sets the rest of her dessert down again. "Really? Why? Won't Eli mind? I'm not a close friend."

I smile at the barrage of questions. "Nah, he's cool with it. He said we could all bring whoever we wanted. Besides, he and Ava both like you. As for the why . . . more tutoring. This could be really useful for you. And me," I rush to add, not wanting her to mistake my offer for charity. "I mean, neither of us are well versed in what to do in uber-romantic situations like a destination wedding, right?"

Lyric considers this, tapping one finger on her pointy chin. "Yeah, but . . . isn't that kind of like jumping into the deep end of the pool before you can float? You saw how I totally bombed at Pepper Tony. If a casual pizzeria we go to all the time got me tongue-tied, what do you think's gonna happen in London?"

I move closer to her. "That's why we should do this. Just get it over with. Once you've learned how to be calm and cool and collected in a romantic city like London, you can do it anywhere. After we practice, you might even be able to go pick up some dude in a pub and have a British fling."

She grins. "Hey, I like the sound of that. A real-life Benedict Cumberbatch, complete with the accent and everything."

I snort and look over at her lemon square. "You gonna eat the rest of that?"

Handing it over to me, she continues, "But basically, I'm in. It'll be good for the both of us, I think. And my passport's up-to-date, so there's nothing to do but buy tickets and pack, I guess."

I fist-bump her. "Hell yeah! Now let me finish this lemon square so I can go forage in the kitchen for something that'll last me more than 5.4 seconds."

Chapter Fourteen

KIAN

"LB. There is an *infinity pool* in this hotel." I point out the large windows in my room down at the pool, which is apparently on the tenth-floor rooftop. Currently, there are a few couples in it, everyone holding drinks as a waiter circles with a silver tray. Beyond the pool lies the city, glistening and beckoning with its peculiar and enchanting mix of ancient and new.

Lyric rushes up to me, jostling to see. "Wow. We are *definitely* getting in there at some point."

I turn around and survey my room again: the big king-size, four-poster bed, the glass of champagne waiting for me on the dresser. Lyric has a similar setup in her room. We got in about an hour ago, and although I'm rumpled and tired from the long flight, I sense the stirrings of excitement I always feel when I'm in a foreign country. All that possibility, the newness of a place you don't know, forcing you out of your comfort zone. "You know, this is my second time in the UK, but doing the whole five-star-hotel thing instead of a divey hostel feels really great."

Lyric laughs. "Yeah, I'll be paying for this with zillions of hours of overtime at the lab but I'm not complaining. Feels good to get out."

I turn to her. She's even more rumpled than me, in a pair of jeans and a pale pink sweatshirt that says PSYCHO THERAPIST hanging off one pale shoulder. "Get dressed, slouchy. We're meeting everyone at the restaurant in thirty minutes."

She salutes me and heads for the door.

Since it's important to Ava, Eli has asked the gang to please dress really nicely—no grad student slumming. I can respect that, so I even went shopping. Tonight I'm wearing a button-down shirt over dark slacks and a tie in a midnight blue color. I even run a little bit of the hotel gel through my hair, though I'm not sure if that does anything for me. A lock of brown hair still falls against my forehead and after messing with it for way too long, I leave it be.

My cell beeps.

> **Lyric:** Running a little late! Tell Ava and Eli I'm sorry and order me a Moscow mule? I'll be there in 15

I head out of the room as I text her back. Sure no worries

There are nine of us, all sitting at the table making small talk—the almost-weds, Eli and Ava, can't seem to keep their hands off each other and I feel both slightly disgusted and happy for them—when Lyric walks in, looking around for our table. I was expecting her to take the dress-up mandate seriously and maybe wear a flowery dress from Target or something.

But holy shit.

She's wearing a red dress that wraps around her body and cinches in at the waist, its hem skimming her midthigh. It's low cut enough that the band of her bra would show, were she wearing one. She's paired it with four-inch glittering gold heels. Every single straight male head in that restaurant turns and follows her as she spots us and makes her way over, her freshly curled blond hair bouncing lightly against her shoulders and arms.

"I'm so sorry I'm late," she breathes, leaning in for a hug from Ava and Eli. Her cleavage is on full display with the angle I'm sitting at, and I can't help it—I look. And not just look, but appreciate. And then I realize what I'm doing, feel like a gigantic pervert, and look away. It must be the half-pint of beer I've already had on an empty stomach.

"No worries," Ava trills. "You look gorgeous!"

Lyric does a mock bow and takes her seat beside me. "Thank you. That's actually what took me so long. I don't think I've attempted to curl my hair since middle school."

The women—Ava brought three of her best girlfriends—all laugh and the guys return to their conversation. But I can't help my eyes from darting over to Lyric every so often. She's . . . glowing. In spite of the jet lag we're all feeling, she looks vibrant, her blue eyes sparkling in the candlelight from the centerpiece on the table. It's like she left the weight of her love life and her thesis back in the US and here she's just unencumbered. Just a beautiful young woman, sparkling with life.

She catches me looking and cocks her head as she picks up the Moscow mule I ordered her. "What?"

"Nothing. You look really nice." I take another deep swallow of my beer. Wait. Is this crawling feeling in my diaphragm . . . discomfort? Why am I so uncomfortable giving *Lyric* a compliment?

She tucks a lock of hair behind one ear. "Oh, thanks. I let Amethyst do my shopping for me."

I half smile. "Kohl's?"

"Where else?" Lyric laughs. "But I have to admit she did a great job. It's comfortable *and* it's pretty."

My eyes flicker over her body without my quite meaning to. "It's definitely pretty."

She laughs and swats my hand. "Are we doing date mode already? You didn't even warn me! I'm jet-lagged!"

I scratch the side of my jaw and clear my throat. "No, right. We can do it later." She thinks I was putting on an act, to tutor her. Good. Because otherwise she'd be completely appalled. The truth is, I was checking my best friend out. *Jesus, Montgomery.*

I might need to get laid in London. Immediately.

LYRIC

I wake up around 3:00 A.M. the next morning, my body clock all messed up. But the great thing is, I don't immediately jump up with a to-do list weighing on my mind. London has taken my emotional baggage and "chucked it" (some London slang I picked up) out the fourteenth-story window of my hotel room.

Grinning, I get out of bed to grab my doggy bag from last night. Then, turning on the TV, I climb back under the covers. I like London. I like it a lot.

About an hour later, just when I'm getting tired of watching TV, my cell phone dings.

Kian: I can't sleep

Lyric: Me either. I'm watching reruns of something called 'Allo 'Allo! while eating leftover fish and chips

Kian: Very British of you. Wanna do something else?

Lyric: sure like what

Kian: I'm looking at that infinity pool and it's empty right now

I grin.

Lyric: meet you there in 10

The infinity pool is where I want to go when I die. I'll just float along on the water, a ghostly martini in one hand. Who needs heaven?

The entire city is in front of me: glittering skyscrapers, light-studded highways, and the London Eye in the distance like a blazing beacon of Britishness. The balmy water laps at the undefined edge of the pool and, just for a minute, I feel like I could easily spill over with it. I imagine tumbling and not being able to catch my breath and the air just whooshing out of my lungs and oh God why am I having this waking anxiety nightmare—

"Hey."

I whirl around to see Kian peeling off his robe and walking into the pool in his palm-motif swim trunks, the water's lights highlighting the sculpted muscles of his pecs and abs, the shadows painting his thigh muscles in stark relief. Just like that, I relax. My best friend's here. I don't feel like I'm falling anymore.

Smiling, I motion him over to the edge. "Check this out."

He swims over and stands beside me, his arms crossed on the glass wall that separates us from the sheer drop off the rooftop. He whistles quietly, then says, "Jesus. That's stunning."

"Welcome to London."

He chuckles softly, the water lapping at our backs. "The last time I was here, the views weren't quite as nice. It pays to grow up and have a little money in your bank account, I guess."

"But also? I can't believe Eli's getting married. That he's *old* enough to get married. The same Eli who fell asleep with his face in a popcorn bowl after one too many tequila shots. Remember that?"

Kian's chuckle turns into a full-on laugh, his Montgomery eye lighting up brighter than the London Eye. "Remember it? I plan to bring it up at his postwedding dinner when I make a toast. Make sure Ava knows what she's getting into."

Turning around, I run my hands through the warm water, my back against the glass wall. The ruffles on my hot-pink bikini undulate in the water and I watch, hypnotized. "They've dated a year. That doesn't seem like long enough to know for sure you want to spend the rest of your days with a single person, does it?"

Kian shrugs. "It seems like madness to us only because we're not madly in love, I think. Everyone always says when you know, you know."

"What if you never know?" I say softly, looking up at him. "What if *I* never know?"

Something soft flickers in Kian's eyes and he puts one heavy arm across my shoulders and pulls me close. "Then you can stay with me. Forever. And I won't even charge you much interest on the rent."

I pound a fist against his side and, in the process, accidentally splash him in the eye with chlorinated water.

"Ow!" he says as I begin to snort-laugh.

"It was an accident!"

He wipes the water from his eye and narrows his gaze at me. "You're gonna wish you hadn't done that, Bishop."

Still laughing, I begin dog-paddling away as fast as I can, which is obviously not very fast at all, considering the dog paddle is the extent of my swimming skills. "Stop!" I laugh-whisper. "We can't get all crazy just because we're jet-lagged idiots who came to swim at four in the morning."

In two quick strokes Kian's at my side, grabbing me by the waist and swinging me around while I try my best not to shriek. Trying to gain the upper hand, I grapple wildly with him, finally securing my legs around his waist and my arms around his neck so he can't swing me around anymore like some kind of wild monkey. We're abruptly face-to-face, chest to chest, body to body. I'm still laughing and so is he, but slowly, steadily, our laughter fades into the quiet, softly lit night.

I should let go. Maybe it's the jet lag or being in one of the most romantic cities in the world, but I don't let go. And neither does Kian.

I'm suddenly aware of his body heat, melting into me. I'm aware of his big hands, pressed into my bare back. His brown eyes, staring deep into mine. Of the drops of water, like diamonds, rolling languidly down his tan and muscled chest.

"We haven't practiced any dating moves since we've been here." Kian's voice is low and husky, his gaze still pinning me like a helpless butterfly.

My heart thuds almost painfully. This is not what he should be saying. "You're right. Maybe we should remedy that." And that is definitely not what *I* should've said in response.

The water moves gently around us as Kian continues, "We

haven't talked about kissing at all." His eyes slide automatically down to my mouth and, nervous, I lick my lips. "That's a very important part of connecting with someone. And as I recall, you haven't been able to keep your mind on *just* kissing, which is a problem."

I nod, riveted. "A big problem." My pulse is so loud I know Kian can hear it. Hell, Eli and Ava can probably hear it in their honeymoon suite on the thirty-fourth floor.

Kian's hands tighten just infinitesimally on my back, his fingers pressing into the ties on my triangle bikini. I'm aware that the knot I've tied is flimsy; he could undo it with just a slight tug. His head inches toward mine, and I notice for the first time how gorgeous his lips are. Full, soft, and firm in equal measure. Kissable lips. And now I don't want to wait another second.

I incline my head, too, and then our mouths are meeting in the middle. An electric spark jolts through me and I actually jump a little in Kian's arms. He tightens his grip on me and my legs squeeze harder around him, secret parts of me coming alive, warming up, liquefying. *What are you doing, what are you doing, what are you DOING, LYRIC* sounds through my brain but then I shut that communication center off completely, just kill the power and leave it in the dark. My id takes over, hungry and raw and selfish, primed for instant gratification and nothing else.

And kissing Kian is nothing if not instantly gratifying. I deepen the kiss.

The Sizzle Paradox

KIAN

Maybe it's the tiny pink bikini she's wearing. Maybe it's this trip, away from the stresses of our grad programs, with Lyric dressing up and acting like . . . like a woman rather than LB, my best friend who never met a pair of tattered, baggy shorts she didn't like. Maybe it's the soft lighting in the pool, the way her body moves through the water, her lithe and supple skin, pale as moonlight. I don't know what it is, exactly, but *something* has a hold of me. I haven't had a drink in over six hours, and yet, I am intoxicated.

She's pressing her lips into mine, harder, and suddenly that's not the only hard thing between us. A layer of flimsy bikini panties and my swim trunks. That's all that's between me and Lyric.

The thought has me brushing my tongue lightly against her mouth, and she opens wider to let me in. Holy fuck, she's hot. Lyric Bishop is an A+ kisser. Her soft breasts are pushed into my pecs, and she lets out a tiny moan, asking for more. My hands slide up from her back, tripping over the insubstantial strings to her bikini top, and tangle in her long hair. I push my mouth harder into hers, and we're tasting each other like we've been hungry for decades. I brush my tongue against her lips, and then gently bite her lower lip. She lets out another hungry moan and my hands are literally shaking from the effort of not taking this further, of not pressing her up against the wall and having my way with her.

A minute later, I pull back. I have to. I can't take this anymore.

I'm breathing hard and heavy, like I just ran the London fucking Marathon. But Lyric—she looks just as discombobulated. Her cheeks are flushed pink, her irises dilated, her lips parted. Her chest heaves and I can't help but stare. This is what every straight man's erotic fantasy is, right here. It's Lyric Bishop personified.

"There," I say, and my voice is tremulous as I set her down. It's the last thing I want to do, but I have to do it or there's no telling what I'll do next. What *we'll* do next. "That . . . uh, that was . . ."

I trail off as Lyric hops down silently and walks off a ways to the underwater stools where people are usually served alcohol. Good idea. I follow her and we both collapse into our own seats, suddenly not making eye contact anymore. Lyric busies herself putting her hair up into a wet bun, blond hair coiling at the nape of her neck. I find myself staring at her and then have to force myself to look away. And then I find myself wishing they really were serving alcohol right now.

She's quiet for so long I begin to worry. "Hey." I wait until she meets my eye, reluctantly. "You okay?"

She gives me a bright smile. "Yep. That was, wow. That kiss, um, was really . . . educational. But it was enjoyable, too. It was infotainment, really."

Infotainment. Educational. Enjoyable. None of those are words I would've chosen to describe the most mind-fucking-blowing kiss I've had in . . . ever. A wet sort of disappointment settles into my chest and I sit back, broadening my shoulders against the hurt. "Yeah. Definitely. Glad, ah, glad it helped." What the *fuck* is wrong with me? All of that chemistry, the sparks, everything I thought I was feeling—it was just one-sided.

Of course it was. This is Lyric fucking Bishop, for fuck's sake. My best fucking friend.

Fuck.

Chapter Fifteen

LYRIC

I'm looking at Kian, but I'm also not looking at him. My mind is reeling, but it's also strangely still.

His face is thunderous and dark, the kind of look he gets when he's upset about something and begins to curse every other word in each sentence he says. But . . . why? What does he have to be upset about right now, except our kiss?

Oh, damn. I must be a totally shitty kisser if it's caused him to look like that. Maybe he's realizing I'm way more of a lost cause than he thought. Maybe he's rethinking helping me. Maybe he felt like I was pressuring him to kiss me or something. Arrrgggh. I felt like I was practically being electrocuted every time his tongue brushed over mine but clearly, *clearly* that was just me.

I blame jet lag.

"Hmm?"

It's only when Kian looks up at me that I realize I've spoken out loud.

Damn. Well, there's nothing to do but blunder forward. Great job, Lyric. Totally winning at this socially competent adult thing.

"Um . . . the kiss. I blame jet lag. We promised we wouldn't get physical and then . . . you know." I laugh a horribly awkward, highly shrill, way-too-loud thing that could be used to carve passes through mountains. "Um . . . anyway. Thanks for the education but I think that definitely doesn't need to happen again. Right?"

Disagree with me, Kian. Tell me you want to kiss me again and then take me in your arms and do it.

SHUT UP, LYRIC.

Yes, brain. Noted.

"Right." Kian pushes himself off the stool and without looking back says, "I'm going to get some laps in before breakfast."

Oh. I've been dismissed.

I stick around the pool for a bit because I don't want to make it even more awkward by scrambling out and running away. I watch Kian's broad shoulders as he freestyles it down the length of the pool, his arms cutting powerfully in and out of the water, his form perfectly straight.

What the hell just happened?

I replay the scene in my head while I hover awkwardly on the stool. We were playing around, like we usually do. And then everything shifted. Kian wasn't just my best friend anymore. In that moment, in the breath before the kiss, he became a *man*. A seriously, painfully hot man. And I wanted to see what it might be like to kiss him. But wait. *He'd* been the one to suggest it, right? So . . . had he been feeling something more, too? I watch him as he swims. On the way back, he catches my eye, but then looks away.

What does *that* mean?

This has never happened between me and Kian before. If I ever had a doubt about what he was thinking, I'd just ask. But now . . . now everything feels horrible and weird and prickly and charged somehow. There's a taste in the air, like the static before a storm. What the fuck is happening?

After an appropriate amount of time has passed, I wave and get out without waiting to see if he saw me. I try not to hurry, but I know I'm practically speed walking to the door as I throw on my cover-up, eager to leave Kian—and all this strange energy—behind me.

But of course I don't leave it behind me. I'm not the kind of cool and casual woman who can just leave things be, let the cards fall where they may. I have to pick at everything like a scab, until I bleed.

I pace around in my room, my hair wet from the forty-minute shower I took to try and sort out my thoughts. Kian and I kissed. As far as I can tell, it was a mutual thing. For science. For my education. But also, as far as I can tell, there was something more there. Something electric. Something I have never, ever felt before in all my twenty-four years on this earth.

Something I want more of.

The thought shoots through my mind with the energy and brightness of a flare before I can quell it. *No*, Lyric. No more kissing. No more physicality. We had those ground rules for a reason and we broke them and already it's been a total disaster. I don't know what came over us—obviously we're delirious from the time difference or the moist British air or crumpets or something. And yes, Kian is a very attractive man, objectively speaking, as we've established before. But he's also *Kian*. Also established before.

I lost my mind temporarily, but it's back now. What I need to do is pretend that everything's fine. I need to get us over this awkward, weird little hump, and tomorrow, after Eli and Ava get married and we're celebrating at a pub, I'm going to pick up the hottest Brit I can find and put this whole thing behind me.

Satisfied with my game plan, I go to my suitcase and pick out a nice breakfast outfit. When I see Kian again, I'm going to give him a high five and compliment him on his freestyle. Nothing happened that we need to talk or even think about.

We're fine. Everything's fine.

KIAN

Watching your best male friend get married is a mindfuck. We're at a pub for the after-party and I can't help looking at Eli and Ava, his hands on her hips, her eyes only on him. They're *married*. Committed for life. They've decided they want to do everything together from now until the end of time, their lives sewn together into one seamless fabric. They may even want kids. What does that kind of love, that kind of surety, feel like?

My eyes unwittingly dart to Lyric, who's dressed in a shiny, low-cut halter top and the same tight jeans she wore on our "date" back in the States. She brought something like this up at the pool yesterday. Before we . . . I clear my throat and take a deep drink of my pint of lager.

Our table is rambunctious tonight. Eli and Ava are dancing off to the side, but the others are tipsy, loud, yelling over the music, laughing at just about anything. Lyric catches my eye in the middle of a story about a hot dog vendor who tried to pressure her for a date. I put on a quick smile, trying to make it look casual. But something about the way her own smile fades and she stutters in the middle of her story tells me I didn't get it right.

The thing is, I can't stop thinking about that kiss. About the way she felt, so weightless and warm in my arms. About that pink bikini. I've had my fair share of sex. But there was something about that single kiss that turned me on more than the best sex

I've had, ever. More than Tatiana, the girl I dated senior year who insisted on blindfolding and tying me up every time she gave me a blow job. And holy shit, that was HOT.

I even thought about the kiss—about Lyric—to get off in the shower this morning. It's fucked up, I know that. Lyric clearly viewed the kiss as an exercise, just like our date at Pepper Tony. She hasn't even brought it up or seemed fazed by it. So why am I still so hung up?

I drain my pint, stifling a groan of frustration. *Goddamn it, Montgomery.*

"Hey."

I look up to see one of Ava's friends, Freya, smiling at me as she scooches closer to me in the booth. There's a bit of lipstick on her front tooth, but she has a nice smile. "Hey."

"Can you believe we're in London and Ava is now Mrs. Delacorte? It's wild."

I shake my head as we both consider the newlyweds, still dancing in a pub where no one else is. But I guess they can hear the music differently than the rest of us. "Yeah." Freya and I turn back to each other and I laugh lightly. "I'm not sure I feel old enough to have a married best friend."

"Right?" Freya shakes out her dark, curly hair and grins at me. "I'm still a *long* ways from wanting to get hitched. But then again, I'm only twenty-two."

"Oh." I study her open face, inhale the fruity smell of her shampoo, and try to feel a spark of interest in the conversation. "So do you go to Columbia?"

"NYU. I'm a Poli-Sci major. Graduate in the summer."

"Right, me too. Graduate, I mean. In the summer."

There's an awkward pause. I *never* have awkward pauses in conversations with attractive women. What the actual fuck.

My gaze flits away and rests on Lyric—her glowing skin, the shimmery stuff she's slicked on her lips. She's walking up to some fit-looking dude in a black leather jacket at the front of the pub. I force myself to look away.

Freya leans in just as I'm racking my brain about what to say next. "You seem distracted," she says softly, moving her arm so it's now resting lightly against mine on the table.

I look back at Freya and smile a little. "Sorry. I . . ." If I tell her it's just jet lag, I know we could be up in my hotel room within the hour. It's probably exactly what I need to stop the thoughts that won't quit swirling around my head. But my brain has other plans. "The truth is, there's someone else," I hear myself say. "Someone I can't stop thinking about."

"Oh." Freya straightens. "Sorry. I didn't know."

Yeah, me neither. I try on another small smile. "It's not your fault." Standing up, I put some money on the table—probably way too much, but I need to get out of here. The damp heat of the pub is starting to make me a little sick. "See you later?"

Freya nods and turns back to her friends. Without looking back at Lyric and the (hot—who am I kidding?) guy she's now laughing with, I slip out of the pub and into the cool, wet London night outside.

LYRIC

This awkward potato is broiled and baked, baby. The ridiculously attractive British guy in front of me—Fergus Tran—is scorching everything around him. I'm surprised his glass of scotch hasn't evaporated into the ether yet.

Out of the corner of my eye, I see Kian talking to Freya, one of Ava's super gorgeous girlfriends. Something inside me shrivels up but I muscle through the feeling. Great! That's really great. He *should* talk to hot girls. Just like I should talk to hot guys. This is all going according to plan and it's all just fantastic and awesome.

I turn my attention back to Fergus in the black leather jacket.

He offered me his barstool almost as soon as I walked up and is now standing next to me, leaning one arm against the bar top. His skin is perfectly tawny, his full, thick black beard glistening with whatever citrus-scented oil he's rubbed into it, his glossy hair pulled back into a low man bun. I can see tendrils of a tattoo peeking out from under his leather jacket, snaking up his neck. Hottttt. "I'm guessing from your accent that you're American."

I bat my eyelashes. I don't even have to pretend to put on feminine wiles. They just come naturally around Fergus. As *I* probably will, later. Heh heh.

A memory of me in Kian's arms, wet from more than just pool water, flashes into my mind and I push it resolutely away. *No. We had a deal, Lyric. Find a hot guy and get that kiss out of your head by replacing it with some random-hot-guy sex.*

I toss my hair and he watches me toss it, his eyes widening just a bit. Yessss. "Yeah, I'm from NYC. Here for a friend's wedding."

Fergus leans in, smiling. Warm citrus mingles with aged scotch and envelops me in a heady scent. "Well, I have to tell you, Lyric, I find American accents quite sexy."

I laugh throatily. "Ditto." At Fergus's slightly confused expression, I rush to clarify, "But with British accents, I mean."

His face relaxes into a smile again. "Really? Well, it sounds like we have quite a lot in common, then."

Smooth. So smooth. Trying to match him in his classy smoothness, I say, "Indeed." And then immediately worry he's going to think I'm a jerk for saying "indeed," which is a decidedly British way of speaking and I, clearly, as we've already established, am American. "Uh, I mean, quite." No, shit. That's a Britishism, too. "Definitely." Ah, better. I relax and take a swig of my wine.

Fergus watches me. Although he's still smiling, there's now a small crinkle between his beautifully groomed eyebrows. "What do you do for work, Lyric?"

"I'm a grad student."

"Ah." Fergus's brow clears as if this answers whatever question was brewing in his head. I'm too scared to ask. His easy smile comes back. "I thought you were a model."

I almost choke on my wine. "Ha ha, no, not even close." I wave a slightly unsteady arm at him. I think this British wine is more potent than what I'm used to at home. "But, I mean, I could clearly believe that about you. What do *you* do?"

He takes a sip of his scotch and says, with a slight preen, "Well, I *am* a model. Strictly catalog at the mo, but hoping to land bigger accounts in the future."

A small part of me wonders if he just said *I* could be a model so he could talk about the fact that he really is one. But I shut that part up by stuffing a mental brownie into its mouth. I'm not going to psych myself out of this one. "Wow." I lean forward and try to look more impressed than I feel. "That's amazing!"

We smile at each other for a "mo." (Stop it, Lyric. Be nice.) Then Fergus leans in closer and says, "So . . . can I safely assume you're staying in a hotel nearby?"

He says it like "assyoom," which is *trés* sexy. But already, I feel like the wind's been taken out of my sails, for some reason. Probably because he's rapidly appearing to be a vain, slightly vapid pretty boy. Which shouldn't really matter, because I'm just looking for a meaningless hookup. And yet, here we are.

"I am." I try to wrangle any last vestiges of attraction I'd first felt toward Fergus, like someone trying desperately to snag scraps of paper from the air during a windstorm. And after a lengthy pause, I add, "Would you like me to show you?"

Fergus's irises dilate even more. "Absolutely."

I'm not exactly forcing myself. But I'm also not exactly *not* forcing myself. I know this isn't the best pre-sex mindset. Here's an actual, literal British model dripping with sex—I couldn't have asked for anyone more objectively, conventionally attractive. So I'm going to stop overthinking and overanalyzing, just like Kian advised me on our practice date.

Kian's hands in my hair. His mouth, sure and strong, his tongue—

STOP IT YOU MORON.

I hop off my barstool and take Fergus's hand. Then I all but march us out the door.

ꝏ

My nipple is in Fergus's mouth. And I'm thinking about Ötzi the Iceman.

Let me back up: Fergus and I undressed each other at record speed once we got to my hotel room, tops and bottoms and jackets littering the floor like bread crumbs in a fairy tale. After taking a moment to appreciate his perfectly modelesque physique—lithe and wiry, so different from Kian's gladiator build—I commented on his tattoos, of which he had many (a disappointing number were acquired when he was "pissed" or "sozzled"). And then he pointed out his very first tattoo, which was a little beer bottle on his calf, which then led me to think about the first tattoo *ever*, which has been attributed to Ötzi the Iceman who died in 3350 B.C. and was discovered frozen in a glacier in 1991.

None of which is germane to my nipple being in Fergus's mouth. I know this.

I try an experimental moan, just to get into the spirit of things. This urges him on to greater frenzied sucking, but now I'm just staring at the side of his face, feeling his beard on my chest, and thinking it probably feels a little like a ferret curled up on my chest. Not that I've ever had that happen; it's just a supposition.

I sit up, push Fergus's head away, and pull the blanket up to cover myself. He looks like someone awoken from a deep sleep; his eyes blink a few times and his face is red where he was nuzzling me. "I'm sorry," I say, biting my lower lip. "I'm just . . . not feeling it."

He sits back and runs his hands through his hair, looking completely befuddled. "Oh. Was it—what happened?"

Kian happened. The pool happened. That damn kiss happened.

"Nothing. You're great, Fergus, really. I'm just not in the headspace for this, I think. Maybe I had too much wine."

"Oh," he says again. "Right." He looks around, as if an appropriate comment to rescue him from this hideous situation might be hiding behind the pullout sofa. "Um . . . do you want me to wait around for a bit? Just in case?"

What? What are we supposed to do while he "waits" for my libido to show up like a tardy party guest—watch *'Allo 'Allo*? Stare at his tattoos? Oil his beard? "N-no, that's okay," I say in a rush. "I think I need to sleep this off, maybe."

He checks his watch. "Right. Well, the pub's still open for another hour, so I'll probably just head back down there."

What he doesn't say but what I hear anyway: *There are probably other chicks there I can pick up. The night's not lost yet.*

I give him a wan smile. "Yeah, sounds good. And um, sorry."

He gives me a watery smile right back as he gets dressed,

also at record speed. "Cheers." His shoes in hand, he walks out the door and lets it slam closed.

I sit back against my pillows and breathe out a sigh. Dammit.

My mind drifts to Freya and Kian, how they were getting cozy in the pub. Is she in his room now? I bet he isn't thinking about Ötzi the Iceman with *her* nipple in his mouth.

Groaning, I pull a pillow onto my face. If even *London* can't help me, I'm 100 percent fucked. And not in the good way.

Chapter Sixteen

KIAN

The day we're due to fly out, I'm eating a giant stack of pancakes in the hotel restaurant when Lyric walks in, wearing a long dress to her ankles and thin straps that hang off her tiny shoulders. I see her look around, notice me, and hesitate for just a moment before she beams and waves. And I find myself hanging on that infinitesimal hesitation like some kind of desperate jackass—what was going through her mind right now? Was she thinking about our kiss? And if so, does she regret it?

The minute I have that thought, I want to stab myself in the eye with my fork. Of course she fucking regrets it. If she's even thinking about it anymore. She probably went home with that leather-jacketed douche from last night and her hesitation was likely just her hangover making her vision fuzzy.

She walks over to me and slides into the chair across from mine. "Yum!" She eyes the strawberries on my stack but doesn't reach over and pick one up like she would've done before. I push it toward her, an invitation, and she bites (pun intended).

Once she's swallowed her mouthful of strawberry—and I definitely *do not* watch her lips as she puts it into her mouth—she smiles at me. "Hey."

"Hey." I continue eating, but I'm also trying to be casual and friendly and my usual self. Instead, I keep seeing her in that bikini in my mind's eye. My mind's eye needs fucking contacts so it can focus on the here and now.

"So," Lyric asks, "are you all packed and ready to go? I could help you if you're not."

"I'm not, but I think I'll be okay." Lyric always packs the night before a trip, whereas I'm more of a "toss everything in an hour before leaving for the airport" kinda guy. My way gives her hives. "Did you have fun last night?"

Why did I ask her that? I kept thinking to myself that I would *not* mention Leather Jacket, but of course that's the first thing that flies out of my mouth the instant she's near. Idiot.

Her smile fades just a tad. "Yeah, it was great."

What does *that* mean? Did that guy know some kinky British sex moves?

But she doesn't give me any more information and I have too much pride to ask.

"Did *you* have fun?" she asks, and there's something in her voice, a pointedness that I don't get.

Did I have fun walking to an empty hotel room alone in the ever-present mist? "Sure." I continue eating but now I'm watching her. "It was fantastic."

She gives me a tight smile and folds her arms on the table. "Awesome. Glad to hear it."

Before I can deconstruct what the hell kind of subtext is playing out here, the middle-aged waiter comes over and takes Lyric's order—just a black coffee. She's upset about something; that's the only time she passes up an excuse to eat restaurant pancakes with extra syrup and chocolate chips and butter. Lyric is made of spun sugar.

Her lips definitely were.

Fuck that, I am *not* going there. Not even in my head.

"You okay?" I ask mildly, my focus shifting to pouring myself some more orange juice from the decanter.

"Are *you* okay?"

I do look at her then. "Yeah, why wouldn't I be?"

"Then I am, too."

The waiter returns with her black coffee, but before he leaves, he beams down at us. "You two are the *loveliest* couple!" he gushes. "I can tell you're newlyweds. Just something about the energy between you." He winks at me. "Congratulations, love. You've nabbed a good one there. She's just gorgeous."

"We're not together," I say weakly, but it's too late; he's already bustled off.

Lyric stirs her coffee (it's black; why is she stirring it?) and doesn't make eye contact with me at all. I wait for her to look up so we can laugh about this, so she can shriek and protest like she usually does when someone insinuates that we're dating. But she doesn't. And the longer I stare at her when she doesn't know I'm looking, the longer I want to keep staring.

The waiter wasn't wrong. She *is* gorgeous. But she's also the only woman I know—hell, the only person I know—who can eat twelve lemon squares in a sitting without puking. And the only one I know who's ever stopped four lanes of traffic to rescue a turtle that was stuck on the highway. She got a ticket for obstructing traffic that it took her a week of overtime to pay. She said she'd do it all over again anyway.

And now I've fucked things up between us. All because I couldn't keep my hands—and my lips—off her. Why the fuck did I go there? Why couldn't I have left her alone?

"Look, I'm sorry I made things awkward."

She jerks her head up to look at me. "What?"

"You know. The pool." There's a mixture of torment and relief on her face that I'm bringing it up. I push my plate aside, two pancakes still uneaten. "That was a stupid idea, and I'm sorry things have been weird between us."

"They're not weird!" Lyric chirps brightly and then, seeing my dubious face, she relaxes into a little lump. "Okay, they're a little weird."

"Mm-hmm." I smile a bit. "But can we both agree that was just London madness and we're ready for a clean slate again?"

She nods enthusiastically before I'm even finished. "Yeah, definitely. Just London madness. And we're going back to the States today, which means we can leave all of that behind."

"Right." I grin at her.

"I love you," she tells me on impulse, her hand squeezing mine on the table.

"Love ya, too, Pound." I slide the plate over to her. "Want my pancakes?"

She considers them and then raises her hand for the waiter. "Can you please bring me extra syrup and butter?"

And I know we're going to be okay.

ꝏ

Except things are not o-fucking-kay.

On the plane, Lyric and I talk and chat and laugh like usual. She's sitting in the middle seat next to me and then I realize I'm making a very big effort not to touch her arm on the armrest in between us and my legs are squeezed painfully together because I don't want to accidentally caress her thigh with mine. This is not easy to do when you're a six-six dude in coach.

And then Lyric turns to me. "Hey. Do you mind if I move this out of the way?" She gestures to the armrest between us. "Just more room to spread out that way, you know? We have another six hours to go."

I smile faintly at her. "Yeah, sure. No worries."

She reads and I work. It's all fine. Until Lyric falls asleep.

Her head comes to rest on my chest. I can smell the pink, fruity smell of her shampoo. But it's not just her shampoo; there's a soft, round, sensual scent underneath that's very Lyric. My heart begins to pound; my fists clench against my thighs. I should move her. Just a slight nudge and she'd turn her head the other way. I could go back to my thesis. But every nerve ending in my body wants her to stay exactly as she is.

When the stewardess passes by, I quietly ask for a blanket and cover Lyric with it as carefully as I can, without moving her. And then I enjoy the weight and warm press of her sleeping on my chest.

I am so fucked.

ꙮ

Thankfully, things return to a semblance of normalcy when we get back to the States and our routines. We've both been jet-lagged enough and busy enough at school that we haven't had the chance to go out on another "date" (and look, I want to help Lyric with her love life and by extension her thesis, but I'm also not stupid and very aware that every time I give her a lesson, I'm playing with fire).

A week after we got back, I get up from the couch where I've been working, stretch, and walk to the bathroom, pushing open the door.

Oh, shit.

Lyric's in a lacy black bra and matching panties, rubbing something that smells like flowers into her hair. Steam from her recent shower envelops her, makes her look like a shimmering mirage in a desert.

I thought she was in her room. We stare at each other for a long moment, and I can't help it—my eyes rove over her body.

Her fragile collarbone, the curve of her breasts and stomach, the soft fullness of her thighs. And then I force my eyes away. "Shit. *Shit*. I'm sorry."

She doesn't say anything. She doesn't move to cover herself. She stands there, her wet hair slicked back, staring at me through the hazy steam.

There's a beat. I have an almost overpowering urge to walk in and shut the door behind me, take her into my arms, and kiss every inch of her pale, exposed skin. But I force myself to step outside and shut the door. Through it all, Lyric never says a word.

LYRIC

As soon as Kian closes the door, I clap my hands over my cheeks and stare at myself in the mirror. My blue eyes are wide, my eyebrows virtually disappearing into my hairline.

Kian walked in on me in my underwear. And instead of screaming and throwing something at him like I would've done even a month and a half ago, I stood there and stared at him with what *felt* like come-hither eyes. At least, my brain was definitely all, *Come hither, Kian*. And what did he do? He shut the door and booked it out of here.

I screw my eyes shut with the absolute humiliation that now burns through every cell in my body. I can tell even without looking at my reflection that I'm a super flattering shade of third-degree burn.

Fuck. Fuck, fuck, fuck.

What's Kian out there thinking? Is he wondering why I'm such a freak? I didn't even say a single word. Not a, "Don't worry about it." Not even a gasp. Nothing. I just stood there staring at him like a psychopath on the verge of her first kill.

I open my eyes and study myself in the mirror. Okay, this is salvageable. I made it super fucking awkward, but that doesn't mean I have to leave it like that. I just need to go out there and be casual about it, just . . . just act like nothing happened. And maybe Kian will be confused enough that he'll forget my empty eyes gazing at him for over ten seconds.

Jesus.

A moment later, I've thrown on my T-shirt and shorts and I saunter out into the living room, even though every one of my "casual" footsteps sounds thunderous and plodding to me. I'm as subtle as a brontosaurus ballerina.

Kian looks up as I walk into view. His expression is mostly guarded, but there's a flash of . . . something . . . on his face that makes my pulse quicken. I remember that, in the bathroom, it wasn't *just* me staring at him. For a split second, Kian had stared at *me,* too. In fact, now that the heavy, flaming curtains of humiliation have fallen a bit, I distinctly remember the way his eyes moved along my body, drinking in every curve.

My pulse beats in the hollow of my throat as I take a seat on the couch, leaving a one-cushion space between Kian and myself. "Um, hi."

He tips his chin, once, but doesn't say anything. I guess it's his turn to be weird now.

"Sorry I forgot to lock the door." Did I forget, honestly? Freud would probably disagree.

"It's okay." Kian turns back to his computer. "No worries." Is it just me or is there the slightest tremble to his hands as he types? I have a sneaking suspicion that if I were to peek at his screen, I'd see him typing nonsense. The thought *thrills* me. Why am I such a deviant?

"Hey, uh, so I was thinking. My deadline to turn something in to Livingstone is right around the corner and . . . I'd really appreciate another lesson." I clear my throat, my cheeks suddenly flaming even though everything I said can be construed as 100 percent innocent. Because honestly, I'm not even being that sneaky. It's pretty clear why I'm asking this.

Our last attempt at fake dating—i.e., London, that tempting seductress of a city—turned out to consist of a hot make out session. Kian just walked in on me half-naked in the bathroom. And now I'm asking for another fake date? Real smooth. The worst part is, I don't even question myself in the moment. I *know* this is a bad idea. That nothing good will come from this. But I'm like a kid with a cupcake under her nose—all about that sweet, sweet instant gratification.

He looks up, studying me for a second before he says, "Sure."

I blink. I was expecting him to try and let me down easy, maybe say he hadn't realized when he first offered to tutor me that I was such a pervert. "Oh, okay. When do you want to do it?"

Kian's gaze drifts across my lips for an instant at the double entendre—or maybe I'm imagining things I want to see. "I actually have to have dinner with my parents on Saturday, and I was wondering if you wanted to come. You're always a good temper diffuser."

We smile. It's true; I have been a good buffer between Kian and his parents in the past, especially him and his dad. "Sounds good."

"And if you want, after that, we could go get drinks or something?"

I shrug, although I'm already planning what to wear. "Yeah, cool." I hop up from the couch. "I'm meeting Charlie for a study session. See you later?"

He barely looks at me as he waves.

Chapter Seventeen

LYRIC

"It's like some weird dance—we're either staring or acting like we can't stand to look at each other. We go out of our way to never casually touch anymore or we're kissing." I cradle my head in my hands and try not to hyperventilate. "It's a total disaster. I wish I'd never agreed to go to stupid fucking London with its dumbass romantic infinity pool."

Charlie and I are in the Columbia Science and Engineering Library, tucked away in a back corner by a giant window-wall, our table littered with textbooks and sheafs of papers and half the inventory of Staples. Now that I'm away from Kian and the soup of pheromones constantly sloshing between us, reality is slamming back in. Have we ruined our friendship completely with that sizzling-but-totally-inappropriate kiss?

Charlie pats my shoulder and looks suitably concerned, as someone watching her best friend descend into a severe state of panicky freak-out (yes, that is, in fact, the clinical term for what I am experiencing) should. "But I thought you said the kiss was just a weird one-off and things were fine."

I lift my head and look bleakly at her. "I was lying. It was wishful thinking on my part, Charlie. Once we got home things seemed okay for a while. But him walking in on me and our bizarre reactions just showed me . . . things are far from fine. Things are, in fact, deeply fucked."

Charlie grins. "I mean, being deeply fucked isn't always a bad thing."

I glare at her but before I can say that I hope she's enjoying my intense emotional pain, someone clears their throat behind us and we turn.

Zoey stands there in a vintage-style polka-dot dress, looking vaguely uncomfortable. "Hey, Lyric." Her eyes dart to Charlie because she has, no doubt, heard the completely ill-timed thing my dumbass best friend just said. It's anyone's guess how much of *my* part of the conversation she heard about the guy *I* introduced her to. Shit.

"H-hey, Zoey." I sit up straight. Not only am I fucking things up for myself, I am also most certainly fucking them up for Zoey. "What's up? You know Charlie, right?"

They shake hands, Charlie holding on to Zoey's hand just a moment too long. "Hi, Zoey. I know you."

Zoey smiles, surprised, her cheeks going a little rosy. "Hi, Charlie. I, uh, I've seen you around, too." She turns to me. "I wanted to see if you'd mind locking up the lab today? I have a doctor's appointment."

"Sure, no problem." I clear my throat, an idea suddenly taking root. "Hey, what are you doing next Thursday night?"

Zoey frowns a little. "I'm not sure . . . probably nothing, considering I'm a grad student." Charlie snorts appreciatively at her joke and Zoey smiles. Turning back to me, she adds, "Why?"

"Kian and I are having some people over around eight. You should come."

I can see Charlie staring at me from the corner of my eye, but I ignore her.

"Okay, I might stop by," Zoey says, after a pause. "Thanks."

Charlie pipes up, "I'll be there, too." And then she actually, literally winks at Zoey, who now full-on *blushes*.

When Zoey's gone, I turn to Charlie. "What the hell was *that*?"

Charlie laughs, looking totally delighted with herself. "I don't know, man. Something about Zoey just . . . brings out the tigress in me. I've *never* felt that confident before, so full of . . . lush sexual Goddess energy. Wow."

I narrow my eyes at her. "You know Kian's trying to get with her, right? Put your lush energy away before I disinvite you from the party."

Charlie shrugs, grins, and leans back in her chair, totally unapologetic. "Hey, she's pretty irresistible. And bi, from what I hear. Also? It sounds like Kian wants to bone *you*, not her, so I don't see a problem anyway."

I throw a paper clip at Charlie. It bounces off the tip of her nose and we both laugh. Then she says, "So I'm guessing that party thing was totally impromptu?"

"Yeah. Maybe Kian and I just need to spend more time with other eligible people to banish this weirdness between us. Can you bring Greg?"

Charlie sits up in her chair. "Greg-my-neighbor-who's-had-an-intense-crush-on-you-for-four-years Greg?"

"The very one." I put my fine hair up in a tiny bun and stick a pencil through it.

"I thought you said there was no chemistry there."

Folding my hands neatly in front of me on the table, I lean in. "Let me explain something to you, Charlie. There is no chemistry *anywhere*. I'm beginning to realize that I'm only capable of being attracted to people who are completely wrong and unsuitable for me on every level. Therefore, I am willing to give Greg a try. Do you understand?"

Perhaps seeing the maniacal, desperate glint in my eye, Charlie nods vigorously. "Yep. Got it, Doc."

"Great." I attempt a serene smile and crack open my laptop. "Now let's get to work."

KIAN

I'm fidgety and grouchy on Saturday, the way I always am when I have an obligatory dinner scheduled with my parents. That's the thing: Neither party really wants this to happen and yet it happens every other month like clockwork. Apparently it's written in some parent-child codebook that we must meet face-to-face in order to assure ourselves and anyone else that we are a normal, functioning family.

That's what my entire childhood was like, and here I am, repeating the same pattern well into adulthood. Maybe that's what makes me an irritable bear in human form. Who the hell knows. I yank grumpily at the collar on my button-down shirt, another formality my father insists on when I am dining in His House, the Hallowed and Opulent Cathedral of Montgomery.

Lyric puts her small hand on mine and squeezes as we walk up the grand stone staircase that leads to my parents' . . . well, mansion is really the only way to describe it. They live in the Old Greenwich neighborhood in Connecticut, and yes, my childhood was ridiculously privileged and wealthy and therefore I have no room to complain about any shitty thing that happened. And yet, my stomach churns as I reach for the doorbell.

A stately gong-like sound rings through the house and then the door is opened by Oliver, my dad's butler. Yes, he has a butler. Yes, the butler dresses in a uniform. No, I don't want to talk about it.

"Master Kian," Oliver says in his clipped British accent (dear God, will the clichés never end?). "Welcome." He bows slightly and stands off to the side as we enter.

Dad hired Oliver last year, but I will never, ever get used to him. I smile at the balding, middle-aged man who has to suffer who-knows-what indignities at the hands of my father and reach out for a handshake, even though I know I'm technically not supposed to do that. I'm supposed to walk to the dining room without acknowledging his presence. Oliver balks a bit at this inappropriate show of friendliness, but then his training takes over and his face goes blank. "Hey, Oliver. Good to see you again."

Lyric smiles radiantly at him. In fact, I have to do a double take—I haven't taken a minute to appreciate how good she looks because I've been stuck in my head all day. But she's made an effort for our fake date later, I see, clad in a dress that puffs out at her waist and is covered in watercolor-like spring flowers. She looks fresh and sweet, her hair in a braid that looks like a crown on her head. "Hi, Oliver!"

In spite of himself, Oliver gives her a slight smile—more than he did for me. I have a sneaking suspicion that Oliver has had a soft spot for Lyric ever since the first time he met her. "Miss Bishop."

"It smells *divine* in here, as usual," Lyric continues, as Oliver leads us to the dining room. "New room spray?"

He cuts his eyes at her, still smiling a little. "Rosemary and Lemon, from Williams Sonoma. On sale at the moment. They say lemon improves focus and concentration. For those who might be academically inclined and working on their theses." Proof that Oliver hears way more than he lets on.

"Oh my God, you're amazing—thank you." Lyric reaches out and squeezes his tux-clad elbow. "I'm gonna stock up on some this weekend."

Oliver looks like he might swoon from happiness. Instead,

he deposits us in the cavernous dining room where I suffered through many a hellacious culinary experience as a teenager, announces us to my parents—who are standing by the bay window having drinks—and leaves.

"Kian." My father turns and surveys me like I'm one of his new-construction McMansions. His mouth turns very slightly downward at the corners when he sees the Gap button-down shirt I'm wearing. He's tall, around six two, but somehow seems taller in his disapproval. Then his blue eyes move to Lyric and crinkle just the slightest bit. There's a sudden warmth in his voice that wasn't present a second ago. "Lyric. How are you?"

We walk forward and take the drinks my mom, silent as usual, is handing us. There's a moscato for Lyric and a scotch on the rocks for me—my father's drink. I hate scotch. But no matter how many times I've requested a beer, they've never accepted such a plebeian libation as "my" beverage.

"I'm well, thank you, Mr. Montgomery!" Lyric chirps. Somehow, she manages to sound both cheerful and respectful, qualities my father wishes I had. She turns to my mom. "Mrs. Montgomery, you look absolutely ravishing. Is that a new skirt?"

My mother smooths down her pastel-colored skirt, her golden-brown skin flushing a little. "It is. Adrienne found it for me. A vintage Chanel." Adrienne is her personal shopper, has been for twenty years now. I have a feeling Adrienne knows more about my mom than my dad or I do.

At a signal from Oliver, who shimmers in and shimmers out (to badly paraphrase P. G. Wodehouse; and yes, as someone with an Indian mother, I was pretty much raised on British fiction), we all move to the dining table. It can seat up to twenty people, but tonight we occupy just a tiny corner, leaving most of it barren. I think about how it's a statement for how my parents occupy this insanely big house—each of them relegated to their own cool corners while the rest sits empty, sad, and unused—but keep that thought to myself.

"Graduation is right around the corner," my father says while we wait. His hands are cupped loosely around his scotch glass, and there are noticeably more lines around his eyes than the last time I saw him. "Have you given any more thought to where you're going to work?"

My own hand squeezes around my glass. "Well, as I said last time, I'm pretty sure I'm going to take a job with the forestry service. If I can get in, that is."

I'm sure my dad has contacts in the forestry department and could get me a job there if he wanted. But it's a testament to how little I want to leverage the Montgomery name and a testament to how little he wants me branching out on my own that neither of us has broached that topic.

He takes a sip of his scotch and considers my answer in silence. My mother has gone as still as a rabbit hoping to elude a predator. Lyric is watching my father with a cautious interest. It's like the whole house is holding its breath waiting for him. As much as I despise his ethics, the man can command a room. "You should give more thought to my offer, Kian. Working for Montgomery Developments will pay a lot more than the forestry department could."

At this, my mother clears her throat and stands. "Excuse

me," she says, to no one in particular. "I need to check on something. I'll be back in a minute."

We watch as she leaves, her skirt swishing around her legs. It's obvious to me that she's just escaping the unpleasantness she knows is going to follow, like it always does when my father begins to make pronouncements about my life. My mother was never very good at confrontation.

My father, unfazed by her retreat, turns back to me. "As I was saying, you have an open offer at Montgomery Developments. And it'll give you the start in life you want."

"Or the start in life *you* want me to have." I stare at him and he gazes back coolly. Under the table, Lyric sets her foot gently against mine, in solidarity or compassion or warning. "We've had this discussion before, and I'm done having it. Helping rich couples design green homes is not how I want to use my degree." The truth is, telling people his son works for the forestry department would probably mulch my father's ego. But that's his problem, not mine.

The cook, Ricardo, dressed in his chef whites, begins to bring soup dishes out with the help of my parents' housekeeper, Moira. "A soup to start. Roasted tomato and sweet pepper, made with fresh organic vegetables from the garden."

Lyric smiles brightly at him. "This looks delicious, Ricardo. Thank you."

My father and I follow suit and murmur our thanks as the rich aroma of the food curls around us. But I know it's going to taste like ash in my mouth.

Ricardo and Moira leave and we dig in, knowing better

than to wait for my mother. My father continues in his cool, quiet voice. "Sometimes we do things we don't really want to do because it makes the most sense. It's part of being an adult."

Lyric stops eating, her spoon hovering in midair between bowl and mouth.

My own spoon clatters into my bowl, splashing the white table linen that probably cost more than what I pay for rent with red liquid. Glaring at my father's complacent face, I lean forward. "Really? *You're* going to lecture me on delaying gratification?"

My father raises one graying eyebrow. "And just what is that supposed to mean?"

I take a breath. "Nothing. Never mind."

My father scoffs quietly. "See? This is the problem with you. You've lacked gumption from the moment you were born. Never ambitious or aggressive enough, never showing any of that Montgomery fire. It's sad, really."

Lyric straightens in her chair beside me. "That is *not* fair," she says, her voice hard.

I look up at my father. "Okay. You want me to finish my thought? What I swallowed back, not because I lack gumption but because I was trying to be civil?" I lean forward as he holds my gaze. "You're a sorry excuse for a Montgomery, Dad. You may have gumption and fire and aggression, but I'm ashamed to share your name. I think it's hilarious *you're* talking to *me* about the evils of instant gratification. Because you and I both know you've been having affairs for twenty-eight of the thirty years you've been married to Mom. You may not want to admit it, but that doesn't make the truth go away."

My gaze catches on a flicker of movement at the entrance to the dining room. My mother stands there, her face ashen. Lyric has gone pale.

Shit. *Shit.*

My mother doesn't move. Her gaze locks on mine for a long moment and then she looks away. She doesn't enter the room, but she doesn't retreat again either. It's as if she's pretending she isn't even here, like she's a wraith. Lyric would know a fancy psychological term for what she's going through. Or maybe it's just plain denial.

Red splotches appear on my father's cheeks. He hasn't noticed her presence, hasn't realized the damage I've done. "You—you are *completely* out of line."

He's never stuttered before, not once in his life. I have to admit, some angry, Neanderthal part of me enjoys seeing his pain. Everyone else has had to suffer in silence around him. It's time he finally pays his due.

For twenty-eight years, he's been having a series of affairs—with secretaries, with subordinates, with women he meets on business trips. I've walked in on more than one amorous phone call over the years. I found old letters in his office drawers when I was a kid messing around where I shouldn't have been. When I was a teen and realized just how fucked up this was, I begged, cajoled, tried to force him to come clean to my mom. But he never did. And that's why I moved out at eighteen and stopped talking to him, save for these bimonthly dinners.

"I may be out of line, but I'm not untruthful. And you and I both know it," I reply calmly now, not breaking eye contact.

There's a deep, cold silence. I can hear Lyric breathing softly beside me, and I take her hand under the table. She squeezes my fingers back and it feels good—like a lifeline, somehow. These people in front of me may be my blood family. But the woman beside me is the family I chose.

"You should leave," my father says finally, his voice trembling like a tuning fork.

"Fine." I scrape my chair back and my mother looks at me again, her brown eyes catching on mine.

I hesitate a second, wondering if she's going to tell me to stay. But she remains quiet, ghostly, insubstantial.

So I walk to the front door, Lyric close on my heels, and leave.

Chapter Eighteen

LYRIC

The rented car is full of a heavy silence as we pull away from Kian's parents' house and down the sloping, tree-lined drive. I don't know what to say, or even if it's my place to say it at all. I sit there, my hands balled on my thighs, staring straight ahead.

It's weird because even two months ago, I would've said something highly inappropriate and irreverent, guaranteed to break the silence and make Kian laugh. But right now, I just keep cutting my eyes at him, looking at the set of his square jaw, the way his hands handle the steering wheel so ably and confidently. And I can't help it, but I'm thinking about how he also held me so ably and confidently in the pool in London and then I'm wondering why the fuck I'm thinking of *that* of all things and that if Kian knew he'd definitely think I was a degenerate and then—

"Hey, LB. You okay?"

I jump as if he pinched me. "Um. What."

He tosses me a bemused look as he rolls down the window for fresh air. Kian is all about the fresh air. What's so wrong with circulated air is what I want to know. "Are. You. Mentally. Physically. And spiritually. Okay?"

I narrow my eyes at his sarcasm. "Yeah, I'm fine." Then I straighten out my face. "But the real question is . . . are you? That was some heavy shit in there."

He chuckles as we get on the highway, though his jaw and the corners of his eyes are still tense. "Is that the clinical term for it?"

"Seriously, Kian. That was a lot."

"Yeah, it was." He's got one hand on the wheel now, the other elbow bent and half hanging out the car window. The wind ruffles his curly brown hair and I watch, fascinated, as the setting sun paints it red and gold. "I feel bad that my mom heard all that, honestly. That's not how I wanted her to find out. But . . . I'm also kind of glad, in a way. As a kid I never knew how to bring it up, you know, or even if I should. And then I felt guilty for knowing and never saying anything. Like . . . like my dad and I were complicit in this thing."

I reach out to pat his thigh, then hesitate, my hand hovering over his leg for the longest moment in history. It was different when we were in that house and he was in the throes of his family confrontation. All the touching and comforting came naturally then; I didn't even think about it. But right now, it's just the two of us off to wherever we're going next and . . . I don't know. I pull my hand back. "You were just a kid."

He shrugs. "Yeah, but then I wasn't. I grew up. I could've called her."

"She leaves the room when you guys talk about your *career*, Kian. How would she have reacted to you telling her about a three-decades-long series of affairs?" I pause, tucking back a strand of hair that the wind has pulled from my crown braid. "I'm not even sure she didn't know all those years. That's kind of hard to believe, don't you think?"

He considers this as the idyllic scenery—white picket fences, rolling greens—rushes past our windows. "I guess. I never really thought about it."

I take a breath. "Now that it's all out in the open . . . do you think she'll leave your dad?"

He shrugs, a small frown knitting his brows together. "I don't know. They've been married more than half her life. It's not going to be easy to walk away from everything they've built. They—"

Kian's interrupted by his phone dinging with an incoming call. He glances down at his screen and then pulls over, the car tires crunching over gravel and dirt on the side of the road. Putting the phone to his ear, he says, "Mom? Are you okay?"

I can't hear her side of the conversation, but after a moment, he nods. "Sure. I can do dinner in the city on Tuesday." He pauses. "Are you sure you're okay?"

He nods a couple more times, and then he hangs up and

looks at me. "Wow. She wants to talk about what happened at dinner."

I raise my eyebrows. "She wants to actually confront what happened?"

"It sounds like it." His brown eyes are wide. "She even said it was about time someone finally told the truth in this family."

"Holy shit. That's good, Kian. That's really good. . . . Right?"

He looks shocked. "I think so. I think . . . I may have helped her with what I said? Maybe? She sounded more confident and . . . younger than she's sounded since I can remember." He blows out a breath, shaking his head.

I grin at him. "I'm glad for you, Montgomery. You're shaking things up."

He laughs, the sound deep and rich in the car. "Guess so." Starting the car back up, he pulls back onto the road and drives.

We listen to the wind and the other cars passing us for another couple of minutes. Then I say, hesitantly, "So . . . I totally understand if you don't want to do our fake date/tutoring sesh next. After all that emotion, I mean. We can just go home if you want."

He glances at me quickly before returning his gaze to the road. "Do *you* not want to do the date?" His voice is carefully neutral but I know Kian. There's something just under the surface that I can't quite see. There's more to the question than meets the eye . . . or ear.

"No, I do." I'm also speaking carefully, trying not to sound overeager. *Am* I overeager? I am, I realize. I'm wayyy overeager.

Distant alarm bells clang in my mind. "But only if *you* want to, too."

"I do. I actually have a whole thing set up."

I turn to face him fully at that. "A 'whole thing'? What does that mean? I thought we were just going to grab a quick drink at a bar or something."

A small smile tugs at the corner of his mouth. "Patience, Bishop."

I turn back around with a huff, feigning frustration at his secrecy. But really, a huge part of me thrills at the fact that Kian has arranged something special for our fake date. I should be worried at just *how* much I'm thrilling, but somehow, I'm not.

ꝏ

We turn at a small gravel road, which Kian gingerly maneuvers the tiny rental car onto. The tires crunch along as we inch past fields and trees and all manner of flora. "You're not taking me farming for a day or something, are you?" I ask, suspicious. It's exactly the kind of thing Kian might think is "fun."

He chuckles. "Relax, LB. I know you better than that. You'd probably fall face-first into a pail of milk or impale yourself on a rake within the first five minutes."

"Hey." I smack him on the arm. Ow. Has he grown even more muscle somehow? "I'm not *that* much of a city girl."

He raises his eyebrows at me as we pull into a small dirt driveway next to what looks like a little house with white siding.

Outside is a sign that reads, TREE HOUSE FARM INFORMATION CENTER.

Kian turns off the car.

"It says 'farm' on the sign, Montgomery." I turn to him with a stern look. "Do you think I'm stupid?"

He lets out a belabored sigh. "Will you shut up and come with me?" He gets out of the car, then walks around to my side and opens my car door.

I smile up at him. "Oh, right. I forgot how courtly date-Kian is."

He rubs the back of his neck, as if he's flustered. "Right. Yeah. It's all part of the package!" He says it like a joke, but it somehow falls flat, partly because he doesn't meet my eye.

Weird.

I don't comment on it, though. Instead, I just get out and walk with him, my ballet shoes crunching on the dirt. It's a little cool now that the daylight is leaching from the sky, and I scooch infinitesimally closer to Kian to absorb his body heat.

We walk past the visitor center and off into a thick grove of trees to the right, through which I can now see a path has been cleared. It's absolutely silent except for our footfalls, a lone owl calling, and the distant sound of rushing water. The stars begin to punch through the darkening sky, glimmering down at us.

"It should be right around . . ." Kian pushes a low-hanging branch out of the way. "Ah. Here it is."

We're at a clearing now, a big circular patch of soft, emerald grass. And dotting the circumference of the circle are magnificent, beautiful, gigantic, elaborate . . .

I stare for a moment and then walk forward. "Are those . . . *tree houses*?"

Kian laughs lightly beside me. "Yep."

But these aren't the rickety tree houses of my childhood that were cobbled together with a few two-by-fours. These are intricately designed, classy, *gorgeous* structures that look like miniature houses. Polished brass lanterns hanging from each tree illuminate the tree house perched in it, as well as the sleek wooden stairs that lead from the ground up to each one. I turn to Kian, shaking my head. "What is this place?"

"This guy I helped with a project told me he was opening New York's first 'tree house restaurant.' Basically guests are served in their own individual tree houses, and they get to rent the tree house for two hours at a time. I helped him with some design elements for the space and in return, he told me I could have a reservation whenever I wanted. I chose today because they haven't officially opened to the public yet, and I wanted to show you first. I have a feeling this place is going to be really popular."

"No kidding." I walk up to the tree house nearest us and get up on the first step. "This is *so* cool. Can we go up?"

Kian gestures with his hand, his eyes crinkling at the corners. "Absolutely."

I walk up the stairs with him right behind me. The tree house has an opening through which I step—and then I gasp. The inside looks like something out of *Architectural Digest* magazine.

Everything is done in natural materials—different types of

woods, mostly. There's a low, rough-hewn dining table with floor pillows around it, a soft fleece throw, lanterns that match the ones outside, and potted ferns in the corners. In the center of the table is a straw tray with two bottles of red wine and two glasses, along with a small silver bowl of chocolates.

"This is *stunning*." I walk to the table and Kian follows behind me. There's a window on the wall across from the door that looks out onto a rushing river in the distance. There's no one around for miles; it almost feels like we're the only two people in the world. "Holy shit, Kian. You helped design this?"

He shrugs. "Ah, just some of it. The main idea was all Josh's."

I put my hands on my hips. "You're just being modest. I can tell. That's your 'I really did a lot but I don't want any compliments' voice."

Laughing, Kian folds himself down onto one of the floor pillows that looks like it's covered in hemp or linen, but turns out to be super soft when I follow suit. "Shall I pour us some wine?"

"Did you arrange for all of this stuff to be set out, too?"

"Yep."

I'm touched. I study his face as he pours me a glass. His expression is calm and neutral, but I can see that his jaw is a little tense. Something in my stomach flutters and I fuss with my hair to distract from whatever it is I'm feeling.

Kian hands me my wine and I take it with a smile. "This is really nice. Thanks for bringing me."

His gaze locks on mine for a long moment, enough so the

backs of my knees get damp. "Thanks for being with me today at the dinner."

"Of course." I take a swallow of the wine. I'm no connoisseur, but it's delicious and fruity—my favorite flavor. "You know I'll always be there for you."

"Yeah." He sips at his wine and then sets it down and looks at me. "About that. I just want to say, Lyric, you . . . you're like my family. No, scratch that. You *are* my family. And I don't want anything to ever get in the way of that."

Touched, I lean forward and put my hand on his on the table. "I feel the same way. I don't want to lose you, ever."

He glances down for a moment, then looks up. Licks his lips. I try not to stare. *I am not a pervert, I am not a pervert, I am not a pervert.* "Good. Because what happened in London . . ."

I take my hand back and look into my wine like it's a crystal ball. "Right. Yeah. London. I thought we already talked about that."

He studies me until I meet his eye again. The lantern light casts shadows across his face. "Do you feel like things have gone back to normal between us since then?"

Sighing, I take a deep sip of wine and set my half-empty glass on the table with a little *thunk*. "No. I don't." My vision is already beginning to fuzz at the corners; I barely ate at dinner.

"I don't either," he says, shaking his head. "And I can't figure it out."

I look around the little room at the wood-paneled walls, the floor decorated with a small hemp rug, the window through which I can see an indigo sky sporting a cut-glass moon. Finally,

I drink down the other half of my wine. Looking at me for a moment, Kian drains his entire glass in three giant gulps. I grin at him, feeling giddy. "Very impressive." I reach for the bottle of wine to pour myself another glass because hey, why not?

"So are you."

I stare at his serious face, the bottle forgotten in my hand. "What?"

He leans toward me across the little table. "You're impressive. But you know that already."

My hand shakes a bit as I finish pouring myself a glass and then pour him one, too. This isn't the Kian I know. This Kian is the same Kian I encountered in the pool in London. This Kian makes me very, very nervous. In a thrilling, terrifying, electrifying way.

"Actually, I don't." Setting the bottle down, I pick up my glass and take another sip, although I most definitely don't need it.

Kian's gaze is steady on mine. "You are, LB," he says quietly, his voice thick with conviction. "You're fucking impressive."

"You're fucking drunk."

He smiles faintly and drinks some of his wine. "Yeah, maybe. But not drunk enough to bullshit you."

I can't think of anything to say. Not one single thing. The thrilling, electrifying feeling is seeping away as the reality of the situation crashes into me. I don't know what to say to Kian. *My* Kian. When did it become this hard to talk to him?

He looks up at me as if I've spoken. "What's wrong?"

I jerk in surprise; it's like he read my mind. "Why?"

"You look like you're going to start crying. Your nose is all red like Rudolph's."

Immediately, I clap my hand over my nose. Damn wine. It's making me labile. "It is not."

"Sure is. So? What's going on?"

Deciding there's no point in lying, I sigh. "I feel like . . . like there's this distance between us. Sometimes it's like I look at you and I see a different person than the Kian Montgomery I've known for almost a decade. Ever since London, just like you said. And I don't know how to fix it."

If I could go back and undo that kiss, would I? The truth is, even with things as awkward as they are, I don't know that I would. It was . . . life changing. It was the best kiss I've ever had, one of the only times in my life when I've felt unquestionably beautiful, sexual, powerful, desirable. It's hard to say you'd erase that, even if you know it would make things easier in the long run.

Kian drums his fingers on the table, thinking. Then, he pulls out his phone. "I have an idea."

"What?"

He swipes the screen. "It's something I saw on TV. There's this app you can use to get to know someone you're dating." I open my mouth to protest, but he holds his hand up. "I know we're not *really* dating, LB, but I think it'll help break the ice. Just to . . . I don't know, get us in the groove of being us again."

I close my mouth. At this point, I'm willing to try anything. "Okay. So what's the app about?"

"It's simple—just a question-and-answer game. We respond

to the questions it pops up on the screen, discuss our answers, and learn more about each other that way. The topics are supposed to be ones you wouldn't necessarily know about another person even if they've been in your life awhile."

I nod and kick off my shoes. "Okay."

"Ready?"

"Ready."

He presses a button and places his phone on the table between us. The screen lights up with a ding and our first question: *If you could gain one quality or ability, what would it be?*

"Ladies first," Kian says, gesturing to me as he takes another sip of wine. He's probably close to being as tipsy as I am at this point. Good. Maybe that's the social lubrication we need to get over this—whatever this is between us.

"Hmm." I chew on my bottom lip as I think. "This is something humans usually do without supernatural help, but I'd want the ability to fall in love with the *right* person," I say finally. "I mean, I'm twenty-four and I've never had the full package—both intense sexual chemistry *and* intense emotional connection at the same time. I think that's kind of sad."

"I don't think it's sad," Kian counters. "You're discerning. You're careful. You're careful and discerning. There's nothing wrong with that."

I snort. "As mentioned previously, I think you're a little drunk."

"I believe the exact verbiage you used before was 'fucking drunk.'"

"Can't forget the fucking," I say, and then I stop and stare at Kian. His eyes darken. I take another deep drink of wine as I feel my cheeks get hotter than the surface of the sun. "Okay, your turn to answer."

He turns his attention back to the screen and clears his throat. "Right. I think I'd want the ability to see my flaws clearly, so I could course correct when I'm making a big mistake."

I sit up in surprise. "Really? But you're already very self-aware."

He shakes his head. "No one's a hundred percent aware of their flaws, LB."

"What are you afraid you might overlook?"

He meets my eyes just for a second before looking away again, out the window at the perfect darkness. "I want to know if I got the cheating gene."

My breath stops for a second. "Kian. You're one of the most loyal, honest people I know."

He looks at me. "Yeah, but I bet my dad's friends probably would've said that about him, too. Hell, my mom probably would've, until the second year of their marriage."

"Have you ever cheated on anyone?"

He shakes his head.

"Ever wanted to?"

"Cheat? No. But I *have* wanted to do something I know I shouldn't."

I lick my lips, my mouth suddenly going dry. "Like what?"

His gaze is heavy, pressing. "Kiss you in that pool. The minute I saw you in that bikini . . ." He looks away, then, and blows out a breath. "I didn't just want to kiss you, Lyric. I wanted to—" He breaks off again, takes another gulp of his wine. My bones go soft. I want to know what he wanted to do. But he moves on from that thought. "Anyway. The point is, yes, I've had urges to do things that weren't wise."

I want to respond, but my voice seems to be stuck in my chest somewhere. I pull it out with a great big effort and squirm, my dress suddenly feeling too tight around me. "Um. Yes. But, ah. Not cheating. Not that."

He gazes into his glass. "No, not that."

"Time for the next question!" I'm drunk enough that I hit the phone with the side of my thumb and it goes skittering across the table. Laughing a little too shrilly, I pull it back and tap the screen. The next question pops up: *Would you ever be naked in public?*

I want to melt into the floor. I don't dare raise my eyes to meet Kian's. I'm frozen.

Chapter Nineteen

KIAN

Lyric seems to have sunk into some kind of stupor, so I take the initiative with the next question. I'd be lying if I said I wasn't looking forward to discussing this particular topic with her. I think about that pink swimsuit again, her London suit. How flimsy the strings were. How the fabric barely covered any of her body at all. How the cold breeze off the rooftop made her nipples press against the bikini top. The wine coursing through my blood makes it a lot easier to think these things without feeling much resistance from the logical part of my brain. My dick appears to be calling the shots now.

"I definitely would," I say. "I think it'd be sexy as hell to be naked in public."

Lyric raises her eyes to me then. "Are you calling yourself

sexy?" A small smile tugs at the corners of her mouth and I don't want to admit I was actually thinking of *her* naked in public. Naked in the woods. Right here, in the tree house.

"Sure, why not." I grin. "What about you? Would you be naked in public?"

As if her dress is listening to me, one strap slips off her shoulder. She doesn't tug it back up but she doesn't meet my eye either. "Kian, I . . ."

I wait. She shakes her head. "I can't talk about that with you." She looks up at me, biting her lower lip. I feel my eyes drift down to her mouth and force them back up. "I'm sorry, I know we're trying but . . . there's something between us. Tell me you don't feel it."

I watch her for a second and then move around the low table so I'm sitting beside her, on the floor next to her pillow. "I feel it."

She rubs her face. "I don't know what it is or what to do about it," she says softly, looking down at her hands, twisted in her lap. She looks back up at me. "All I know," she says, her voice almost a whisper, "is that I miss you."

I cup her cheek with my hand, my thumb stroking along her jaw. Her skin is silk under my hands. "I miss you, too."

We're getting closer as we talk. Lyric is leaning into me, her blue eyes soft, her chest rising and falling with each breath. The dress is low enough that I can see a hint of cleavage. She smells like wine and chocolate. "What are we going to do?"

I keep caressing her jaw. She turns her head slightly so my

thumb caresses her lower lip. "I have an idea," I say, aware that my voice is two octaves deeper than usual.

She waits.

"Maybe we need to get this out of our systems."

Lyric cocks her head a little, and my thumb brushes more of her mouth. Her eyes flutter closed for just a second before she refocuses on me. "What do you mean?"

"Maybe that kiss in London wasn't the reason we can't move on. Maybe that kiss in London was an indicator that there's a glaring obstacle between us that we need to take down before we can progress any further."

She frowns. "I don't follow. You're doing your drunk professor thing. What are you talking about?"

"Sex. I'm talking about sex, Lyric."

She pulls back, but her pupils dilate, turning her blue eyes black like ink dripped in a pool of water. Her breathing comes faster. "You want to have sex with me?"

"And I think you want to have sex with me."

Her eyes deceive her; they rove down my body and back up to my face. "Yes," she breathes, and then stops suddenly. "Holy shit. I'm drunker than I realized. I only meant to *think* that, not say it."

I laugh a little and move closer to her again. She doesn't back up this time. Cradling her jaw in both hands, I murmur, "So tell me. Have you ever wanted to be naked in public?"

She nods, staring into my eyes. "I think I have a little bit of an exhibitionist side. But I've never given in to it."

I smile a half smile. "Now's your chance."

There's a long pause. We're both breathing faster, shallower. I'm afraid she's going to say no. I'm afraid she's going to say yes.

"Okay. But only if we strip together," she murmurs finally, leaning forward and slipping the first button on my shirt from its buttonhole.

"Deal."

Her small hands slip from the first button to the second and the third. She slides my shirt apart and runs her hands over my chest; my breath catches at her touch. She smiles, recognizing the power she has over me. She's breathtaking.

Leaning over, I reach behind her—my face inches from hers—and unzip her dress halfway. My fingers graze the curve of her spine, skin lighting on fire. She isn't wearing a bra.

Lyric licks her lips, her eyes on my chest. She unbuttons my shirt, moving lower, toward my waistband, toward my lap. As she pulls away, her hands graze the hardness there and I groan. Her eyes glitter with heat, twin blue flames.

Without saying a word, I reach behind her again and unzip her all the way. The straps of her dress slip down her shoulders, and her neckline falls lower, exposing the tops of her breasts—full, pale, silken. She watches me watching her.

"God, you're beautiful." I'm aware my voice is husky, my breathing harsh. Aware that I can't stop staring at her.

In answer, she stands and lets her dress slip down her body and puddle at her feet. She steps gracefully out of it and her underwear, donning nothing but a slim silver necklace at her throat. It winks in the lantern light. "Your turn," she says, and her voice, too, is deeper than usual.

I stand and shrug off my shirt as she watches every move. It's like I'm her private strip show. The thought thrills me, ignites a fire deep in my chest. There's a caveman inside me who wants to lunge at her, to pull her to me and ravish every part of her body. To feel her wetness, to plunge into her, to watch her cry out in pure hedonistic pleasure. I manage to contain that part, but barely. The leash I'm holding the caveman back with is fraying, though, and quickly. I unbuckle my pants, slide them down, and slip out of them. My boxer briefs follow.

We stand before each other, fully naked. My eyes are hungry, roving, touching her with my gaze while my fingers cry out for her body. Lyric Bishop is *exquisite.* She has small, perky breasts, a flat but still soft stomach, and legs that go on for miles. What I saw when she was clad in her bikini? That was just the preview. This . . . I could never have prepared myself for this.

"Kian," she murmurs, and I notice for the first time that her eyes, too, have been roving my body. "My God, Kian."

She doesn't have to say any more. I know exactly how she feels.

LYRIC

I am a walking paradox: Every part of me is trembling, but every part of me is flourishing, confident, glowing. I'm drunk, but I've never been clearer about what I want. I want to run and hide, I want to ask myself exactly what the hell I think I'm doing, but I also want to throw myself at Kian. I want to wrap my legs around his waist, I want the hard length of him inside me, again and again and again.

"What next?" he asks, his voice barely a rumble. There's a fire in his eyes and I know what he wants because I want it, too. But he's letting me take the lead a little; he's making sure I want it. The thought makes me wetter than I already am.

"Outside," I say, a tad breathlessly. "I want to go outside."

A small smile licks across his face. He looks positively feral and oh God, that expression makes my knees go completely weak.

"Okay." He turns and begins to stride out the door, looking every bit like a Roman emperor who commands his kingdom easily and confidently. Helpless to do anything else, I follow.

We walk out onto the grass in the clearing. It is almost completely pitch-black now, save for small pools of golden light thrown by the single lanterns that hang from each tree house. I move to the center, the soft grass bending under my bare feet, tickling. There's a cool breeze in the air, but I'm hot from the wine and sheer lust, my blood ambrosia.

Kian follows silently behind me, but I can feel the heat of him wrapping around me, teasing me, curling around every curve. I ache for his hands to touch me the same way; I've never been this weak with want.

I turn to him and he walks up to me, that expression of feral determination and lust on his face reducing me to a puddle of desire and nothing else. The moon shines down on us, casting silver shadows and dusting his hair and shoulders with light.

"Are we really doing this?" I whisper, wondering if I'm going to wake from a dream again like I did eons ago. I remember what Kian was doing to me in that dream and feel the blush seeping onto my cheeks.

"If you want to," Kian replies, and I can tell he means it. In spite of him being clearly aroused and ready, he would back down if I expressed a shred of uncertainty. But there isn't a shred, not a speck of doubt inside me. I want this. I want him.

I step closer to him, tip my head back and gaze into his eyes. "I want to."

At that, he wraps his hands around my waist and pulls me to him, his hardness pressing into my stomach. Bending lower, he presses his mouth to mine, claiming me with his tongue, his teeth, his lips. His hands rove up my back, cup my ass, move up my arms and over my shoulders and neck as if he can't get enough, as if this is all he's thought about, as if he's a starving man who's finally given a scrap of bread.

I let him devour me.

KIAN

If the kiss in London was the match, this one is the explosion.

I cannot believe Lyric Bishop is once again in my arms, and that this time, her bare velvet skin is hot and flushed against mine. The curve of her breasts pressed against my chest, the flat of her stomach against mine, the lean muscles of her thighs—everything is driving me wild. She smells of moonlight and wildflowers and sex. I kiss her shoulders, trail my tongue against the bowl of her collarbone, dip my head and take a nipple into my mouth.

She gasps, her hands tangling in my hair too hard, and I relish the pain. For too long, we've been far apart, a distance between us that shouldn't have been there and felt wrong on a molecular level. Wanting more, wanting to touch her in places I've never touched before, I slip a hand from her waist down between her legs, feeling the wet heat of her core, letting my fingers slide in deeper, inch by inch. She moans and presses herself against me, closer and harder.

"Fuck, Lyric," I gasp, my desire a tsunami threatening to engulf us both. I slip my fingers out of her and circle her swollen clit. She gasps and shudders, her knees going so weak I have to hold her up. "Does that feel good?" I murmur, needing to hear it from her mouth. To see this hidden, shadowed side of my best friend, to see her raw and wild and wanting.

"Yes," she whispers, then louder, "oh God, Kian." I can feel that she's close, she's about to come already. I pull back a little.

"Not yet," I say, smiling against her mouth. "Not so fast."

She's smiling, too. "Montgomery. You absolute tease."

"Is that a bad thing?" I ask, laughing a little, my fingers tracing lightly against her inner thighs now, spreading that delicious wetness everywhere. I'm outwardly cocky, even blasé, but my mind is going *HOLY SHIT, MONTGOMERY. LYRIC*

BISHOP IS IN YOUR ARMS, YOU LUCKY FUCKING BASTARD.

She gives me a look, her blue eyes sparkling with mischief. "Two can play at that game."

I'm about to ask her what she means when she drops to her knees. Then, in one smooth movement, she takes me in her mouth, her hands cupping my ass.

It's like I've swallowed the sun. My blood is fire; my veins glow. Everything in the entire universe shrinks to this one precise point of pleasure—the feel of Lyric's soft, wet mouth on me. The knowledge that we've crossed the line, that there's no going back. No matter what happens now, this is a link that'll tie us forever. We'll always know what the other tastes like.

Her tongue licks me slowly, deliciously, until I'm nearly doubled over and begging for mercy, for relief, my hands in her hair, pulling her braid out so her strands blow wildly in the night. The moonlight turns her golden hair silver.

She hums against my skin and I groan out loud, pushing her against me, shuddering and so, so fucking close to the edge.

Then she pulls away and smiles up at me, nearly knocking me over with the mischief, the wanton playfulness, of that smile. "Not yet."

"Touché," I gasp, and then I kneel, too, pushing her gently down so she's lying on her back.

I spread her knees open with my hand, positioning myself between her legs. "My turn." I can feel the devilish smile on my face and I'm powerless to stop it. This is what I want. Her. Now. Like this. "Do you know how many times I've wanted to do this?" I growl as I settle between her legs, feeling the wet heat from her core wrap around me. I kiss her clit softly, my tongue circling it, and she gasps and trembles under me. "Every time I've seen you in a dress since London. Every fucking time."

"Really?" she asks, her voice breathy, gasping.

"Really. And maybe even a few times before then." I look into her eyes, finding myself being honest. "I've had dreams about you, Lyric. Vivid, graphic dreams. Even before we started fake dating. I think there was a part of me that always wanted you." They were more than sex dreams, but I don't tell her that. In my dreams, we were a couple, hand in hand at the farmers' market, me licking strawberry juice off her fingers later, in bed.

She laughs a little, shaking her head in what looks like wonder. "And I thought I was the only pervert," she muses. But before I can ask her what she means, she looks at me again, her eyes glittering. "What did you want to do to me? In your dreams? When you saw me in a dress?"

Half smiling at her, I bend my head down. I trail my tongue lightly against her core, not quite reaching her clit. "This." Then I nip at her clit, gently but with enough teeth so she gasps again. "And this." I press the tip of my tongue into her, feeling her tighten against me. "Fuck, you taste so good."

She arches against me as my tongue works against her, licking and tasting and moving slowly up and down and up again. My hands move up to her breasts, and I pinch her nipples, making her cry out, making her writhe. I watch her for a second, a Goddess in the moonlight. Then I bend my head down again and make her come.

She crashes into me, over and over and over again, gasping, shouting my name, trembling and shaking. I plunge my cock into her, rocking into her, my thumb rubbing her and she goes up to the crest with me again. My heart's pounding, I can't stop staring at her, head thrown back in ecstasy, legs spread for me and only me. I drive into her again and again and soon we're both going over the edge, and I'm holding her as we come together, wave after wave after wave of pleasure with this Goddess who's rendered me speechless in my devotion.

Chapter Twenty

LYRIC

When Kian and I are both done, thoroughly spent, he kisses my eyelids and lies beside me in the grass, panting. Waves of heat roll off him and cover me, which is good, because I'm suddenly cold. I roll closer to him and he wraps his arms around me, cradling me against his broad chest. He smells like me and I smell like him and we smell like sex, a curious mixture of the two of us that never before existed in this world. I've never been happier. In fact, I can't stop grinning because I'm feeling exquisitely self-satisfied.

That's how you have sex that's just sex, people. No-strings-attached sex. Get-it-out-of-your-head-and-move-on sex. Masterfully executed by both Montgomery and Bishop. I imagine a crowd of spectators cheering us on and I laugh quietly. Talk about exhibitionistic.

Kian looks down at me. "What's so funny, hoss?"

I snort. "Hoss. Who says that?"

"Me?"

I nod and kiss his chest. "You. Only you."

"So, did that scratch the exhibitionism itch for you?" Kian plays with an unruly strand of my hair, coiling and uncoiling it around his finger that, just moments before, was in a number of interesting places.

I feel a shiver go through me that has nothing to do with the temperature and snuggle in closer to him, naked skin pressed against naked skin. "Oh, yeah. Better than I could've expected."

I can hear the smile in his voice when he answers, "Yeah, for me, too. Hey. How'd I rate on the SPS?"

Raising my chin so I can see him, I ask, "You really want me to rate you?"

"Sure. I can take it." He thumps his chest in a very Tarzan move and I laugh.

"Okay, let's see . . . the invitation to kiss—really to fuck, in this case—was incredibly well done. Stroking my jaw, running your thumb over my mouth?" I squirm a little; I'm getting wet again just thinking about it. "Mm, it was good. Very good. I give you a solid 5 out of 5."

"Wow." I can hear the glee in Kian's voice. "That's pretty great."

"And then we have the pre-sex sexual chemistry. Asking me

about exhibitionism. Telling me we should get it out of our systems. That was all delicious, Montgomery. You definitely got me hot."

"Did I?" His voice is a bit husky and he pinches my ass.

I find myself hoping his hand will continue doing other things, but no. Playtime is over. I refocus on the question at hand. "A 5 there as well, no question. Ah, let's see. Hooking up and actual sex were all part of the same package here, so I give those a 5 as well."

Kian mock gasps. "Are you telling me I just got a solid 5 on the SPS?"

I laugh. "Don't get so cocky." After a pause, I add, "It's great, because now when I have other sexperiences, I have a solid 5 to judge them against. So thank you."

I'm expecting Kian to enthusiastically agree or even get cocky again about his perfect sex score, but he . . . doesn't. Instead, he makes a noncommittal sound in his throat that could be anything. It could be a hiccup.

I feel a small spike of alarm—my brain telling me this is something to look deeper into—but I ignore it. Kian's probably just tired, lost in the postcoital glow and all. That's it. Nothing more.

We're silent then, me still propped up on his chest looking at the ring of tree houses, him flat on his back, gazing up at the stars.

"I wish I could see this every night," he says, a weight around the edges of his words that belies his casual tone.

I study the stars, the blackened silhouette of the trees, trying to see them through his nature-loving eyes. "Which part?"

"All of it." He looks at me then, and there's something about his gaze that sets my pulse thumping. "Every single bit of this."

Pushing myself off his chest, I lie on my back, my heart thudding, and gaze up at the sky without really seeing it. "Well, you can't. There's too much light pollution in the city." Purposely misunderstanding what he's saying. Or, at least, what I *think* he's saying. There's silence for a moment. Then I add, in a careless tone, "Do you think we got it out of our systems?"

There's a tiny hesitation before he says, equally carelessly, "Oh, yeah. For sure. We can go back to normal now."

I try to smile. "Good."

But the intense high I felt only moments ago is seeping away fast. Serious doubts clot out the stars in the sky that, just a moment before, felt so clear.

KIAN

We're back home now, back in our apartment and lives, post sexual experiment. I'm hiding the biggest secret I've ever hidden, holding it close to me like a deck of cards I'd never let Lyric see: Sex changed everything. At least, it did for me.

That night, something happened. Something shifted. When I look at Lyric now, I don't see my best friend. Or at least, I don't see *just* my best friend. I see Lyric Bishop as a whole universe—a woman I want to take to bed *and* spend all my time talking and joking with. Instead of leaving the sexy, romantic-partner-potential Lyric behind, I seem to have brought her with me. She's in everything I do now. She's everywhere.

I held Lyric under the moonlight; I caressed every curve; I became one with her, as ridiculously cliché as that sounds. In some primitive part of my brain, she's mine now. I *know,* okay? I know that makes me sound like a total asshole. But it's how I feel, in a part of me that evolved millennia ago. When she talked about using the information she gathered from the sex we had and extrapolating it to other men . . . I wanted to pummel the fucking tree houses to the ground. Because I don't want *anyone* pleasuring Lyric the way I did. That's my job. That's my privilege.

At least, that's what my inner caveman says. And hence the reason I'm totally fucked.

I'm keeping up my usual routine. It's marginally easier to avoid her now that my defense is only a week away. I'm sequestering myself in the library a lot, even though it's not my favorite place to work. (Home is. But home has Lyric.)

But there are moments throughout the day when I'm sure, I'm *certain,* I'm wearing my feelings on my sleeve. It actually takes my breath away when she walks by me and I smell her sweet floral shampoo. Once, I was getting myself a cup of coffee in the kitchen and she came to make herself some tea. Her hair was loose and when it brushed my arm, I got actual goose bumps. When I see her lying on the couch reading, I want to slide my hands up her shirt, distract her from her book, have her smile at me like she did under the moonlight, all sinful and mischievous and pulsing with desire.

This is my best friend we're talking about. Sex with her was supposed to be just sex. She's kept up her end of the bargain but for the life of me, I can't seem to keep mine.

ꝏ

I meet my mother for dinner at Eleven Madison Park, her favorite place to eat in the city. I don't question how she managed to get a reservation so quickly at a perpetually sold-out establishment; my mother has her ways and those ways have a lot of money. And naturally, she's paying for us. The plates run hundreds of dollars per person, something my grad student budget would protest mightily. I offered to meet her at a more reasonably priced restaurant, aka the taco place with bottomless guac and chips Lyric and I love so much down the street, but she refused.

It's Tuesday night, but Eleven Madison Park is completely packed with mostly genteel middle-aged people in a sea of gray and black suits and dresses in jewel tones. I'm wearing my only suit, which I'll be wearing again at my dissertation defense next week. Hopefully I won't get a stain on it tonight.

My mother's dressed in a well-cut dress in her favorite color—pastel pink. Her graying hair has been pulled into a tight bun at the nape of her neck, but she looks younger, somehow. She looks up and smiles over her water glass as I enter and am shown to her table.

"Kian." Her brown eyes twinkle like they haven't in . . . ever. "Sit. You're looking well."

"Well, you just saw me a couple days ago, so that's good." I laugh and then lean forward, getting serious. "How are you, Mom? How have things been at the house?" My father is not a physically violent man. But if he ever so much as breathed wrong on my mother, I'd pummel him into a shapeless mass without a thought.

"Fine," she says, her nail-polished finger tracing the crisp edge of the tablecloth. "Your father left on a business trip the night you were over, and I haven't talked to him since."

I wait. The waiter brings our dishes and drinks without us having to order—they know what the Montgomerys like. We thank him, and then my mother seems ready to speak.

"Before you ask, I'm not sure I'm going to leave him."

I look at her. "I wasn't going to ask."

She studies my expression for a moment before nodding. "Okay. Do you judge me for it?"

"For not knowing if you want to leave? Absolutely not." I press my fingers to her forearm before moving them. She's not one for public displays, no matter how subtle.

"You really helped me that night at dinner, you know. I always knew—how could I not?—that he had others on the side. I always knew he thought that was his birthright. He made the money, he was the reason we had all we had. I had no right to tell him how to spend his time and energy when he wasn't working. So, yes. I knew. But you bringing it up . . . I realized it wasn't normal. People in our social circle—we're look-the-other-wayers. It comes as naturally to us as breathing. But now I think . . . maybe I can go do some of the things I've always wanted to do, too."

I smile at her. "Like what?"

"Take a painting class in Italy. See the Louvre. It's been years since I've been there alone, without your father rushing me. Maybe I'll even start an interior decorating company, an idea I've toyed with since you were a child." She looks up at me for a second and then down into her lap. "It's hard to walk away from your life after thirty years. So maybe . . . maybe it'll be easier to just adapt it more to what I need instead. I can imagine that looks incredibly weak to you, Kian, but I promise you, it's what I think will make me happiest."

It hurts my chest to see her looking so afraid of my judgment. "Hey. Mom." I wait until she meets my eye again. "Your life's your own. I think maybe it's easy to forget when you live with a strong personality like Dad's, but this is your decision to make—or not make. And I'm in no position to judge you. No one is."

She swallows. Neither of us have touched our food yet. "You've become quite the young man when I wasn't looking."

My jaw twitches and I look away. "I don't know about that. I think . . ." Breathe in, breathe out. "I may have more of Dad in me than you think."

A small frown knits her carefully manicured eyebrows together. "Why on earth would you say that?"

Lifting my glass of fine, imported beer, I take a deep swig. Setting it back down, I feel the warmth travel down my throat, loosening the words from behind my teeth. "I have a tendency to want things I shouldn't want, too." Really just one thing. But her name sits between us, unsaid.

"And who told you you shouldn't want these things?" My mother's eyes are clear, sharp.

I shake my head. "I guess . . . I did. It's just—it's a bad idea, me wanting this thing. Nothing good will come from it, I can see that from a mile away."

My mother smiles a little. "Sometimes we tell ourselves we *shouldn't* want something when really, we're just *afraid* to want it. Afraid of what it means that we want it. And afraid of both success and failure—what if we get this thing we desperately want? What if we don't?"

I rub my jaw, frustrated. She's saying all the things I've spent nights tossing and turning and asking myself. "So what do you do about that?"

She spreads her hands, her diamond bracelet winking in the muted light. "You walk through the feelings, Kian. You grasp for that thing with both hands. And you worry about the consequences later."

Shaking my head, I pick up my fork and make a half-hearted attempt at eating my fish. "The consequences are *all* I worry about," I murmur, too low for her to hear.

LYRIC

I have my own family crisis when Kian's at dinner with his mom. I know where he is because he told me over his shoulder on the way out the door. And I'm pretty sure that's the most he's spoken to me since this past weekend.

Oh, yeah. Our little experiment didn't work. It doesn't take a genius to see that. Ever since we . . . ever since our . . . ever since *that night*, Kian and I have barely been able to look at each other. Things changed almost instantly. The ride back to the city was painful. I felt like I was being held hostage in a car with a stranger who hated me and was secretly hoping we'd get into a wreck just so the Lyric problem would be taken care of.

I don't understand this sudden 180. I can understand being regretful of what happened. I am, because it's made things completely horrible between us. But why is he acting like he can't stand me anymore? Was sex with me really *that* bad?

But I can't just blame all of this on Kian. Something's wrong with me, too. Eye contact with him has become excruciating. Smelling his fully clothed, soap-scented body after a shower has become maddening. We can't stand to be in the same room at the same time. Anytime I sit on the couch and he walks in, we watch TV awkwardly for a few moments before one of us makes an excuse and leaves. I tried lying with my head on his lap yesterday in a desperate attempt to prove to the both of us that nothing had changed, and . . . let's just say we both got "excited" and it was very obvious.

It's a fucking disaster.

But I can't think about any of that now because I just got an SOS text from Opal. All it said was: That's it. I'm done. Can't do this secret relationship shit anymore.

I texted back and told her not to do anything rash and rushed out the door. And now I'm outside her apartment, knocking. Actually, I have to knock three times and then practically thump the door down with my fist because they can't hear me over their arguing. But I can hear them, clucking like angry geese.

Finally, the door opens and Arthur stands there, his face red, his hair sticking up all over the place. His hands are on his hips and he looks equal parts angry at Opal and ashamed that I'm here, overhearing his epic battle with my boneheaded sister. "Hey. Lyric."

"Hey, Arthur." I try to peek around him—he's two inches shorter than me—but don't see Opal. "Where's—"

Before I can say her name, he thrusts an irate hand behind him, toward their bedroom. "Packing. She's leaving."

I frown. "Can I come in?"

He stands to the side and I rush to their bedroom. Arthur wasn't kidding; Opal has a suitcase open on the bed like some scene from a movie, and she's throwing things into it haphazardly from her dresser.

"Hey."

She looks up at me, her pale face red and tear streaked. Her hair has been pulled into a hasty ponytail, but I don't think she realizes she forgot half of it on her shoulder. "Hey." Her voice is wobbly, thin and high. "You didn't have to come."

"Like hell I didn't." I gesture to the room at large. "What the hell's going on, Op?"

She stops packing and thrusts her hands into her hair, pulling loose the other half of her ponytail. The hair tie goes flying across the room and hits the window, but I don't think she notices. "I can't do this anymore! It's too much! It's all—it's all just, I can't . . . I should never have . . ."

Walking forward, I put my hands on her shoulders. "Okay, breathe. In . . . and out . . ." I breathe with her until she's calm. I can feel Arthur hovering at the doorway, watching us. Probably worried out of his mind.

When Opal is calm, I nod and step back. "Tell me what happened."

"I'm . . . this is all a big mistake. A three-year-long mistake." Opal looks down at her feet. "I should never have let it get this far."

I glance over my shoulder to see Arthur's hurt face watching us at the threshold. My heart squeezes for him. "You don't mean that," I say quietly to my sister. "You love him, Opal."

"Yes, I do! I love him!" Opal yells suddenly. "And you know what that gets me? Nothing! If I told anyone I'm in love with Arthur, they'd laugh their asses off! I had a plan, dammit. I told everyone I was getting engaged at thirty-seven to an accountant who could help me run my business because it makes *sense*. This"—she gestures between herself and Arthur behind me—"makes absolutely no fucking sense.

"I have *always* done everything according to plan, Lyric. That's who I am. And the moment I stop doing that, things are going to go to shit."

"This is ridiculous!" Arthur says, apparently unable to take it anymore. He steps into the room and I'm caught between them with no way or space to extricate myself. Awesome. "Tell Lyric what brought this on."

But Opal just turns back to her suitcase, and so Arthur decides to enlighten me. "We were sitting on the couch surfing our phones when she got an email from your mom. And it had a sample of the wedding invitation for Max and Camellia." Arthur turns to look pointedly at Opal, who's avoiding his gaze. "And *all I said was*, 'Those are nice. I wonder what ours will be like.' The next thing I know, she's jumping up from the couch saying how this is all a mistake and thanks for the three years, but she's jetting now."

I turn slowly to my older sister. "What . . . um . . . Opal?"

She sets down a T-shirt and turns to us, her hands on her hips. Her eyes are red and watery again. "Arthur, you're *twenty-six*. You're ten years younger than me. A whole decade."

"Yeah, I know. I was aware when I asked you out three years ago."

"A lot can change in ten years, especially going from your midtwenties to your midthirties. How do I know you won't change your mind about me? Maybe you think you want marriage and kids now, but what if you really don't? I don't have that much longer, Arthur." Her voice hiccups. "To have kids, I mean. And I really want them. I really, really want them."

Arthur puts his hands on his head with the air of someone who's had to repeat himself more than a dozen times. "Then let's have them! How many ways can I say this? Opal, *I want to have kids with you. I want to marry you.* Can you understand that?"

My sister blinks, and fat tears roll down her cheeks. "You're just saying that because it's what I want."

"When have I *ever* been someone who just goes with what you want? Besides the 'not telling your family' thing, because, okay, they're your family and that's your shit. But you told me not to tell my family, and I told them two and a half years ago. They all love you. You were in our Hanukkah card!"

I turn to look at Opal. "You were in the Kohens' Hanukkah card?"

Opal shrugs. "Yeah. I didn't want to tell you because it sounds so fucking serious and committed."

Arthur sighs. "Sweetheart, we *are* serious and committed, whether you want to admit it or not. And that's not going to change whether we live together in secret or get married and have kids."

Opal turns to me. "Can you believe this? Tell him, Lyric. You're almost the same age. Do you want to get married and have kids?"

"Not right now," I say, and Opal throws her hands up in sad triumph. I can feel Arthur's eyes boring angry holes in the back of my head, so I rush to add, "But that's just *me*, Op. I mean, there are plenty of people in this country and the world who have two or three kids by the time they're Arthur's age. And they're perfectly happy. I want to finish my doctorate and get a career going, but Arthur already knows what he wants to do. And so do you. You're both set up already."

She turns to me, her blue-green eyes narrowed. "What are you saying?"

I look at Arthur and shrug a shoulder. "I'm saying, what's the holdup? You're freaking out because you think Arthur will change his mind. But that's a nonissue because, a, he's telling you what he wants, b, as explained, he has never changed his mind to suit you, and, c, you're not being fair to Arthur by speaking for him just because you're ten years older than he is. You'll *always* be ten years older. Does that mean he doesn't get a say in any big life decisions simply because you'll always have more life experience than he does?"

Arthur actually, literally claps. "Hear, hear!" he says, and looks at Opal, his eyes brimming with love. "Honey."

She turns to him.

"I love you," Arthur says, his voice deep and sure. "I have loved you for three long years. For a young one like me, that's a long time."

They both laugh. When she throws a shirt at him, he catches her elbow and pulls her to him. I have to plop down on the bed to get out of the way, but I don't think either of them is worried about me right now.

Opal sniffles into Arthur's chest. She has to bend down to reach it, because he's shorter than her, too. "You really mean it? You want to get married and have babies with me?"

"Hell yeah," he says, stroking her hair. "You're *it* for me, Opal. You're my happily ever after. I've just been waiting for you to realize it, that's all."

She looks up at him, smiling. "I think I just have."

From my vantage on the bed, I cheer.

Since Tuesday night, Opal has sent me a thousand texts re: telling our parents about Arthur: What will they say? What should *she* say? How should she react to negative reactions? To positive reactions? What if she throws up from anxiety while she's telling them? etc. etc. All of the drama has made it easy for me to overlook one very big thing: It's Thursday. The day of our house party.

It honestly came rushing at us, and I'm not sure if that's a good thing or a bad thing. I really haven't had a lot of time to mentally prepare for this.

"Does this look okay?" I ask Kian now. I'm hanging paper lanterns as a decoration. I want to give this 110 percent.

"Yep." He barely looks up from his computer. He's lounging on the couch in a T-shirt and jeans, tapping away, putting the finishing touches on his thesis. He defends it next week and even though we've only talked about it a couple of times, I can tell he's nervous. Not that he'd tell me that. Not anymore.

That's why I have every hope hanging on this house party. This has to be it. This has to be when he asks Zoey out and she says yes and when I ask Greg, Charlie's neighbor, out and *he* says yes. Then we'll have a legit reason to get over our interpersonal weirdness and I can finish my thesis and all will be right with the world.

Oh, speaking of my thesis: I emailed Dr. Livingstone with an update. I told him I'm starting to get a handle on the data and how I'm going to analyze it. He seemed pleased.

Of course, I'm a liar. I have no idea about the data. I'm no closer than I was before to a relationship like the people I've studied have—strong on both the sexual and emotional connection fronts. And now, to add to it, I'm an emotional maelstrom of confusion and despair, thanks to what happened with Kian.

But what else am I supposed to do? Throw away five years of work because of an extreme and total mental block?

It's kind of depressing to realize I'm still just as fucking confused and clueless as ever. I mean, case in point. I'm over here hanging paper lanterns and Kian's doing his best trying to pretend I don't exist.

Sometimes I swear I feel him staring at me from over his laptop. But when I look over, he's just staring at his screen again. And dammit. I've been looking at him again and now I've hung the stupid paper lantern in the wrong spot and I can't reach it to pull it back down.

"Um, Kian?"

He looks up for real this time. There's a five-o'clock shadow on his jaw, and I have a crushing, pressuring need to run my hands through it. "Yeah."

"Would you mind?" I'm standing on a step stool, and I swipe at the bottom of the paper lantern. "I can't reach the tape."

"Sure." He sets his laptop down and comes over to me, standing closer than he has since the tree house for any extended period of time.

Immediately, my pulse kicks up. It's like a Pavlovian response. I smell his scent—soap and something heavier and darker and intoxicating—and I'm wet. My bones are liquid. I want to bury my nose in his neck; I want him to grab me around the waist and hoist me onto his lap, pressing his hardness into me while we're fully clothed.

"Lyric?" I blink and he's holding the paper lantern out with an uncertain look on his face. "Here you go."

"Oh." I shake my head a little, trying to clear it. Our fingers brush as I take the lantern from him, and is it just me, or does his hand linger for longer than strictly necessary? "Thanks."

"Yep."

But he doesn't move away. We stand there, staring at each other. On the step stool, I'm about half a head taller than him. I feel overdressed in my T-shirt and shorts. I want to be naked again, skin to skin, on a bed of grass with a blanket of stars covering us.

"Do you need help with any more of your lanterns?" Kian asks, his voice low. It's definitely not my imagination; his eyes fall briefly to my lips.

The idea that he might be thinking about that night, too, about all the things my mouth did, is driving me wild. I begin to breathe faster. "Maybe this one." I twist and reach for a high-hanging lantern that definitely doesn't need adjusting.

It feels like a setup, but I swear it's not. Somehow, maybe because my feet are cold and I'm wearing socks, I lose my footing on the step. I fall backward with a shriek, my hands flying out to hold on to something, the paper lantern tumbling lightly to the floor.

Kian catches me. It's a movie moment, with me in his arms and him looking down at me, our faces just a breath away. His dark brown eyes are like melting chocolate, hot and sweet. "I got you."

He stands there with me like I weigh nothing. His hands press into my body, and I can feel the strength in his forearms, muscles like corded steel. "Th-thanks."

My phone dings and vibrates on the coffee table and we both startle. The moment is broken. I feel a wet rag of disappointment slap me in the face as Kian places me on the floor, no longer making eye contact. His jaw is hard, his mouth a straight line, his hands tense now, as if he's struggling mightily with something.

Sighing inwardly, I walk to the phone and check it. It's Charlie.

Greg is a go! He's really reeeeally excited

I manage a half-hearted smile, even though she can't see me. Great! See you guys this evening

I look up at Kian, who's back on the couch working as if nothing at all happened. "By the way, Zoey's coming tonight." I meant to say it perkily, but it comes out sort of bitter and annoyed. As if this is somehow Kian's fault.

"Okay." He doesn't sound too enthused, but he doesn't say anything else about it either. "Is Charlie bringing Greg?"

He heard us talking about it the other night when Charlie was over. "Yeah. She just texted."

He nods once, curtly, and returns to his work.

So that's that.

Chapter Twenty-one

*
*

KIAN

The first guests begin to arrive to our house party, and I greet them all, but only half of me is actually paying attention to anything they're saying. I find myself constantly checking on Lyric, as if my attention is a homing pigeon and she's home. It's fucking annoying, it's irritating as hell, and as much as I'm trying not to, I can't get myself to stop.

It doesn't help that she looks absolutely delectable tonight. She's dressed up a little—probably for Greg, I think, my jealousy a sudden green veil over everything—in a little white dress that ties around her neck and leaves her shoulders bare. The hem barely comes to midthigh on her, leaving most of her legs on display. I remember those legs. I remember them wrapped around me.

I force my mind away from that memory. At the time, having sex seemed like a brilliant idea. We'd get it out of our systems and be able to move on with our friendship. No more awkwardness, no more stiffness (pun intended). Yeah, genius plan, Montgomery.

But I'm pretty sure I'm not the only one who was affected by our night at the tree house. Ever since we got back, Lyric has been distant. She seems skittish, dancing around me, staring at me when she thinks I'm not looking, tearing her eyes away the instant I look at her, too. She can't bear to be in the same room as me.

Not that I blame her—anytime we're together now, there's a sexual tension that simmers in the air, bubbling and hissing and popping, begging us to pay attention, to do *something*. It's not one-sided; that's pretty clear. Sex has ruined our platonic bond, it's twisted it into something unrecognizable.

Which is why, right now, Greg is walking up to Lyric and she's smiling at him like she's delighted to see him. My hand tightens into a fist around my glass of beer.

"Hi."

I turn to see Zoey. We haven't really talked since that night at Central Park when I walked her home. I've been distracted. And, to be honest, she hasn't reached out either. "Hey. You look great." I lean over and give her a hug.

She looks down at her cargo pants and top printed with tiny daisies and makes a face. "I couldn't decide what to wear."

"Me either."

We laugh because I'm wearing what I always wear, an old T-shirt and shorts with flip-flops. I happen to glance over Zoey's shoulder and see Lyric watching us, her face set and slightly annoyed, but when she sees me watching, she pastes on a smile and waves.

I wave back, conflicted. I'm not trying to hurt Lyric. But I don't know what else to do. We're stuck in limbo, a limbo that I created by proposing this dating-tutoring scheme in the first place. I have to fix it, and this is the only way I know how. To give her—and myself—some distance until this blows over and we figure out what we need to do.

I turn back to Zoey.

LYRIC

I'm not jealous. "Jealous" is such a strong word, anyway, and what does it really mean? Nobody knows.

I'm just . . . mildly interested in the fact that Kian's talking to Zoey and they're laughing together like good friends. They've probably got inside jokes now. Which is nice. What am I saying? It's *great*. It means our plan is working. Kian's going to date her and get out of his rut. He'll get what he wants. Woo-hoo and a happy dance.

I turn back to Greg. He's got a slightly bigger nose than I remember, and bushier eyebrows, but that's not a deal breaker. I can tell he made a real effort tonight: He's wearing a polka-dotted bow tie that would make Dr. Livingstone proud.

"I like your bow tie," I say, when there's a lull in the conversation, and sip my wine. The taste brings me back to the tree house, but I bat that memory away like a balloon. *No.* I'm here now with Greg.

Greg leans against the kitchen counter and grins. "Hey, thanks. I make them now. Did Charlie tell you? I have an Etsy shop. I also make dog bow ties, so people can match with their dogs."

I smile. "That's cute. Do you have a dog?"

"Do you have a dog?" This is really low-vibe small talk, Lyric. But Greg doesn't seem to notice. "Yeah, I have three, actually. Two pugs and a husky. It gets a little cramped in our apartment, but we're happy."

I continue to smile because I have no idea what else to say. What's a good segue from two pugs and a husky?

"Heyyy!" Charlie, dressed spiffily in a black moto jacket and jeans, slings her arm around me. "How's it going here? Hey, neighbor," she says to Greg, even though they walked in together twenty minutes ago. I suspect she could tell things were flagging a bit.

"Greg's telling me about his bow tie business," I say brightly. "And his dogs."

Charlie's sharp eyes study my expression. "Ah. That's awesome."

Still smiling like an overly happy dumbass, I take a sip of my wine again. "Yep."

"Greg, you don't mind if I borrow Lyric for a minute, do you?" Charlie asks her neighbor sweetly. "There's a situation in the living room I need help with."

"Not at all," Greg says magnanimously. "I'll get myself a glass of wine."

Charlie walks me to the living room, one hand pressing on the small of my back. "Hey." She turns to me when we're in a little deserted corner by the floor lamp. "You okay?"

"Sure," I chirp brightly. Then I glug my wine.

Charlie narrows her eyes. "I hope you don't think I'm that much of an idiot after six years of friendship, Lyric."

Sighing, I look over my shoulder. Kian's still engaged in conversation with Zoey by the TV. Turning back to Charlie, I say quietly, "I fucked up. Big-time."

She's immediately concerned. "What? What happened?"

"Kian and I had sex."

Her eyes practically shoot out of her head and land in my glass of wine. Appropriate, because my life has turned into a Halloween special. "You *what*?"

"Shh." I grab her elbow and squeeze. "Nobody knows. We're keeping it to ourselves."

"When was this?" Charlie says in her I'm-panicking-but-quietly voice. "I thought the kiss in London was the last of it!"

"Yeah, well, so did I." I take a morose drink of my wine. "It was on Saturday. We had another date tutoring session and Kian took me to this tree house restaurant thing. It was deserted; just us. And . . . one thing led to another. We had too much to drink and he said maybe having sex would get it out of our systems since things were so weird between us after the kiss in London, and Jesus. It sounds so incredibly stupid when I say it out loud."

Charlie blows out a big breath, but her eyes are sympathetic. "Look, I'm not going to pretend to understand you heterosexuals. But I'm guessing from your face and the fact that you and Kian haven't exchanged a word all evening but keep stealing glances at each other that things aren't working out as planned?"

Immediately, I look over my shoulder. "He's stealing glances at me?" When I turn back around, Charlie's looking at me with a raised eyebrow. My cheeks burn. "Right," I say sheepishly. "Anyway, yeah. Now things are even weirder. That's what this party's about. I need to get on another horse pronto and that horse is named Greg and has an Etsy bow tie shop."

Charlie massages her temples as if my straightness is too much of a burden to bear. Which, to be honest, it probably is. I need to take her out to dinner to thank her for putting up with it. "Are you sure about this, Lyric? I mean, Greg doesn't really seem like your type and he doesn't deserve to get hurt."

"I don't want to hurt him," I say quickly, because I've spent a lot of time thinking about this. "This isn't just something I'm doing to get over Kian or make him jealous. I genuinely want to move on and find a new relationship. And Greg not being my type is a good thing. Maybe I just need to date a wider variety of people, you know? Maybe *that's* where the solution to the Sizzle Paradox lies."

Charlie shrugs. "Okay, sure. If that's what you want." Her eyes drift over to Zoey and she smiles a little dreamily. "She looks good in flowers, doesn't she?"

I turn and look at Zoey's daisy top. "Yeah, she does. Are you going to try and pursue something with Zoey?"

Charlie adjusts her moto jacket and stands up straighter. "Well, it doesn't look like she and Kian are going to be a thing anytime soon." Turning to me, she adds, "A girl's gotta act when she sees an opening, you know?"

I wish I had a third of Charlie's big ovary energy. "I know. You have my blessing, but I have to warn you: Zoey's not easily impressed."

"Challenge accepted." Charlie grins, her eyes on Zoey again.

I take a rallying breath. "Well, I better get back to Greg." Giving Charlie a quick hug, I return to the kitchen.

KIAN

The party ends around 1:00 A.M. After the last of the drunken stragglers have left, Lyric and I move around the apartment, cleaning up the most egregious of messes. She hates leaving them for the next day.

Things are quiet, except for the occasional car honking or siren from an emergency vehicle going by. I get a trash bag from under the kitchen sink and begin to put empty drink cans and plastic cups into it for the recycling bin. Lyric picks up plates and mostly empty boxes of pizza. We work in silence for a few minutes before I can't stand it anymore and have to go and break it.

"So. I liked Greg's bow tie."

Lyric stiffens a little. "Thanks. So did I. He sells them. On Etsy."

"How creative of him." I don't know why I'm being an asshole about it. Kudos to the guy. But suddenly all I want to do is rip Greg's bow tie off his neck, wherever he is.

She gives me a look but keeps picking up the trash. Then she says, "Looks like you and Zoey were having a good time."

"Yeah, we were."

"Good."

"Uh-huh." I glance at her out of the corner of my eye as I pick up a beer bottle. "Did you know she has a butterfly collection?" I don't know why I tell her this, except that I don't want Greg to be the only one who does something interesting.

Lyric makes a noise in her throat but doesn't say anything.

After a beat of silence, I ask, "What does that mean?"

She shrugs and aggressively pushes a box of pizza into her trash bag. "Oh, nothing. I didn't know you were such a fan of people collecting dead animals that were once beautifully alive."

I frown at her. "Firstly, butterflies aren't animals. And secondly, you used to have a cat skull."

"That cat was already dead when the artist harvested its skull!" Lyric shoots back. "I think encasing butterflies into Lucite boxes is just weird and gross and sad."

I'm a little taken aback by the passion with which she says this, but I play it off. "Okay. Well, I think it's cool. Way cooler than bow ties."

Lyric glares at me. "Stop talking about Greg's bow ties."

I drop the trash bag and raise my hands. "Sorry, didn't know you were so protective about him."

Her mouth is a hard line. "Well, I am. I guess I'm just as protective about his bow ties as you are about Zoey's butterflies."

I grab the trash can off the floor and stalk to the front door. "I'm going to put this in the trash chute."

She doesn't respond.

ꟷ

I stay gone for a while. It's not smart because I have to see my advisor early the next day, but I need the time and fresh(ish) air to cool off.

I'm not sure why I fought with Lyric, and about something so silly. But I'm still angry. I'm still fucking jealous about fucking Greg with his fucking bow ties.

As I walk past shuttered shops and sleeping homeless people on the steaming sidewalk, I stick my hands in my pockets and wonder why I'm having such an oversized reaction. Yeah, so the line between friendship and something more has gotten ridiculously muddled with Lyric because we were fucking stupid and slept together. But why am I so jealous I can barely think straight? Why have I felt depressed every day, knowing I can't sit with her and watch *Friends* reruns because things have gotten too weird now? Why do I still think about the kiss in London and her under the moon at the tree house farm, her golden hair gleaming silver?

It all feels so heavy. And nothing with Lyric has ever felt heavy before.

I turn the corner, intending to circle back around the block and head home. There, around the bend, is a lone homeless man sitting on the stoop of a liquor store. He's fallen asleep with a cardboard sign propped up in his lap. It reads: THIS IS YOUR SIGN TO FACE THE TRUTH YOU'VE BEEN DENYING.

It's like I've run into a brick wall. I come to a dead stop, staring at the sign. Something about it tugs at my brain. If I were Lyric, I'd say the universe was speaking to me. I rewind back to all the thoughts I've had about her recently.

That she's my family.

That she looked like a Goddess under the moon.

That I'm insanely jealous at the mere thought of her showing interest in someone else.

That kissing her and making love to her was an experience I've never come close to having before.

And then I think about what my mother said the other night, that sometimes the things we think we *shouldn't* do are actually just things we're afraid of. What am I afraid of?

Face the truth you've been denying, Montgomery, I think, my hands loose at my sides, my eyes fixated on the sign. What do all those things add up to?

"Holy fucking shit," I murmur to myself as a light, cool spring rain begins to fall. The droplets bead on my skin like crystals. "I'm in love with Lyric."

LYRIC

I lie in bed, awake, after Kian leaves. I don't even know what we were fighting about. I mean, yes, it was about bow ties and butterflies, but that's ridiculous. Kian and I never fight, least of all about fucking butterflies. Why did I have to say they were weird and gross, anyway? What do I care if Zoey collects them?

I turn to face my window, my hand curled around a quartz crystal point for clarity. The lamppost outside throws an orange stripe of light across my face, but I don't move away. I feel physically sick, my body bruised and hurting as if I've fallen from a great height. I don't understand what's happening to me.

Chapter Twenty-two

*

KIAN

"I'm on track to defend my thesis on Tuesday," I tell my advisor, Dr. Simmons, a brown-bobbed white woman in her midfifties. We're seated at the desk in her tiny office, me across from her with a Starbucks coffee in my hand after my sleepless night. The walls are lined with her many degrees, all from Columbia. It doesn't matter that today's Saturday; Dr. Simmons is at work more often than she's home.

She waves me away, her round face bright and happy. "I'm not worried about that, Kian. I know you're ready. The reason I called you in today is about something different." She leans forward, her eyes shining. "Your effort with the greener greenhouse has not gone unnoticed. I've been speaking to someone from the US Forest Service. They're actively recruiting for top-notch environmental engineers."

I sit up straighter, my tiredness and near-constant inner turmoil dissipating momentarily. "Really?"

She smiles. "Really. In fact, they want to meet up in Burdett this weekend and show you some of the work they're doing at Finger Lakes National Forest. Tell you a little bit about what they're looking for, let you tell them what you want from a career with them. I told them you were interested. Was that okay?"

I laugh. "Absolutely! This is incredible!"

"Good. Now, go home and pack your bags. I used department funds to get you a hotel room up there tonight and tomorrow."

I stand and shake her hand. "Thank you. Thank you so much."

She sits back, satisfied. "Anything for my favorite student."

Still grinning, I walk out the door, forgetting all the other shit going on in my life for just a few minutes.

I pack in record speed. This is it. This is everything I've been working toward. Every time I didn't want to go to a lecture and I went anyway; that time my dad offered me a mid-six-figure job if I'd forget my plan to apply to grad school and start at his company and, in spite of a million misgivings, I turned him down; all the times I had to subsist on ramen and water . . . this was what it was all for.

When I'm done, I walk to Lyric's closed bedroom door and knock. She doesn't answer, probably because she's at the lab, like I expected her to be. Feeling a little relieved that I won't have to face her just yet after my earth-shattering revelation last night, I pull out my phone and text her.

Kian: Hey I'm going upstate for the weekend

Her response comes a minute later.

Lyric: Oh. Everything okay?

Kian: Yeah just some engineering thing. See you monday

Lyric: k see you then

She doesn't ask what engineering thing like she would've a few months ago. She's just letting me go.

I put my phone away, feeling that familiar sad tug at my heart that I've come to abhor. This is what it's come down to. Seven years of friendship and we're just a handful of awkward texts and ridiculous arguments. But maybe this trip to Finger Lakes will help clear my head, give me some clarity.

I pick up my bags and leave.

LYRIC

I knock obnoxiously on Charlie's door, over and over and over again until she finally opens it.

"Doc?" she says, her glasses crooked and her hair all mussed. "Are you okay?"

"No," I say, my voice wobbling. "I think I'm going crazy."

It's 7:00 P.M. and I've just left the lab, the last one out of there. Zoey left two hours ago, but I couldn't even bring myself to say bye to her. This is what I've become—a twisted, angry, bitter person, and I don't know why. I don't know why the sight of Zoey annoys me so much. I don't know why I want to simultaneously punch Kian in his stupid square jaw and bite his bottom lip.

I follow Charlie into her living room and flop down on the ancient black pleather couch, putting my head in my hands. "Charlie, I'm so fucked up. I can't. I don't. I'm not. Help."

She sits beside me and rubs my back in soothing circles. "Hey. It's okay. Breathe."

So I try. I breathe in and out, three counts each, blowing out each breath. A few moments later, I'm a lot calmer. I look up at her. "Thanks."

"'Course. Want some coffee? I've got decaf."

I nod and she bustles off into her tiny kitchen. A moment later, she returns with two steaming coffee mugs. I take one and take a deep sip, even though it burns my tongue and throat.

"Now." Charlie sits back down beside me and gives me the

mom look. "Want to tell me what's going on? You're not into drugs, are you?"

I snort and laugh a teary laugh. "I wish. I think that'd be a lot less complicated. At least I'd know what the hell is wrong with me."

"Okay, honey, start at the beginning," Charlie says. "Does this have to do with Kian? What we talked about at the party?"

I nod, running my finger around the rim of the mug as I watch the white steam curl and bend in the air. "Things have just gotten more and more fucked up, Charlie. We can't even talk to each other without fighting. I feel physically ill, like, all the time. Last night after the party, we fought about fucking butterflies. *Butterflies.*

"And then he left and I haven't seen him since and he just sent me a text this morning saying he was going upstate for some engineering thing. And you know what? He didn't even tell me what engineering thing. He didn't say anything else. And I just . . . I didn't know what to say. We're like two uncomfortable strangers forced to share living quarters; we don't even know each other anymore."

I stop to take a breath and Charlie studies me. "Wow. That is a *lot*."

"Yeah, it is." I feel choked up and frustrated and too hot and too cold all at once. Setting my coffee down, I get up and begin to pace around the tiny living room. "And I don't know what the fuck's happened. The only thing I can think of is I've ruined everything with my stupid Sizzle Paradox and being so selfish and wanting his help with it. I didn't even stop to really think about what might happen if we lost our friendship. And then to kiss him and sleep with him and expect things to just go back to normal? I've been a total idiot." I throw my hands up. "I can't sleep, I can't eat, I can't even fucking *think* without his face flashing into my brain constantly. I feel like I'm going to vomit anytime I imagine him moving away after graduation. But when he's near me, I can't even sit on the couch with him anymore without thinking about his mouth on mine. So what is it? Am I a pervert? Or just a bad friend? Or both?" I walk up to her and put my hands on my hips. "Give it to me straight, Charlie. I need to hear it from an objective third party."

She takes a deep sip of her coffee and then clears her throat. "Um. Well. You're not going to like what I have to say, Doc."

I throw my hands up in the air again. "At this point, how bad can it be? You can't tell me something I haven't already thought about myself. So lay it on me. Come on."

"Okay." She sets her coffee down next to mine and pats the seat next to her. I sit and turn toward her. She puts her hand on my knee and says, "Lyric, I think you're in love with Kian."

It takes a full five seconds for her words to penetrate my brain. I blink. And then I laugh. "Stop. I'm being serious."

She doesn't return my laughter. "So am I."

I blink again. I try to unhear her words. And then I let them rattle around my brain for a minute. "You . . . you think I'm in *love* with Kian Montgomery?"

Charlie nods carefully. "Yeah. All the signs are there. You're thinking about him constantly. You want to be near him but you're terrified. You're arguing with him because of your unresolved feelings. I mean, I'm no psych nerd, Doc, but it seems pretty obvious to me. You tried to sleep with him to clear your system, but it just made things worse between the two of you." She makes an apologetic face. "I think, somehow, in the course of all the fake dating-slash-tutoring sessions . . . you've fallen for him. And hard."

I put my hands on my head. "Oh my God."

She nods at the look of shocked but indubitable acceptance on my face. "Yep. That's what I thought."

Tears begin to run down my face. "But I can't love him. I simply can*not*. It'll ruin everything."

She puts her arm around me. "I know, sweetie."

I sob into her shoulder. "I'm such an idiot. I'm such a stupid, dumbass, fucking fool. Why Kian? Why, of all people, *Kian*?"

"Because it makes perfect sense?"

I look up because it isn't Charlie who's spoken. It's Zoey.

She's standing on Charlie's other side now, dressed in a T-shirt and nothing else. I blink the tears from my eyes. "Um . . . am I dreaming?"

Zoey gives Charlie an apologetic look. "Sorry. I couldn't sit in there anymore when I heard what was going on."

Charlie reaches out and squeezes her hand. "No worries. We could use another opinion in here."

I look between the two of them. "You two are . . . are you two together?"

They nod in tandem and share a secret smile.

"Yeah," Zoey says finally. "I was going to let Kian know.

Um . . . we walked home after the party and one thing led to another." Her cheeks glow an endearing pink.

I laugh. "No, this is great! Charlie's been—" I catch Charlie's warning look and amend what I'd been about to say ("Charlie's been pining after you") to something a bit more pulled back. "Charlie's a really great catch."

Zoey gives me a look like she's not stupid. She knows Charlie's head over heels for her. And from the way she's looking at my other best friend, I think Zoey might be on her way there, too.

"Anyway," Zoey says, coming to sit next to me on my other side. "I was saying it just makes sense for you to have feelings about Kian. Honestly, when I first met him, I wondered why you two weren't dating. You just . . . belong together."

"That's what everyone always said," I reply miserably, wiping my cheeks. "And I always told them they were completely wrong. And now here I am—" I choke back another sob. "I've ruined everything. Our friendship is over."

"Wait a minute," Zoey says. "What makes you think he isn't into you?"

I shake my head. "I just know, Zoey. It's all been pretty one-sided. I mean, yes, we slept together and Kian was into that. But . . . I think it was just sex for him. And clearly, for me, it was way more than that. He hasn't given me any signs that he feels differently."

"But you don't even know that. You haven't even tried to tell him how you feel," Charlie counters.

I look at her, my heart beginning to beat faster. "Are you saying—you think there might be a chance . . . ?"

"Of course there's a chance," Zoey says, shaking her head. "You guys are best friends. You've kissed. You slept together. Of *course* there's a chance he has feelings for you, too. You just have to ask him."

I rub my face, my heart twisting with a painful hope. "Shit. Shit. Really?"

"Yeah, and you should do it soon. He's defending his thesis next week, right? And then he'll be graduating. You don't have much time."

I look into Charlie's kind brown eyes and realize she's right. "Okay. Yes. I'm going to do it. I'll tell him when he gets back from upstate."

Charlie grins at me. "Atta girl. Now that we've got that sorted out, who's ready for something a bit stronger than coffee?"

Both Zoey and I raise our hands.

Chapter Twenty-three

*

KIAN

"And that about concludes our tour of the research station," Trent Goldberg, one of the forestry department employees, a bald man in his sixties, says. We wander over to the glass front doors, and he leads the way outside into the warm sunshine. "As you've seen, we have a lot of lab equipment available to you and your team as an environmental engineer. But a lot of your time will also be spent outdoors—collecting soil samples, gathering data on shrub and ground cover vegetation, that kind of thing, depending on what exactly the project is at your particular research station. Of course, I'm not an engineer so I can't speak to that side very technically, but we'll get someone to sit down with you if you decide to proceed with us."

"I onboarded as a civil engineer when I first began twenty

years ago, and I can say that this is hands down one of the best places I've ever worked." Sheila Rasmussen, the other employee I've been speaking with who's now the VP of her department, smiles at me in the sunshine. Her brown hair is threaded with gray and pulled back in a no-nonsense ponytail. "If you enjoy being outdoors like you've told us, Kian, you're going to love the balance of engineering and, to be honest, tromping around in nature." She laughs. "Beats being a desk jockey at any of these other firms for sure."

"We don't have to tell you, your résumé is incredibly impressive," Trent puts in. "We'd love to have you aboard if this sounds like something you're interested in."

I gesture toward the Finger Lakes National Forest that sprawls behind us. "This is my dream job," I say, shaking my head. "Still can't quite believe it's real, to be honest."

Sheila and Trent laugh heartily. "Believe it," Sheila says. "We were really floored by your greenhouse design. That's the kind of innovation we're looking for here."

I turn to look at the research station again. "So would I be working at this exact station or somewhere else . . . ?"

Sheila and Trent exchange a look. "Well, actually," Trent begins, "the job we're thinking about for you isn't in New York."

I pause. "Oh. Where is it, then?"

"Washington State," Sheila replies.

"We'll pay for you to relocate, of course," Trent puts in quickly. "And you'll be paid a relocation bonus as well; I don't think you'll be unhappy with the amount. Really, Kian, you'll love Washington State. And the sky's the limit once you join us out there."

Sheila studies my expression, her weathered face careful. "Dr. Simmons told us you don't have any attachments here in New York. You're young and unmarried, at the beginning of your career. So relocation shouldn't be a problem, right?"

I take a deep breath of unpolluted air, so rare where I currently live. Washington State could be a new start. A new slate. Leave behind the mess I've made in New York, start over. Breathe in this rich, fresh, forest air every day. I turn to them. "How long do I have to think about it?"

"One week," Trent replies.

LYRIC

By the time Kian returns home Monday morning, I've rehearsed what I'm going to say about a thousand times. I even take the morning off from the lab, something I didn't even do when I had a tailbone fracture from when Kian took me on that mountain hike and I fell off a boulder. Because Charlie and Zoey are right; this needs to happen now. I need to say what I feel or I'll wonder about it forever. How do I even know how Kian's going to respond if I don't give him the chance?

I'm in my room rehearsing in front of the mirror again when I hear him walk in. His footsteps fade as he goes into his room. My heart thumps in my chest, but I shake my hair out, take a few deep breaths, and then stride out into the living room to wait on the couch.

He comes back out a minute later, looking down at his phone.

"Hey."

He looks up, startled. For just a moment, his face softens and his eyes crinkle. And then it's like he remembers how things have changed. I can practically see the wall going up in real time. "Oh. Hi. Why aren't you at the lab?"

Right into it, then. But I don't think I'm *quite* ready to dive in yet. I need a warm-up first. So I say, "Um, how was upstate?"

Kian slips his phone into his pocket and then comes to sit across from me. "It was good. I . . . I have a lot to think about."

I nod, unsure. I don't know what he means and he doesn't volunteer any more information, so I try a different tack. "Are you ready for your thesis defense tomorrow?"

"I am," he says carefully.

"Great. Because I was thinking I could come and provide moral support, if you want—you know how you asked me before, and—"

"Lyric," he interrupts, looking into my eyes. "I have something to tell you."

I sit back. For a moment, my heart starts pounding furiously. What if Kian wants to tell me he's in love with me, too? What if this is some cosmic happy ending, playing out right here in our minuscule, crappy living room? I twist my fingers together, not daring to breathe.

Kian looks down at his hands, which are hanging loosely

between his knees. Then he looks back at me. "I'm moving out."

"Yeah, I know, you told me. After graduation."

"No, not after graduation. This afternoon. And I've been offered a job at the forestry department in Washington State. I think I'm going to take it."

I study his face, confused, not yet heartbroken. "What? But . . . why?"

He runs a hand through his hair, leaving it mussed. "I think it's pretty clear that this"—he gestures between us—"isn't what either of us wants."

It's like watching a car crash. Everything slows down. It takes my brain a second to let me understand that yes, all of my hopes and dreams *are* being pulverized right before my eyes. I appreciate my brain trying to protect me for that split second, but when the pain hits, I can barely move. It feels like every bone in my body is broken.

Charlie and Zoey were wrong. My own idiotic hope was wrong. Kian doesn't want me. He doesn't want this. In fact, he *so* wants nothing to do with me, he's running away to Washington State. And I'm too proud to let him know that, actually, this—us—is exactly what *I'd* wanted. That it's exactly what I'd been planning on.

I straighten up, trying to blink away tears that may give me away. "Okay," I say, my voice only the tiniest bit strangled. I'm proud of myself for that, for keeping a grip on my emotions even as I'm drowning. "Of course it isn't. Everything that happened between us has been a huge mistake." I pause, trying to choke out the next words. "And Washington State will be a nice change for you. Congrats."

Something flashes in Kian's eyes but it's gone before I can tell what it is. "Right. Since you feel that way, I think you can see that me moving out right away is the only solution. We need space from each other."

Every word is like a splinter under my skin, slicing me to shreds. Death by a thousand truths I don't want to hear. "Space. Yeah." I'm barely coherent, but I don't think he notices.

"I'm going to stay with Templeton for a bit, until after graduation. I'll come back when you're at the lab to move my stuff out a bit at a time. I should be done by the end of the week."

I can't look at him anymore. I can't believe he's saying this to me. I can't believe this is how it ends. "Okay."

"Lyric."

There's a long pause and then I realize he's waiting for me to look at him. So I do. My eyes burn because his face is still the single most beautiful thing I've encountered in my lifetime.

"This is all my fault." His voice is rough, so deep it's barely a rumble. "I should never have suggested tutoring you." His fists are tight against his thighs, as if his regret is so great, he can barely hold it in. "I'm sorry it's ruined our friendship. I'm . . . I'm sorry."

So much regret. So much he wishes had never happened. And that's the difference between us. Even knowing what's happened, I would never take a single second of it back. "It's fine," I say, trying to keep my voice casual. I stand. "I have to get to the lab. So . . . good luck. With everything."

Without waiting for a reply, I sweep out of the room and out of our apartment and out of our lives together. I run down the stairs that I can't see anymore because my tears are washing the world away.

KIAN

After Lyric leaves, I sit in the absolute silence of our apartment for ten minutes without moving. I've been in here alone before, of course. But it's never felt this empty.

She didn't deny any of the things I said. She didn't tell me I was wrong, that this wasn't a mistake. She didn't ask me to stay. It's like I suspected: My falling in love with her ruined everything. It changed our friendship fundamentally in the worst way possible. And there's no taking it back.

I get off the couch and walk to her room. Her door is wide open, so, ducking under the ever-present and slightly hazardous crystal chandelier, I walk inside, breathing in the scent of freshly washed sheets and Lyric's own smell: feminine and sweet and soft. Walking to her crystal-adorned windowsill, I reach into my pocket and pull out the stone I got her from a little spiritual shop in upstate New York. Morganite, to help with emotional healing and forgiveness. It's also the stone of unexpressed feelings.

I place the orange-pink stone next to her other crystals. It winks at me in the sunlight.

Then I turn on my heel and leave, walking out of the

apartment where we built our friendship, our selves, our lives together, knowing I'll never be back.

The door closes with a final click.

LYRIC

It's Tuesday afternoon. Kian is done defending his thesis. Ava sent me a text to let me know. He passed, obviously, like I knew he would. He's officially Dr. Montgomery now. The walk across the stage next week is just a formality. And then he'll be gone completely. He'll be across the country in Washington, starting his new life. One that won't have me in it.

I lean back in my chair in the lab. I've been staring at my computer for the last two hours, but I've written a total of one whole sentence. Nothing makes sense. Nothing feels good. I'm wondering if I should just pack it in and head to our empty apartment when a thought occurs to me. And before I can change my mind, I'm up out of my chair and walking down the hall to the fMRI room.

The fMRI room, as one might guess from the name, is where we store the fMRI machine that the Columbia psychology department is intensely and aggressively protective of. There's a very intricate sign-in procedure and no one from any other department is allowed to breathe on it without a psych doc student present. But since it's Tuesday afternoon, I know it'll be empty except for Daniel Fuhrman, the undergrad student I recommended to Dr. Livingstone. I push my way in and stand in the cool, quiet room, the fMRI machine humming quietly under the fluorescent lighting like a mechanical sleeping beauty.

Daniel looks up from the bank of computers on the right and flashes me a big, bright smile. "Hey, Lyric!"

I manage to conjure up a smile. "Hey, Daniel. How's it going?"

He leans back in his chair. "Really good. Thanks for convincing Dr. Livingstone to let me access the fMRI data on these computers. He's weirdly possessive about it."

I snort. "Yeah, get used to that. Around here, the fMRI machine is God. It cost them about three years worth of their budget, I think."

He grins. "Good to know, good to know."

There's an expectant silence, and I know Daniel's wondering what I'm doing in here. I wasn't signed up to use the fMRI.

"Daniel." I clear my throat. There's no other way to say this than to just say it. "I wonder if you could run the machine on me?"

He frowns. "On *you*?"

"Yeah. I, uh, I need to collect some data."

Daniel raises his thick eyebrows. "On yourself?"

I understand his confusion. When I got the data on my ex-boyfriends Hamish and Samuel, I was testing out the software. Everyone in the lab did it. But I have all the data I need now, and there's no reason for me to run the software on myself again. Except I want to. I need to know.

"Please." I walk forward and place my phone in front of him. "And . . . I need you to feed that into the machine so I can see it when I'm inside."

He looks down at Kian's picture on my phone screen and then slowly up at me, realization dawning on his face. He knows what I'm doing. He knows I want to test my reaction—my sexual and romantic connection to Kian. My cheeks burn, but I don't explain. I have to believe that Daniel, being the decent human being he is, will keep this to himself. That he won't tell Kian.

"Gotcha," Daniel says softly.

I divest myself of all metal. And then, taking a breath, I walk forward and climb into the waiting machine.

Daniel helps me get set up and hooked to everything in silence. But his eyes are kind and sympathetic; I feel like he can sense my inner turmoil. "Any problems, just let me know," he says and then, nodding, steps back and over to the computers.

Daniel gives me a verbal cue and then the machine starts up. Its noisy racket is familiar and comforting, in a way. And then Kian's smiling face flashes on the internal screen and I can feel myself react ferociously, even though I'm lying still.

It's a picture I took of him at the beach last summer—he's shirtless and smiling, his brown hair ruffled by the ocean breeze, gold flecks of sand glinting on his broad, tawny shoulders. Even as my body reacts, my scientist's mind takes note of my reaction with a cool, calculating mind: My muscles tense up while, simultaneously, there's a curious rush of release in my blood; I am calm and keyed up all at once—my body's on fire but also bathed in silky, honeyed tranquility. Neither Hamish nor Samuel brought out this response. Not even close.

A few moments later, the machine goes quiet.

"All done," Daniel says.

I get up and get myself put back together without meeting his eye. Then I walk up to him and hold out a hand. "Printout, please," I say quietly.

He hands it over without a word.

Not able to wait, I look at the results.

My dopamine levels, indicating sexual attraction: bright green, the highest level possible.

My oxytocin levels, showing emotional connection: bright green, the highest level possible.

I have a near-perfect score. I've cracked the Sizzle Paradox. Kian Montgomery, it turns out, was the key all along.

ω

The printout is laid on my desk and I sit across from it in a chair, my hands laced over my stomach. I haven't stopped staring at it since I got back from the fMRI room, over an hour ago. These results are extraordinary. Even among the thousands of participants in my study, this level of sexual and emotional connection was only present in .05 percent of the population. And Kian and I have it.

Well, I have it with Kian. But he doesn't feel the same way.

He's my key, but I'm not his lock. I'm not sure what to do with that.

There's a knock on my door, interrupting my reverie. I look up to see Dr. Livingstone peering in at me.

"Hello, Miss Bishop."

"Dr. Livingstone." I barely feel any fear or discomfort at his presence at all, which just shows how fucked up I am.

"The end of the academic year is upon us, and I cannot help but notice that you haven't provided me any updates on your thesis since the last one about two weeks ago."

"Right." Flipping the printout over, I ball up a nearby Post-it Note and toss it from hand to hand. "That's because I actually don't have one for you." I'm so beyond trying to cover this up or act like I care, it's not even funny.

Dr. Livingstone studies me for a long moment and then comes in and sits in the empty chair across from me. It squeaks in protest as he sighs and leans back. "Miss Bishop. May I be frank with you?"

I gesture expansively with my hand, feeling generous.

"You've been working on your thesis for several years, and yet, as I sit before you now, it seems you have very little enthusiasm for the topic. Am I wrong?"

I look into Dr. Livingstone's wise eyes—eyes that would've once given me a panic attack were they waiting for a response to the question he's just posed me. But in this moment, I feel absolutely nothing. I'm numb from the tips of my hair to the soles of my feet. "No," I say quietly. "You're not wrong."

"Hmm." He props his elbows on the arms of the chair, steeples his fingers, and considers me over them. "Then the logical follow-on to that is: Is this the right field of study for you?"

I swallow, aware that I probably should feel humiliated. "You don't think I have what it takes?"

But he's shaking his head before I'm even done with the question. "Far from it. The reason I took you on as my student is because I saw a spark in you. You're one of the brightest people I've worked with. You've come up with a study that has almost single-handedly funded this department over the last five years. I'm asking the question because I don't want to be the reason for the extinguishing of that spark. And I certainly don't want *you* to be the reason for the extinguishing of that spark. Miss Bishop, nothing will dim your shine faster than working in a place that plunges you into darkness."

I rub my face, barely able to even register the compliment from Dr. Livingstone. "It's not this place," I mutter, gazing at the floor. "It's me. I'm . . . lost."

He sits back and raises an eyebrow. "Then isn't it up to you to find yourself again? Look at your internal compass. What does it tell you?"

My internal compass is telling me to run into Kian's arms. Obviously, it's broken. But maybe I can use that. If my internal compass is telling me to run to Kian and it's broken, the logical thing to do is the exact opposite of what it's saying.

I straighten as a sudden idea occurs to me, so obvious I'm shocked it never occurred to me before now. "Of course. That's the answer. I . . . I need to drop out of this program. I have enough credit to earn a master's in sociology next year; maybe I can transfer over to that department."

He raises an eyebrow. "You've never talked about sociology before."

"Maybe that's why it's perfect. Maybe it's the change I need. I minored in sociology as an undergrad, so it's not like I have no concept of the subject matter. Plus, psychology and sociology are sister disciplines. Maybe all the time I've spent studying won't be completely wasted this way."

After a pause, Dr. Livingstone bows his head a little. "If that's what you want. Only you can decide. I'm happy to write you a recommendation, whatever you need. Of course, you will be missed."

I want to cry. Working with Dr. Livingstone has been a dream of mine since I was sixteen years old. I've been working toward it for the last eight years. I don't know how this is happening, why everything around me is crumbling. But I have to believe there's more for me on the other side of this devastation. I have to.

"I'll miss you, too," I mumble. "Believe it or not."

Grunting, he stands and makes his way to the door. On the way out, he turns and looks at me over his shoulder. "By the way, thank you for referring Daniel Fuhrman to me. He's turning out to be an excellent lab assistant, and possibly a very good grad student when the time comes. He reminds me a little of you."

I smile weakly. "That's good to hear."

Then Dr. Livingstone raises a hand to me and is gone. He never was one for elaborate speeches.

And just like that, my career as an experimental psychologist is over.

Chapter Twenty-four

KIAN

I have my doctorate and I feel . . . strangely empty. I'm still in my robes, just an hour after walking off the stage at the outdoor ceremony, when I run my eyes over the dissipating crowds of families.

My mother was here; we're having dinner later. My father is in Europe and didn't come, which wasn't a surprise. Eli, Ava, Templeton, and Jonas were all here; we're meeting up for drinks in a bit.

But what still is a surprise and really shouldn't be is that *she* didn't come. I know I essentially told her not to. I know we're not friends, not anything, anymore. But still. I thought Lyric would be here anyway. I could've sworn, at one point, that I saw her blond hair glinting in the sunlight, at the back of the crowd of families. But when I looked again, the illusion was gone. Wishful thinking.

My heart crumples in on itself as I realize just how little I mean to her now. My mind flashes back to our last in-person conversation, when I told her I was moving out. How calmly she accepted it. How she chose not to fight for us at all.

"Dr. Montgomery."

I swallow my heartache and turn to see my advisor smiling up at me, her glasses glinting in the sunlight. "Dr. Simmons."

"Congratulations."

I manage a smile. "Thank you. For everything."

She brushes me away. "So, as I understand it, you're off on a grand adventure now."

I take a deep breath and tip my head back to look at the cloudless sky. "Yeah. Fresh air, plenty of trees, the whole thing. I think it'll be good for me."

"A brand-new start." Dr. Simmons beams, looking very much like a proud parent. "You're going to fly, Kian. I just know it."

I'm in Templeton's apartment, packing the last of my things and putting the pullout couch back into position as the sun sinks lower in the sky. I leave tonight for my new place, my new job, my new life. Eli and the others asked if I wanted to stick around, what's the rush, why don't I stay. I told them I was eager to get started at the new job, learn the ropes. But the truth is, what do I have left to stay for?

I pick up my phone and my social media app reminds me that this time last year, Lyric and I were at our favorite taco restaurant, wearing sombreros together. I look at the silly picture, Lyric with her eyes crossed, her hair shorter than it is now. I'm grinning and looking at her, not the camera, my entire face lit up with happiness. I don't remember that particular night, but I do remember that feeling. Lyric's the only one who can make me feel that way—completely free.

I take a breath and grab my wallet off the coffee table. I'm not leaving without saying goodbye, dammit. We can at least manage that after seven years of friendship.

I ring the doorbell to our—her—apartment, which feels all kinds of wrong. But I wait patiently until I hear the lock sliding back, the doorknob being turned. My heart thumps painfully as I stand there, waiting for her to open the door and ask me what the hell I'm doing here.

"Hey." It's not Lyric's face peering up at me; it's Charlie's. The door opens wider and there's Zoey, standing next to her, looking just as confused to see me as I am to see them.

Not to see them together—Zoey sent me a text about a week ago saying she and Charlie were dating and hoping there were no hard feelings. Of course there weren't. Zoey and Charlie make more sense than Zoey and I ever did. What I'm confused about is why they're answering the door *here,* in Lyric's apartment, when she's nowhere to be seen.

"Hey." I frown a little. "Is Lyric here?"

They exchange a look. "No . . ." Charlie looks back at me. "Lyric is . . . Lyric left, Kian."

Zoey stands aside. "Why don't you come in?"

My mouth suddenly dry, I follow them inside to the living room.

The house is empty. I stand rooted to the spot just inside the door, staring at our small space. The couch we snuggled together on is gone. The tiny kitchen is devoid of Lyric's waffle maker, her bullet blender. I walk past Charlie and Zoey to Lyric's bedroom. There's no crystal chandelier I have to duck to get under anymore. The windowsill is bare. Her room is just a box.

I feel like someone's punched me in the gut. Leaning against the wall, I attempt a deep breath but it keeps getting trapped somewhere in my chest. It's like she was never here. It's like *we* were never here.

A small hand presses against my arm. Charlie's looking up at me in concern. "You okay?"

I begin to nod and then shake my head. I can't quite form any words just yet.

Zoey walks in and looks around the room. "It's depressing, isn't it?"

"Where . . . where is she?" My voice is a croak.

Charlie hooks her thumbs in the pockets of her jeans. "She left a couple of hours ago. She's on her way to Houma."

Confused, I ask, "Who-ma?"

Charlie shakes her head. "Houma, Louisiana."

That I wasn't expecting. Are she and Greg eloping or

something? Is Houma a beautiful, romantic wedding getaway that I haven't heard about? The thought makes me physically ill. "What the hell's in Louisiana?" I sound angry. I shouldn't, but I do. I am. I ache and it comes out as irascibility.

But then Zoey's next words bring me back to confusion. "She quit her program, Kian. She's not working with Dr. Livingstone anymore."

"What?" I stare at Zoey. "Why not?"

Zoey shakes her head. "I'm not sure . . . she didn't tell us all the details. She was kind of in a hurry to leave. She switched over to the master's program in sociology, working with Dr. Perez. Apparently Dr. Perez was looking for grad students willing to spend a year in Louisiana for a study she's conducting there. Lyric volunteered." She pauses and gestures around the apartment. "We were just helping her clear out the last of her stuff. She said if we wanted any of it, we could have it, but she wants the rest in storage until she can sell it."

Charlie fixes me with a glare. "She needed to get away. You know, after everything. Kind of the same thing you're doing."

"Me?" My brain is all kinds of muddled.

"Yeah, she told us you were going to Washington State."

I push a hand through my hair. "That's not—I'm—wait. So she's competing with me? Seeing who can get farther away?"

Charlie sighs. "I don't know, man. I'm just as confused as you. Straights are exhausting."

"Right." I push off the wall I've been leaning against, a sudden determination coiling in my limbs, infusing me with energy. "Do you have Lyric's travel itinerary by any chance?"

Charlie and Zoey look at each other and then Zoey nods. "Yeah, of course. We wanted to make sure we could check on her in case anything went wrong."

I smile a little. "Zoey, would you mind giving me a copy?"

LYRIC

As soon as I board the Greyhound bus from NYC to New Orleans, I turn off my phone and stick it in my messenger bag that I then place in the empty seat beside me. The fMRI printout's in there, too. I couldn't bring myself to toss it out.

The Greyhound is going to take me thirty-eight hours and a transfer, and then another bus ride into Houma from New Orleans. I could've flown and made it easier on myself. But I need the extra time to *feel* myself putting physical distance between my past life and the new one waiting for me in Louisiana. I need the extra time to detox, to let my feelings slip away with every mile under our tires. Because right now, I'm a mess.

I went to Kian's graduation earlier today. I watched him, tall and handsome and confident, stride across that stage to applause. I thought my heart would pop with pride. It was everything he'd ever wanted, and I wanted to be there to cheer him on, silently. Even if he didn't want me to. Even if he didn't know I was there. Now I'm vacillating between numbness and devastation, anger at myself and Kian. There's a painful longing that feels like my chest is being cleaved in two, one half left behind with Kian, wherever he goes.

I shake my head a little as the bus's tires hiss on the road. We've been on the road about ninety minutes and just finished a quick break at the gas station where everyone except me loaded up on Taco Bell. My stomach churns at the smell of fried food all around me. I haven't eaten in a while, and I don't think I can. I wonder if grief can make you really ill. Because right now, every cell in my body feels sick. And the only one who could help me heal is the one who won't.

Reaching into the front pocket of my bag, I pull out the morganite stone I found on my windowsill the day Kian moved out. It glitters in my palm with the movement of the bus, an orange stone with threads of pink shot through. It feels a little like holding the sun in my hand. I don't know where it came from; I was tempted to think Kian left it behind, but I know that's just wishful thinking. Kian doesn't believe in crystals. Plus, why would he want me to have this? But neither Zoey nor Charlie admitted to leaving it there either.

I'm still staring at the morganite, pondering its mysterious origins, when the driver yells out and stamps on the brake. Startled, I look up. People are murmuring and pointing, some of them standing for a better view. What the hell is going on? I lean to look out the window, but from this angle, I can't see anything.

Then I hear a deep voice say something insistently from outside the bus. There's a knock on the bus's folding doors, which the driver opens with an expression somewhere between confused and flustered. And suddenly, Kian is standing at the front of the bus, his brown eyes searching, searching, searching.

Until they land on me.

I'm frozen in my seat, watching him walk forward, his ridiculously perfect face serious. There's scruff along his jaw, like he hasn't shaved in a day or two; I didn't notice when he was onstage. My hands itch to touch it, so I hold them tightly in my lap.

"May I?" he asks quietly, gesturing to the empty seat next to me.

After a pause, I nod, moving my messenger bag so he can sit. He does, looking laughably large in the cramped space, his legs folded almost to his chest. It's Kian origami and almost makes me smile in spite of my shock.

"Lyric," he says, and it's a breath, a prayer.

I don't move. I can't.

"Are you running away from me?" he asks.

"I thought *you* were running away from *me*," I reply, my voice hushed. "To Washington."

A half smile tugs at his lips. "I didn't take that job."

I blink. "Oh."

"They managed to find me one upstate, at the research station in Finger Lakes. They'd offered me one in Washington because they thought I had no ties to New York. I agreed with them, at first."

I'm quiet, barely daring to breathe.

"But I realized I have one very important connection to New York." He grazes my jaw gently with a finger and I want to weep at his touch. I've missed this. I've missed him. "You."

I lick my lips. The bus is hot. I'm vaguely aware there must be people staring at us like we're live entertainment and that we're putting everyone behind schedule, but in this moment, no one exists except Kian and me. "What are you saying?"

He takes my slightly damp hands from my lap and holds them between his big ones. Looking right into my eyes, he says, "I've fallen in love with you, Pound. That's what all this has been about. I was an idiot to deny it for as long as I did. It's always been you. Always. But if you don't feel the same way about me, that's okay." He squeezes my hands gently. "If you'll have me, I still want you in my life as a friend. As my *best* friend. Because it's not life otherwise."

Tears spill down my cheeks before I'm even aware I'm crying. "Really?"

He looks at me in concern. "Yeah, LB."

"I was going to tell you I'm in love with you the day you moved out. But when you said . . . what you said—I just assumed you were letting me down easy. Because I'd ruined everything between us."

A sob hitches in my chest and he gathers me to him, rocking me slightly, one hand cupping the back of my head. Chuckling lightly, Kian says, "You seemed so unfazed when I said I was moving out, I thought there was no way you felt the same way I did."

"I was pretending!" I say, indignant. "Don't you even know when I'm acting?"

He laughs and kisses the top of my head. "You're a better actress than you think, Bishop."

I look up at him, through tear-soaked lashes. "Is this real? You love me?"

He is completely serious now. "I love you."

"I love you, too."

The Kian Montgomery grin is back, big and happy. It is sunshine itself. "Good. So what do you say we get off this bus and figure our lives out?"

"Yeah, get off the bus so I can get these people to their destinations!" the bus driver, who's looking pretty grumpy now, calls out.

But all around us, the other passengers are beaming, laughing, whispering. My cheeks flaming, I stand. Kian is more confident, unfolding himself easily. Even though he's in the aisle seat, he stands off to the side to let me go in front of him.

"Hey, thanks," I say, tipping my face up and smiling at him.

He tugs on a lock of my hair and kisses the corner of my mouth. "I'd follow you anywhere."

Epilogue

ONE YEAR LATER

LYRIC

It is tradition within the graduate experimental psychology department at Columbia for each advisor to read a little bit about the graduating student. It doesn't take long, since there are only three to five of us in each cohort. As I walk across the stage in the late spring sunshine, I hear Dr. Livingstone's deep baritone ring out.

"Dr. Lyric Bishop graduates summa cum laude and is the youngest woman to ever do so in this program's history." The audience breaks out in applause. I hear Kian wolf whistle and look into the crowd right at him and grin. He winks and blows me a kiss.

Beside him, Charlie's clapping so hard, her hands are a blur. I know Zoey's right behind me, so I hope Charlie doesn't injure herself before she gets the chance to clap for her girlfriend. And right behind *them*, the entire Bishop family of eighteen is cheering their hearts out, their joy and pride a deafening tsunami of sound.

There's Max, with his arm around Camellia, now his wife. My mom, dressed in a peacock blue tunic, is sobbing and clinging on to my dad, who has tears running down his smiling face. Amethyst is dabbing her eyes with a tissue with her husband Brandon's arm around her shoulders, while their daughter Lapiz is busy eating a lollipop, completely unfazed by the ceremony around her. Opal and Arthur sit close together, and even at this distance, I see the enormous engagement ring on her finger glinting in the sunlight and her swollen belly like a full moon in her lap. My other sister Willow is with her boyfriend Damien, grinning like a loon.

I take a breath. I am truly, truly the luckiest girl in the world.

Dr. Livingstone clears his throat disapprovingly and continues, louder, "Dr. Bishop has published a portion of her thesis in the prestigious, peer-reviewed *Journal of Sexual Psychology*. I will now read you one of my favorite passages from her conclusion:

"'In analyzing the data from thousands of study participants who all scored well above the mean on oxytocin and dopamine levels, I arrived at the following conclusion to explain their strong, multifaceted bond.

"'There are many unknowns in this world, and the vagaries of romantic and sexual chemistry are undoubtedly among them. However, it is the opinion of this writer that, as with anything, it is *true human connection* that makes any attraction richer, deeper, truer, and longer lasting. That human connection can only be found when we look outside our own prescribed notions of what is right and perfect and well suited for us. True human connection is often found in the most unexpected of all places—perhaps with a mate who doesn't fit neatly into our carefully planned-out lives; maybe with a person who, until now, was thought of only as a best friend and nothing more.

"'Perhaps we are all born alone and will die alone; however, if we are lucky, there are many years between one and the other. What better way to fill those years than with an enduring love?'"

Dr. Livingstone pauses and looks at me. I could swear his eyes are teary. Or maybe it's just the sun's reflection on his glasses making me see things. "I have been an advisor to many students in the course of my teaching career. I can truly say that Dr. Bishop has been one of my favorites . . . and most challenging. I am proud—and more than a little relieved—to present her with her doctorate today."

Laughing, I take the diploma from him as the crowd once again drowns us in noise. He holds out a hand for a handshake, but I hug him. "Thank you for taking me back," I say into his ear.

After a moment, he pats me on the back. I hear the smile in his voice as he replies, "You were my boomerang pupil, Dr. Bishop. They're always the best ones. Keep in touch, now."

I know I will.

The Sizzle Paradox

KIAN

"I can't believe this is our last night here in our apartment," she says, twining her fingers with mine.

We're lying on Lyric's bed together, having celebrated her graduation on multiple levels. Now our pajamas are back on and we're snuggling, neither of us wanting to let the other go. I pull her closer into my chest, breathing in her floral shampoo. Luckily, after we got off the Greyhound bus last year, Lyric was able to keep her lease and the apartment. And every chance I got, I drove down to spend the weekend with her. At other times, she drove up to sleep under the stars with me.

"I'm so happy you got the teaching job at the University of Rochester. Now we can be together all the time, not just on weekends." I pause, rubbing my thumb along hers. "If you want to."

Lyric trills a laugh. "I love that you still ask me that. As if the madness we went through a year ago wasn't a temporary hiccup." She rolls onto her stomach and looks at me. "I love you, Kian Montgomery. And I will always, always love you. Just accept it."

I look at her seriously. "Always is a long time, you know."

She replies, equally seriously, "I know."

I take a deep breath and look past her at the crystal-bedecked windowsill, lit only by the streetlamp outside. "Hey . . . is that a new rose quartz crystal point?"

Frowning, she turns around. "Oh. Weird." Reaching out, she grabs the thick, tall crystal point and looks at it. "I don't remember getting this. I know the morganite was a gift from you, but seriously . . . I feel like my crystals are reproducing behind my back or something."

"Hmm." My heart is pounding so hard, I feel my teeth vibrating. "Is that . . . a seam running along the center?"

Lyric's frown gets deeper, blond eyebrows pulling together, her pink mouth pulling down. In spite of my nerves, I want to laugh at her expression. She looks like a little kid, trying to figure out a difficult math problem. "What the hell?" She snaps the box open. Stops short. Looks at me and gasps so softly, I can barely hear it. "It's . . . it's a ring."

I look steadily at her. "Rose quartz for an unconditional, never-ending love. I got the stone from your mom. Remember when she tried to give it to you at Max's engagement party? I had a jeweler set it earlier this year. I've been waiting for the perfect moment."

"Oh my God. Kian." She's beginning to cry now, and can't speak anymore.

My turn. Taking the box gently from her, I get off the bed and down on one knee. She claps her hands to her mouth. "Lyric, if there's one thing this past year has taught me, it's that I can't stand the thought of life without you." I clear my throat. "Perhaps we are all born alone and will die alone; however, if we are lucky, there are many years between one and the other. What better way to fill those years than with an enduring love?"

"Hey," she says, through a teary laugh. "Those are my lines."

"And they speak to my heart." I smile at her, my best friend, my true love. "Lyric Rae Bishop, will you marry me?"

"Yes, yes, yes!" she yells, laughing and crying and laughing again. I take the ring from the box and slip it gently onto her finger. It's a perfect fit.

"I hope you know you've made me the happiest man in the world," I tell her. I've barely gotten the words out when she launches herself at me and we both fall to the floor, laughing.

Between kisses, Lyric says, "Thanks for helping me crack the Sizzle Paradox, Kian."

"Dr. Bishop, it was truly my pleasure."

And then we lose ourselves in magic, the kind only love can create.

Acknowledgments

It's such a giddy feeling, knowing that my second adult romance is out in the world! I'm so grateful for the incredible team at St. Martin's Griffin that made this possible, even during a pandemic. Thanks also to my super-agent, Thao Le, for saying Lyric was one of her favorite contemporary heroines.

My family has all my gratitude and hugs for being so tolerant of my weird writer quirks, of which there are many. No, I don't plan to stop embarrassing you anytime soon. Sorry-not-sorry.

A big, fat thank-you to my readers for buying and reading this book! I wouldn't be able to do my dream job without you, and I'm so grateful. I hope Lyric and Kian made you giggle and swoon as much as they did me.